Praise for
KNIGHT'S CURSE

"Rich with action, romance and sensory overload, the story goes places I never expected and delighted me every step of the way. Duvall is a writer to watch for!"
—C.E. Murphy, author of *Urban Shaman*

"Duvall's heroine is an endearing mixed bag of coiled emotions, and the other characters are a collection of good and evil that readers will want to know more about."
—*RT Book Reviews*

"This is a spectacular story. The urban fantasy world that Karen Duvall has created feels genuine and fully realized and best of all, the places and characters in this book are just flat out fun to read about."
—Bonnie Ramthun, author of *The White Gates*

KAREN DUVALL

DARKEST KNIGHT

LUNA™

LUNA™

Recycling programs
for this product may
not exist in your area.

DARKEST KNIGHT

ISBN-13: 978-0-373-80344-6

This edition published by arrangement with Harlequin Books S.A.

For questions and comments about the quality of this book
please contact us at Customer_eCare@Harlequin.ca.

www.Harlequin.com

Printed in U.S.A.

Dear Reader,

I had so much fun writing about Chalice, a modern-day knight,
in the first book that I knew her adventures would continue.
After all, she has unfinished business to take care of, namely getting
Aydin back to his old self again. He changed into a gargoyle to save
her life, so she promised to find a way to make him human again. The
senseless murder of her sister knights by an unknown attacker is an
unexpected foil to her plans, but she won't let that stop her. Against
all odds, she vows to catch the killer as well as restore Aydin to the
man he used to be.

Knight's Curse, the first book in Chalice's harrowing adventures,
is available in print and ebook formats. Please visit my blog,
www.karenduvall.blogspot.com, for updates on my future books.

Karen Duvall

This book is dedicated to my five adorable grandchildren:
Kai, Zach, Adam, Andrew and Bella.

My heartfelt thanks go to my amazing literary agent,
Elizabeth Winick Rubenstein, who's a great listener and extremely
supportive. I also appreciate her assistant, Shira Hoffman, who
always makes herself available.

I'd also like to thank my editor, Ann Leslie Tuttle, and her helpful
assistant, Dana Hamilton.

Rocky Mountain Fiction Writers deserves my thanks, as well. I've
benefited greatly from this professional organization devoted to
writers of novel-length commercial fiction.

DARKEST
KNIGHT

one

"YOU'RE COMING WITH ME, RIGHT?" I ASKED
Rafe when he opened the silver veil that separated the
physical world from the realm of angels. This misty oth-
erworld was home to Rafael, my guardian angel, but not
to me. I think I'd overstayed my welcome.

Rafe towered above me and scowled. "No."

I leaned forward to peer through the filmy curtain.
"I'm not ready to go there alone. It's too soon."

"Chalice, it's been over a month." Rafe closed his eyes
and sighed so deeply I thought he'd collapse a lung if he
had one. "But if you prefer to wait a while longer…" He
held his palm flat against the transparent veil and the sigil
on his hand glowed. The surface began to solidify.

I grabbed his arm. "Wait."

His sigh came even louder this time. "Make up your
mind."

I narrowed my eyes at him. "You have no idea how hard this is for me."

The deep creases in his forehead smoothed as his eyes crinkled with the start of a smile. It made him appear almost human. "I can imagine."

"No, you can't." The memory of my last day of bondage to Shui, a homicidal gargoyle, remained clear in my mind. The gargoyle's death had freed me of the curse that once threatened to take my humanity and turn me into a winged devil as horrible as Shui. But my freedom had come at a price. In order to save me from my fate, Shui had to be killed by another gargoyle. Aydin, who was also bonded to a gargoyle, had allowed the curse to change him so that he could fight Shui to save *my* life. But, by doing so, I'd lost the only man I'd ever loved. It was time for me to bring Aydin back, to make him human again. The only way for that to happen lay on the other side of this veil, at the Vyantara fatherhouse. Home of my nightmares, where failing a heist used to mean a beating by my master or a death threat from Shui. Lucky for me the gargoyle died before getting his chance to feast on Chalice tartare.

I sucked in a breath. "I can't face another gargoyle."

"Then don't face it. Just kill it." Rafe's hand stayed in place against the veil, but he didn't reopen it. He waited for my okay.

"Come with me," I told him, trying to make it sound like an order. He was usually good at following orders.

"You know what would happen if I did?" he asked, raising his eyebrows. "My presence would set off every alarm and ward in the house."

I winced. "That would defeat the purpose of sneaking in, right?"

"Mmm-hmm."

I heaved in a fortifying breath and blinked. Even after a month, it felt strange not to wear my contact lenses. Or the filters for my ears and nose. I'd worn these protective devices practically all my life. For being half angel, even if that half was the fallen kind, my unusual abilities helped keep me out of trouble. Unfortunately, they helped get me into almost as much. Rafe had been forbidden to meet me until after my curse was broken, so only recently was he able to teach me control over my hypersensitivity through meditation. Now I could turn my powers off and on as easily as a light switch, though I hadn't practiced under stressful conditions. I was about to test my new skill big-time.

"I'm ready," I said. "Open the veil."

"One last thing before you go—"

"No!" I glared at him. He was about to deliver another lecture about staying focused and making safety my first priority. I'd heard it over a dozen times. "Do it now before I lose my nerve."

"As you wish."

The veil opened and I stepped through, my booted feet landing on a dark Oriental rug as wide and long as the room I stood in. I glanced behind me. Rafe and the veil were gone.

My heart did a brief tap dance against my ribs before I reminded myself that Vyantara fatherhouses fed on fear. I knew from experience that this building would suck out my energy like a baby sucks milk from a bottle, and I'd end up too weak to do what I'd come for. I had to kill the gargoyle Shojin and take its heart for Aydin. Before he had turned into a gargoyle, Aydin had been bonded to Shojin and now only Shojin could save him. I knew the gargoyle was here because on the last day Aydin and I were together, this is where the Vyantara had said he would be.

I thinned my mind's sensory defenses just enough to get a sense of the place. Straining against the silence, I listened for signs of life and found two beings upstairs. Whether they were human or not didn't matter. I only cared about hearing one heartbeat: the rapid bass drum pound that belonged only to a gargoyle.

It didn't take long for me to detect it. One gargoyle was in the basement and it had to be Shojin. No two gargoyles could occupy the same space or there was sure to be a fight.

Mouth dry as parchment, I swallowed my fear and sniffed the air. The kitchen smelled close by and I knew I'd find a door to the basement there. That's how most fatherhouses were laid out due to the spell-casting needs of their magic-users.

I crept down the narrow hall toward the scent of herbs and cooking oil. Squinting in darkness that appeared gray as fog to my sensitive eyes, I detected no ghosts. Most likely the house's warding spells kept them out. Good. Ghosts were annoying distractions and the last thing I needed right now. My focus had to be sharp as a gargoyle's talon.

The vibration down my spine told me I was surrounded by curses and charms. I sensed a huge collection here, possibly even bigger than the fatherhouse in Denver before it blew up. It reminded me of one more task on my to-do list: steal back every magical object in the Vyantara's gallery of hellish artifacts. After I'd been kidnapped from a monastery in Lebanon at thirteen by the leaders of this nasty black veil group, I'd been forced to steal many of these artifacts for the Vyantara. I had my work cut out for me.

The wooden stairs creaked with my slight ninety-eight pounds of body weight. If Shojin didn't hear me coming, he'd surely have smelled me by now. A gargoyle's senses were nearly as keen as mine.

I sniffed the air and it chilled my lungs, which came as no surprise considering this was a Canadian fatherhouse in the dead of winter. But it didn't lessen the scent of damp feathers and unwashed fur. When I reached the bottom step, a plume of steamy gargoyle breath seethed out of the darkness and enveloped me like a blanket.

Shojin's eyes glowed red and I listened for his heartbeat to speed up, but he remained calm. His breathing came slow and steady despite the billowing clouds of hot air that puffed from his flared nostrils. I didn't know Shojin well, only that Aydin had been bonded to him and that their eight hundred years together had forged a rare friendship. I did a mental eye-roll. In the thirteen years I'd been with Shui, we had shared only hatred. Gargoyles were assassins for the Vyantara. I could never befriend a murderer.

The gargoyle growled. Oh, there we go. That was the behavior I expected. I didn't deal well with the unpredictable. Monsters should act and react in accordance with their vile and murderous nature.

I slid my balisong blade from its sheath on my back. The knife glinted a glorious purple in the red light that shone from Shojin's eyes. No ordinary blade, this balisong could do something no other knife could. It could kill an immortal gargoyle because it was created from the dead body of one.

"I know you and Aydin were good buddies, Shojin. And I'm sorry to have to do this." I brandished the blade and stood poised to strike. "But you have what I need to make Aydin a man again."

The gargoyle hissed and lunged at me. It was an ancient creature, possibly the oldest one on earth, but you'd never know it by its speed and agility. Shojin's wings spanned the width of the room and with just one flap, I was airborne and sailing toward the stairs. I landed on my back, the air whooshing from my lungs like a deflating balloon. I managed to roll sideways just as the gargoyle pounced. He missed me by a hair.

I wanted to yell but I didn't have enough breath to make a sound. It was all I could do to stay conscious. We were both in full battle mode and my intent to win replaced any fear I might have had. There was no room in my mind to be afraid. My head filled with tactics and strategy, driven by instinct to survive.

Shojin matched my intensity. He wanted to win just as badly. He knew what I'd come for and wasn't about to let me take it from him.

One clawed hand the size of a grizzly bear's paw sliced through the air to backhand my head and send me sprawling. My arms and legs flailed as I slid across the dirt floor to slam into a wall. I hit so hard I didn't see stars, I saw planets. I wasn't so fast getting back up this time. And Shojin took full advantage.

He grabbed me by the throat and lifted me up off the ground. I swiped the blade toward the arm holding me, but dizziness kept me from seeing straight and I connected with nothing but air.

I wanted to scream at him that he owed Aydin his heart. Killing me wouldn't bring Aydin back, but killing Shojin could. Struggling to breathe, I gritted my teeth and tried forcing my will on the gargoyle. He stared hard at me, his ridged brow deeply creased with age, his curved raptor's beak parted as if to bite. I fisted a clump of fur on his arm and hung on tight, sucking in what air I could while watching the edges of my consciousness fade to black.

Fury in his eyes, Shojin lowered me to the ground. His grip on my neck lessened, but I felt something warm trickle down the collar of my shirt. I vaguely wondered how badly I'd been wounded, and if it even mattered. For the second time in less than two months I was about to become gargoyle chow.

If I hadn't been so weak from lack of oxygen I'd be slicing through his thick chest right now and cutting out his beating heart. As it was, my legs couldn't even hold me up. I hung from Shojin's claws like a bloody rag doll.

The gargoyle growled and squawked as if trying to talk. He shook his head and clacked his beak. What would he say if he could speak? *Thanks for the quick snack, and I'll have your guardian angel for dessert?*

He pried the balisong from my hand, his clumsy claw gouging my arm in the process. Who knew a gargoyle preferred to cut his meat with a knife? But instead of peeling me open like a ripe piece of fruit, he plunged the blade into his own chest.

Shojin's grip on me weakened as he sawed through his flesh in search of what lay beating underneath.

I knew in that moment that he loved Aydin as much as I did. His adoration for a mere human stunned me. I wasn't sure I could grasp the concept of compassion coming from a fiend.

His eyes glazed and filled with tears. I could imagine pain had caused this reaction, but I had to give him more credit than that. Aydin had told me many times that Shojin was different. That his beast wasn't a homicidal killer like others of its kind. I realized now that he'd been right.

A tear dripped from the corner of Shojin's eye and slid over the coarse surface of his beak. I bit my lip to stop my own tears from flowing. I wouldn't dishonor him by showing pity. He'd done an honorable thing for a friend and it was costing him his life.

He dropped the knife, which quickly dissolved to dust after having done its job, then closed his eyes while reaching inside the hole he'd cut into his chest. When he opened his clawed hand, a glowing lump of purple flesh lay centered in his palm. He offered me the still-beating heart.

We both fell to our knees and I caught the heart before it could hit the ground. It was warm and wet and mine.

Shojin gasped and collapsed forward, his dense body

falling hard and shattering in more pieces than I could count. When a gargoyle died, it always turned to stone. So his lifeless body breaking apart was no surprise. What surprised me was that his heart continued its rapid bass drum beat. A minute later the organ went still in my hands.

The heart was still warm, still glowing, but solid and shiny as a purple gemstone. Now I understood why Shojin had fought me so hard. If I'd killed him like I wanted, his heart would have shattered along with the rest of his body when he died. He'd known I would come and had planned all along to end his life this way.

Shojin had proved himself more angel than demon; he was a creature with a soul. His sacrifice would mean new life for Aydin.

two

AS MUCH AS I WANTED TO MOURN SHOJIN'S passing, I had to get the hell out of the house before a flood of Vyantara magic-users descended on me.

I gulped a shaky breath and glanced at the pink scar on the palm of my hand. My sigil was new, only a couple of weeks old, but that made the young scar no less effective. Eyes still stinging with the tears I held back, I smeared blood from my neck onto the scar and flattened my hand against the wall, waiting for the fluttery buzz that came with opening a veil. The tension in my shoulders increased with each passing second. The veil usually opened immediately. What was taking so long?

I clenched my jaw and listened. No thundering footsteps on the floor above, no wards sending out rays of lightning or demon warriors to take me out. No veil opening for my sigil, either. I began to wonder if I was in a time warp. I'd seen something like that done once. In fact, it was my fallen angel father who had made it happen.

I tried my sigil again. Nothing. What the hell?

I looked at the stone heart I still held and rolled my eyes. Of course the veil wouldn't open. Gargoyles, and anything associated with a gargoyle that wasn't angel-blessed, was not allowed through the silver veil. As long as I had the heart I was stuck here.

But that didn't explain why the Vyantara hadn't come running at the sound of battle. I went back to the basement stairs and stepped cautiously up to the top. That's when I saw the halt charm. About six inches tall, it was the figure of a hand woven with strips of bark from an ancient oak tree. I recognized it because I'd stolen the charm from a museum in Wales about five years ago for the Vyantara. It was one of many magical artifacts I'd been forced to steal as their indentured thief. The charm's fingers were spread out in a stop gesture and its palm faced the door. Someone had placed it there to soundproof the basement.

Charms don't work on me, which is why I could hear Shojin's beating heart when I was on the other side of the door. I suspected Shojin himself had placed the charm here, and not to keep me from finding him, but to keep others away once I did. And it had worked.

But that didn't solve my current problem. The only way I knew out of the house was through the house itself.

I wasn't doing myself any favors by standing still, so I freed the spare butterfly knife from my ankle sheath and opened the basement door. Greeted by silence, I took it as a good sign and continued making my way through the kitchen. Getting to the basement in the first place had been no problem, so chances were good I'd get out of the house just as easily. A lot could be said for positive thinking.

I crept through the main part of the house where glass-lidded tables displayed dusty old relics tagged by yellowing strips of paper. Each one had a typed word and number that referenced it for the Vyantara's catalog. They made their money by selling off these cursed and charmed antiques to the highest bidder. There were hundreds of them in this room alone.

I stopped and listened to the silence, hearing only the low thrum of slow heartbeats and the smooth breathing of those in sleep. No one would miss an object or two… or three. Along with the bottle of salt water I used for destroying spells, I always carried a special pouch that hid magical objects from detection. I'd simply toss a handful of these in the pouch and be on my way.

A pocket watch inscribed with a protection spell would be useful for my sister knights in the Order of the Hatchet. Our knighthood shared a bond of nearly a thousand years, starting when our ancestors fought side by side in the Crusade Wars. Each generation gave birth to daughters spawned by their guardian angels. My sisters still fought together, and though the war had changed, the goal of vanquishing evil remained the same. I was proud to be one of them.

I dropped the watch in my pouch along with a fountain pen filled with invisible ink that made the writer disappear instead of the words. Then I found something

I wouldn't mind having for myself if I weren't immune: a dove's feather that enabled the user to fly.

Treasures in hand, I headed for the front door, which appeared farther away than it had only minutes ago. In fact, the faster I walked the more distance I created between the door and me. Déjà vu.

The same thing had happened to me on my first night at the Denver fatherhouse. I suspected a similar ward had been triggered here and the apparition of my demon foe would appear any second. A fuzzy image took shape in the foyer and a zigzag of energy wiggled through it like a weak signal on a television screen. Blackish-purple and bald, green eyes glowing, the Maågan demon offered me a menacing grin as if it knew me. Perhaps it did. I had severed the arm from one of its cousins a few weeks ago when it tried to stop my escape from a building that was about to explode.

I was fresh out of gargoyle blades and I doubted the knife I had would even make a dent in that thing. Its hide was strong as iron. At the moment it was only a projection from the hellish realm of the black veil, like the warning growl of an attack dog. If provoked, the creature would pop through to this side and kill me on the spot.

The last time I'd tried running from one, its claws had sliced my ankle and the venom had made me sick. I'd rather not repeat the experience, especially since the venom could be lethal. The Maågan didn't know I had taken any magical objects because I'd hidden them inside the pouch.

I suddenly realized what had sparked the demon's interest. Shojin's heart. Shit.

The heart still felt warm in my hand, which I knew was stained purple with Shojin's blood. Holding the pouch behind my back, I carefully slid the fist-size stone in with the rest of my booty. The Maågan continued to glare. I gritted my teeth and stalked toward it as I knew the creature respected anyone who confronted it head-on.

The distance closed between us, and the front door was now a mere few feet away. I didn't make eye contact, but the demon's gaze bored into me like twin lasers. Malice oozed from it like a septic sore. I lifted my chin and marched toward the exit.

I admit I was afraid. Not terrified, as I'd confronted much worse in recent weeks, but fearful enough to attract the house's appetite. I felt my energy begin to drain. Between the Maågan's murderous instinct and the building's hunger, my hyper senses couldn't do jackshit to keep me safe. I needed a miracle.

Knowing a sudden rush for the door would only kill me faster, I kept my movements slow and precise. My fingers curled around the door's knob and relief overwhelmed me. As the door opened, a whoosh of frigid air cooled the sweat on my skin. I smelled snow. I could hear leafless branches rattle in the winter wind. An overcast sky opened briefly to allow a faint ray of moonshine to struggle through.

A quick tug on my jacket let me know I'd deluded myself into believing I was safe.

It jerked me backward, but I grabbed on to the door frame to hold fast. The fabric tore, but I felt no stinging pain from the Maågan's razorlike claws as it searched for the pouch.

Still holding the pouch in one hand, I fisted the top to keep its contents from spilling out. The fingernails of my other hand dug into the door frame to anchor me in place. I'd lose this battle before long, but I refused to give up easily. I kicked backward, connecting with what might have been the demon's head. It screeched and a roar of voices filtered down from the floor above. The home's residents had awakened and they didn't sound happy.

I was losing my grip and the threatening voices inside the house grew louder. A flap of giant wings forced my gaze upward and I half expected to see Shojin sweep down for the kill. But Shojin, whom I now thought of as a gentle giant, was dead. This must be another gargoyle. A hungry house and a demon weren't enough for these guys? Give me a break.

I squinted up into the darkness and saw nothing but gray clouds and falling snow. Yet my nose detected more. Damp fur, old blood, and dirt that smelled like a farm. As well as a familiar scent that hurt my heart.

I barely had time to think when I saw the set of enormous curled talons appear inches from my face. They latched onto both my arms and lifted me aloft with the Maågan's claws still gripping my jacket. I released my hold on the door frame and the jacket slipped free from my body. In a burst of speed, my rescuer surged upward, away from the fatherhouse and into the snow-filled sky above.

I was hardly conscious by the time my feet touched

solid ground. Icy cold cut through me like a blade and my skin had turned numb. Frostbite would soon follow. The thought had barely touched my mind when a thick woolen blanket fell across my shoulders. Only one person knew me so well that he practically read my mind.

"Aydin." I whispered his name, which was difficult to say with a nearly frozen tongue. He stayed out of my line of sight, but I heard him shuffling around in the dark. I took a minute to gaze at my surroundings. The crackle of a fire gave me tingles as I anticipated the warmth it would offer.

This structure must be his temporary home, a hidden place relatively close to Shojin. I imagined the Vyantara were still looking for Aydin, as he'd be a valuable asset if caught. Gargoyle assassins weren't easy to come by. They were ancient creatures, but new ones could be made by binding humans with a curse that would transform them into winged devils. I'd been cruelly bonded to one named Shui, but the monster's death had set me free. Aydin hadn't been so lucky.

I sniffed the air. That's where the farm smell had come from. This old farm looked abandoned, the barn's walls rotted and boards missing, though it appeared Aydin had tried making repairs. His dexterity compromised by claws, he'd been ill-equipped to wield a hammer.

The scent of roasting meat wafted through the air. Rabbit. I grinned in spite of my situation. He'd never cooked for me when he was human.

"Thanks for coming to my rescue," I said to the hulking shadow by the fire. This was the first time I'd noticed he had a tail and I watched it twitch like an irritated cat. "I'd be dead if not for you." *Again.*

He grunted. That's all he could do. The ability to speak wasn't included in the gargoyle transformation package. He could, however, rip someone apart with his bare paws and chew through bones like they were jawbreaker candies.

"I've missed you, Aydin," I said softly to his back. His bat wings were folded at his sides and they shifted as if in a shrug. "Did you miss me?"

He seemed to ignore me, but I sensed he was listening. So I prattled on. "I haven't been back to Denver since, you know…that day."

He growled low in his throat.

"I couldn't agree more." Though *I* had benefited from my experience, he had not. I wondered if he resented me for that. I wouldn't blame him if he did.

"I've been staying with the Arelim since then," I told him, and waited for his reaction. Guardians were Arelim angels from the twelfth order of the angelic hierarchy, sworn to protect the Hatchet knights. But Aydin had been my real protector. He had explained to me my role in the knighthood and showed me how magic could be good if used in a good way. He even taught me how to fall in love.

Aydin turned sideways to peer at me. His eyes were still that lovely shade of jade, clear as ice. His face, however, looked like that of an oversize cat. That didn't matter because I would recognize him no matter what he was.

"The silver veil is kind of nice, but it's too solitary—

even for me. And to be honest, I felt claustrophobic most of the time. There's nothing to do there but meditate."

Aydin pulled something from the fire he'd been tending and blew on the flame that engulfed what was on the stick. Charred rabbit. So much for his cooking skills.

He gestured for me to come closer, which I eagerly did. I could hardly feel my feet and I stumbled. Aydin caught me before I did a face-plant on the hay-strewn ground. He was surprisingly gentle for a gargoyle, but he let go of me so quickly I nearly fell anyway.

"Thanks." I sat on one of the logs positioned around the fire and he handed me the skewered rabbit. "Aren't you going to have any?"

He glanced away, then turned his wedge-shaped head to stare at me. He placed both paws on his belly.

"Ah, I see. You've already eaten." And no doubt his had been rabbit tartare.

Feeling warmer already, I pulled a leg off the rabbit and peeled away its burned hide before taking a bite. Not bad. Not bad at all. I devoured the meat as though I hadn't eaten in days. Come to think of it, I couldn't remember my last meal.

I didn't like the awkward silence between us. I'd always felt comfortable with Aydin, and though I realized he couldn't speak, it wasn't a lack of words that made our meeting so uneasy. We were both different now and we hardly knew each other anymore. I hoped we still shared the same goals when it came to my sister knights in the Order of the Hatchet. In spite of everything, I still loved Aydin; claws, wings, fangs and all.

I cleared my throat. "Anyway…" I gently swung my

pouch of ill-gotten gain between my knees and the few objects inside clattered against one another.

Aydin lifted his chin and wiggled his feline nose. He sniffed and jerked his head at the pouch in my hands.

It was time to tell him what was inside.

"This? I've begun reclaiming stolen artifacts from the Vyantara." I held up the bag. "My sisters can make good use of these." Our original plan had been for Aydin to help me steal back the magical objects from all the fatherhouses, then help me teach my sister knights how to use them to protect themselves.

I pulled out each item, one by one, starting with the pocket watch. I slowly withdrew the halt charm made of oak bark. "There's an interesting story behind this one." I held it out to him and he nodded as if he recognized it. I smiled. "It was actually Shojin who found it."

Aydin's cat whiskers twitched.

I nodded. "Yep. I saw him today. He gave me something to give you." My heart hammered so hard against my ribs I thought they'd break. I tossed the empty rabbit stick in the fire. "Shojin loved you very much."

Aydin straightened and backed away from me. Though fur covered his face, I could still see his scowl. I think he guessed what I was about to give him. He shook his head.

"He made the ultimate sacrifice, Aydin." I lifted the beautiful glowing heart from the pouch and held it up. "Shojin died so that you could become a man again."

Aydin's chest rose and fell like he had trouble breathing. He pointed at me.

"No!" I gave my head a quick shake. "It wasn't me, I

swear. He harvested the heart with his own claws because he loved you that much." And so did I.

Still frowning, Aydin gently took the heart from me. My shoulders slouched in relief. Once he ate the heart, I'd have him back the way he used to be. We'd be together again, both free of our curses, both ready to start new lives. My eyes felt hot and I realized they'd filled with tears. Tears of hope.

Aydin's paws rubbed over the heart as if cherishing a precious gem, which it was. Rare and beautiful. Then he threw back his head and roared. His anguished cry tore through me and I stood to hold my arms open to him. To comfort him. But he tossed the heart at my feet.

I crouched down to snatch it, unbroken, from the frigid ground. "What are you doing?" I yelled.

His lips peeled back from fangs sharp enough to pierce glass without making it crack. He fisted his claws and spread his wings before abruptly vanishing from sight.

three

"AYDIN!" I RAN OUT OF THE BARN AND GAZED
up at the dense clouds that had dumped buckets of snow.
I didn't see him, but I sensed him up there. Invisible, and
he was flying far away from me.

I clutched the gargoyle heart to my chest and whispered, "Shojin, you didn't die for nothing. We'll get him
back. I promise."

"I see he didn't lose his ability to vanish like a thief in
the night."

I spun around to see Rafe standing behind me.

"How long have you been here?" I asked, blinking
hard as I tried to figure out what was wrong with this
picture. He looked so…different.

"Long enough to hear him roar and see him vanish,"
Rafe said, sounding annoyed. "As I suspected he would."

I squinted at him. "Rafe, what have you done to your-self?"

He placed both hands on his chest. "Me? Oh, you mean the clothes."

I nodded and stared, openmouthed. "The clothes, the hair, the skin, and the fact you cut about a foot off your height."

He turned his back to me and I gasped.

"Oh, my God! What happened to your wings?"

"Relax." He faced me again. "This is a disguise. We can take human form whenever we wish. It's often neces-sary when we interact with mortals."

His hair was no longer white but a wheat-blond that looked as natural as the stubble on his tan cheeks and chin. What a change. His skin was normally porcelain-smooth, and he was usually taller than a pro basketball player. I had to give him credit for his choice of clothes. Acid-washed denim from top to bottom, but his jacket looked thickly lined with fleece, his gloves leather and his muffler cable-knit. Even his boots were stylin'. He looked like he'd walked straight out of GQ *Magazine*.

"Wow," was all I could say.

He scowled, looking uncomfortable, and glanced down at himself. "Did I miss something?"

I shook my head. "Not a thing."

He smiled. "Good." Squinting up at the sky, he said, "Now that it's gone, we can leave."

Though Aydin's rejection of the heart was a setback, I wasn't angry, just disappointed. He needed time to grieve for his old friend and I could be patient. After everything Aydin had done for me he deserved at least that much.

"Rafe, Aydin is a he, not an it. And by the way, I still have the gargoyle heart so we can't travel through the veil. I already tried and it wouldn't open for me."

"Of course not. I made an attempt to warn you about that, but you cut me off, remember?" Lips pressed firmly together, he added, "This is why I acquired a motor vehicle for our transportation."

Like any good Boy Scout, Rafe had come prepared. This kept getting better and better. "Tell me you're kidding."

He scowled again. "Why would I kid you? Don't you think I can drive?"

"Um. No?"

Shaking his head, he stalked past me and rounded the corner of the barn. I followed. Parked out back in a foot of snow was a shiny black Cadillac Escalade.

Pointing at the tires, I said, "You put the chains on yourself?"

He sighed. "Just get in. Thanks to the trophy you just acquired, we have a long drive ahead."

Ah, yes. I was finally going to meet my sister knights and my grandmother for the first time. A Hatchet knight herself, she lived with my grandfather—an angel who chose to become mortal—in the very state I'd fled from a month ago. Colorado, here we come.

"Are we there yet?" I sounded like a petulant child, but I didn't care. We'd traveled over two thousand miles and as nice as this SUV was, I wanted out.

Rafe glanced at his watch. "That's the second time

you've asked me in the last fifteen minutes. My answer is still the same. Two hours to go."

"Correction. That should be one hour and forty-five minutes."

"Traveling with me hasn't been that bad, has it?"

I slumped down in the seat and uncrossed, then re-crossed, my ankles on the dashboard. "I'm bored and I'm tired and my back hurts." I wished we'd park in one spot long enough for Aydin to find me. I glanced out the window and peered up at the overcast sky. He had to be up there somewhere.

Rafe followed the direction of my gaze. "Still on the lookout for your winged devil, eh?"

"Don't call him that." I understood angels and gargoyles didn't get along, but for crap sake, this was Aydin. One of the good guys. "He's on our side, remember?"

Rafe grunted.

I stared at his resolute profile. He looked mortal, but he didn't behave like one. He'd hardly eaten anything in over thirty hours and he never slept. Not once. The only time we stopped was to gas up and for me to eat and use the bathroom. I wanted a shower in the worst way.

Feeling grungy, I gave myself a sniff. "Do I stink?"

He scowled. "No, you don't stink." He shook his head. "You smell fine. You smell like…you."

I didn't know if that was good or bad. He had no odor whatsoever and if anyone would know it would be me. "How do you stay so clean without taking a bath?"

"I'm an angel."

"Duh. I know that." I rolled my eyes. "But you're

mortal at the moment. You've got mortal parts, right?" I looked pointedly down at his crotch.

He dropped a hand from the steering wheel to his lap as if to hide his manly bits. "Of course I do."

Leaning toward him, I looked closely at his face. "I don't believe it. You're blushing."

"Look, there's a truck stop. Hungry? Need to use the facilities?"

"Sure," I said, settling back in my seat again. "I could eat and take a pee. Don't you have to pee?"

"No."

I jutted my chin toward the hand that covered his package. "Then what good is that?"

"It's plenty good, I assure you." He turned the wheel a bit too sharply and I slid across the seat. I nearly landed on top of him.

I moved over to hug the door on my side.

"Sorry about that," Rafe said, and a shadow of a grin touched his lips. He wasn't sorry at all. He'd done that on purpose. "Don't pout. It's unbecoming for a knight."

"I'm not pouting." Crossing my arms firmly against my chest, I sat up straight and looked longingly at the coffee shop ahead. Hungrier than I thought, I wondered if it was morning or afternoon. I'd completely lost track of time. "Waffles. No, make that French toast. Two eggs over easy and order me extra bacon." He parked the Escalade and I hopped out to make a beeline for the restrooms. "Thanks, Rafe. You're an angel."

I gave myself a whore's bath in the restroom sink, using generous amounts of hand soap in the process. The hand dryer was an awkward way to dry off, but I was used to it. I'd done this countless times on the road during my thieving days so I was no stranger to prancing around a public bathroom in the buff. Luckily no one came in while I indulged in my trucker's toilette.

Moderately refreshed, I got dressed and strode inside the restaurant to find Rafe. He sat in a booth looking worse than dejected. He looked lost.

"Hey," I said softly, sensing something was wrong. I slid onto the bench seat across from him. "You okay?"

He blinked at me. "I just received a message."

I cocked my head. "Yeah? Who from?"

He swallowed, his Adam's apple making a deep bob in his human throat. "The Arelim. It's bad news."

My heart sank into my stomach. Rafe had a telepathic link with his angelic brothers, who were never chatty without good reason. An angel with bad news always meant trouble. I waited for him to tell me what it was.

"Your sister knights," he said slowly, his human eyes shining brighter than they should. He closed them and his hands curled into fists on the table. "Almost all of them are dead."

four

"WHAT? *NO!*" I STOOD UP AND NEARLY TOPPLED the table. I'd waited so long, struggled so hard to finally join my sisters in the knighthood. My mission was to train them in self-protection. I refused to believe it was too late. "It must be a mistake."

Rafe gazed down at his fists and shook his head. "No mistake," he whispered. "It happened a few hours ago. I was just told that those who didn't perish were either out of the country, in a warded area, or on sacred ground. That's the only common link the Arelim have found."

I blinked over dry eyes that stung from the effort to control my sensitive vision. This news was too distracting. Lights became too bright, I saw people's auras spike with the colors of their emotions, and smells from the kitchen roiled what little I had in my stomach. I no longer had an appetite.

"How?" I asked.

"Suffocation." Rafe leaned back in the booth seat, his handsome face looking haggard, as if defeated. Angel or not, the dark circles under his eyes were proof he needed sleep. "How they suffocated is unclear, but it happened as they slept."

It was mildly comforting to know they hadn't suffered. I grieved for Shojin and now I added my sisters to what seemed to be a growing list. I hoped this wasn't a sign of more to come. "What killed them?"

"Unknown, but the cause appears unnatural," he said. "And by that I mean supernatural."

That didn't surprise me considering each knight had a supernatural ability of her own. "Magic?"

Narrowing his eyes, Rafe said, "Not exactly. The Arelim detected no spells, charms or curses."

"Yet they weren't strangled or smothered?"

He shook his head. "It's as if their breath was snatched right out of their lungs."

Now I was really puzzled. "What could do that? A demon?"

"Possibly." He gave me a long look. "Or another knight."

Wow. "Don't tell me my sisters are prone to killing each other."

"It's been known to happen in the past, but that was hundreds of years ago. The motive had always been jealousy, usually of another knight's abilities, or if her guardian angel chose to become human after mating. It's very rare within the order to have an angel for a husband."

Yet my grandmother had wedded her guardian after

my mother was conceived. Had her sisters been jealous? Was her life ever threatened? There was so much I still didn't know. "Are the surviving knights under suspicion?"

"No one is above suspicion, Chalice. Not even you."

"Me?" That surprised me. "Impossible. I've been with you this whole time."

"Perhaps it was someone you know." His eyes became hard. "Someone who can enter a body and make it do whatever he wants."

He was talking about Aydin. Even though he had that ability, Aydin would never use it to harm a living soul. Just because gargoyles were assassins for the Vyantara didn't automatically make him one. "I know who you're talking about and he's not like that." I felt my ire heating up. "What reason could he possibly have to hurt my sisters?"

Rafe shrugged. "He's a beast of darkness now. Who knows what he would do, or why."

I glared at him. "You're wrong. Aydin took a vow to Saint Geraldine that he would protect the Hatchets. He'd never go back on his word." Saint Geraldine was one of the very first knights in the order, but she was a mummy now. Or at least her head was a mummy. Suffice to say she still lived despite existing over nine hundred years without the rest of her body.

Rafe blew a blast of air out his nose. "How can you be so sure? You hardly even know each other."

"I know him better than I know you."

He looked stunned for a second, but quickly recovered. His eyes hooded as if he were bored. Though we hadn't ordered anything, Rafe threw a couple of bills on the table and stood. "Let's not keep your grandmother waiting longer than she already has. She needs you. And you need her."

What I really needed was to be away from Rafe for a while. He'd been wearing on my nerves ever since we left Quebec and after seeing his hostile attitude toward Aydin, I'd rather be alone. Rafe's ego was big enough to fill a small planet.

We finished our drive to Golden, Colorado, in awkward silence. I was angry and Rafe was...who knew what. Angels were hard to read. He appeared deep in thought, but he also seemed to be sulking.

The long, snow-packed driveway leading to my grandmother's home had tall pines on either side that sparkled with frost. It looked like a fairy winter wonderland.

Rafe stopped the car. "We're here."

My gaze wandered over the majestic ponderosas and skeletal aspens that had lost all their leaves. No house in sight. "We are? I don't see anything but trees and a few big rocks."

He opened the car door and stepped out, his boots squeaking on the snowy ground. "That's because it's protected by a privacy ward." His hand waved through empty space and like a mirage, the air rippled and gradually formed the image of a house.

No ordinary house, its size made it more like a mansion. Yet it still looked like a classic mountain home of exposed cedar logs and natural stones set into the walls. Awesome.

"Wow," was all I could say.

"After you," Rafe said, making a slight bow.

I stepped gingerly over the invisible barrier between the seen and unseen. A massive door on the front porch opened and out walked a woman who could have been my mother's twin. On closer inspection I saw she was much older, with gray streaks running through her wavy ebony hair, and her frame was more generous than my mother's had been. My grandmother had meat on her bones.

"Rafael!" she called to angel-man beside me. "And oh, dear lord! Is this our Chalice?"

I felt my cheeks grow hot.

"Yes, Aurora. It sure is," Rafe said, a genuine smile in his voice. He liked her, I could tell.

"She's the mirror image of Felicia, rest her soul." My grandmother pranced down the steps, her breath steaming in the icy air. She hugged a thick wool cardigan closed against her chest and the knitted muffler at her neck trailed behind her. As she came nearer I got a good look at her eyes. Turquoise and gold. Just like mine.

Smiling, she stopped about a foot from me and opened her arms. I knew she expected a hug, but I wasn't a hugger. I made only one exception, but getting to hug Aydin wouldn't happen for a while. For my grandmother I compromised, leaning forward to touch my cheek to hers. She smelled like vanilla and cinnamon.

Eyes twinkling, she seemed satisfied with that. "Chalice, I'm so happy you've come."

I was about to say how glad I was to be here when an enormous figure appeared at my grandmother's back.

"So this is the granddaughter I've heard so much

about." The man stood slightly taller than Rafe in his human form, and his hair was black as Aurora's. He looked mature, but it was hard to tell his age since there wasn't a speck of gray in his hair. Signs of years gone by and exposure to the elements creased his handsome face. This must be my grandfather.

"Zeke, say hello to Chalice," my grandmother said.

"Hi, sweetheart," he said to me, a grin tweaking the corners of his mouth. It made me feel like a little girl again. As happy as I was to finally meet my grandmother, my heart swelled at seeing my grandfather. I knew the sacrifice he'd made. He'd been an angel before deciding to become human just so he could marry the woman he loved and be a father to his child. His courage and commitment took my breath away.

"Honey, are you all right?" My grandmother placed a hand gently on my shoulder.

I blinked and sniffed, then rubbed my nose. "I'm fine. Just cold. Can I get a tissue, please?"

Eyes wide, she said, "Of course! Grab that angel of yours and let's get you two inside to warm up."

Rafe drew to my side and I jumped ahead before he could touch me. I wanted nothing to do with him right now.

"Welcome to Halo Home," Zeke said.

I stood at the entrance and stared, wide-eyed, at the vast interior of the first floor. The foyer opened out into the living room, which opened to the dining room, which opened to the kitchen. One great room with a giant round fireplace in its center. This house was way too large for only two people.

Aurora nodded. "I know what you're thinking. Yes, it's too big for Zeke and me, which is why we have other Hatchet knights live here with us. This house has become something of a sanctuary over the years, mostly for new knights in training."

I nodded, though I was puzzled by something Aydin once told me. "I thought it was too dangerous for the knights to live together. Made them vulnerable."

Rafe studied my face. "Turns out it was more dangerous for them not to."

My grandmother lifted both eyebrows in agreement. "It's true that keeping the knights together can make them a target for black veil crackpots." She shook her head. "Young knights come to us as orphans from time to time and we care for them until they're ready to go out on their own. It's a sad but necessary part of being a Hatchet knight. We're prone to losing the people we're close to."

I'd been an orphan too, except I'd had no one to help me but a monastery of monks in Lebanon before I was kidnapped by the leader of the Vyantara.

She tipped her head to one side and said, "Follow me to the kitchen, Chalice. You can help me finish making cookies." She frowned at the two men and made a shooing motion with her hands. "I'm sure these two can find something to do with themselves."

Zeke rolled his eyes. "Sure, steal our grandchild so you can have her all to yourself. When is it *my* turn?"

"When I say so." She marched toward the other end of the house and I followed.

"I'm sorry to tell you this," I told Aurora as I watched

her tug cookie sheets from a lower cupboard, "but I can't cook."

She winked at me. "There's nothing to it, honey. Have you ever mixed a spell?"

I thought about the summoning ritual I'd performed to bring my fallen angel father across. "Sort of."

She set the pans on the counter and placed a large mixing bowl filled with dough beside them. "A pinch of this, a dash of that, stir it all together and presto. You're a cook."

It couldn't be that easy.

She handed me a spoon. "Scoop up a teaspoon of batter and plop it on the cookie sheet. Keep doing that until the bowl is empty."

I stuck my finger in the batter for a taste. Peanut butter. Yummy.

Aurora smacked my hand. "None of that now. You're as bad as your mother was."

Wiping my hand on a towel, I asked, "What was she like?"

"Your mother? Headstrong, fearless, determined. A lot like you, I suspect." She dumped two cups of flour into a large mixing bow. "Felicia was an amazing woman. I wish you'd had a chance to know her."

"Me, too." But all I had was one photo. Aydin had rescued it from a fire and saved it for me. It was a precious gift I'd cherish forever.

"You're very lucky, you know," Aurora said as she cracked an egg on the side of the bowl. "I don't know of anyone who's ever survived the gargoyle's curse with their humanity intact."

"I'm guessing you know the whole story about what happened to me?"

"In great detail."

Of course she knew. She must have her finger on the pulse of the entire Hatchet order no matter how scattered they were. I guessed that Rafe kept her well informed about everything having to do with me. Everything he knew, anyway.

"I also know about the newly made gargoyle who used to be your friend."

"Aydin is still my friend." The flutter in my belly reminded me how my feelings ran deeper than mere friendship. "He may look different on the outside, but he's the same man on the inside."

My grandmother made a huffing noise. "Don't be so sure."

Her too? I plopped a glob of dough onto the pan. "You sound like Rafe."

She looked at me and arched both her eyebrows. "Oh yes, you gave Raphael a nickname." She chuckled. "Rafe. It suits him."

I dug the spoon into the bowl. "I don't get how he can be so judgy," I said, then clamped my mouth shut before I could accuse her of being the same. We were just getting to know each other and I wanted her to like me. "I thought angels were supposed to be open-minded."

"He worries about you, Chalice."

I frowned, unused to anyone worrying about me unless they had an ulterior motive. It made me wonder if Rafe had one, too. "He's a bit late, don't you think?"

"Don't be so hard on him. Your enslavement by the

Vyantara wasn't his fault." Her voice sounded soft, but I heard the steel underneath.

"I've been on my own for a long time, Aurora. I know what's best for me."

She shrugged. "Maybe you do, but you have us now. Isn't it time to let those who care about you into your life?"

I looked at her. "I've done that. Aydin cares about me. He saved my life."

Aurora's chest heaved with a sigh. "Okay, I'll give you that. We would have lost you if not for him."

Nodding, I said, "Exactly my point. Aydin's a good man."

"But he's not a man anymore. And that's *my* point."

"Rafe isn't a man, either."

"Touché." She scooped a glob of peanut butter out of a jar and dropped it in the bowl she was stirring. "But he could be. It's what he wants."

I blinked. "The only way that can happen is if…"

My grandmother gave me a hard look. "Your grandfather and I have been happy together for over fifty years. He was a wonderful guardian angel, and he's an equally wonderful man."

My skin heated at the thought of Rafe and I doing the wild thing. I didn't think of him that way and it wouldn't be right. It was hard enough being friends with the guy. He was more like an overprotective big brother than anything else.

I rapidly dropped more dollops of dough onto the pan. "He and I don't really know each other."

"That will change with time."

"He's not my type."

"You two are more alike than you think."

This conversation was making me more uncomfortable by the second. "Don't get your hopes up. I have other plans."

She folded her arms across her chest and waited for me to go on.

"Aydin won't be a gargoyle much longer."

Her expression softened when she said, "Honey, I know it's hard to accept, but once humans have transformed—"

"They can become human again by eating the heart of their bonded gargoyle."

Her eyes squinted in thought. "That old myth? Chalice, you'd have to kill a gargoyle to take its heart. The creature would turn to stone so fast you'd never get hold of it in time."

I glanced behind and around me to make sure we were alone. I peeled back the shield on my senses and heard murmurs from both men in the other room as well as three distinct heartbeats somewhere else in the house. I knew my grandparents had other knights living with them and the three I sensed were far enough away they couldn't see us.

I reached inside my inner jacket pocket and touched the warm chunk of polished stone that was Shojin's heart. It seemed to pulse in my hand, though I knew my imagination got the best of me. The heart was just as dead as the gargoyle it came from.

Treating it like a fragile piece of glass, I held it out for my grandmother to see.

She looked puzzled before recognition brightened her eyes. "Oh, my."

I smiled, feeling warm affection for the gentle monster the heart had come from. "This is the heart of Aydin's gargoyle. All he has to do is eat it and he'll become human again."

"But how...?" She swallowed. "I don't understand. It should have shattered along with the beast when it turned to stone."

I slipped the heart back into my pocket. "I know, but there's a reason that didn't happen. It's a long story."

The mixing bowl I held grew suddenly warm. Glancing down at the lumps of dough on the pan, I saw steam begin to rise as if the cookies were baking. What the hell? The edges were turning brown and they weren't even in the oven.

The wooden spoon in my hand exploded in flame.

"Oops," said a quiet voice from the doorway.

I threw the spoon onto the stone-tile floor and stomped on it to put out the flames.

"Rusty! What have I told you about using cloaking spells in the house?" My grandmother soaked a towel under the faucet and tossed it over the smoldering spoon. "I hate it when you sneak up on me like that."

Sneaking? I was more concerned about the fire. Even so, the very idea of a cloaking spell that could evade my senses had me worried.

Aurora crouched down and mopped up the mess of burned wood and ashes. "Honestly, Rusty. What were you thinking?"

"It was a joke," said the young woman who stood

leaning against the counter. "I didn't mean for anything to catch on fire." Her hair was the color of flame, long and wavy, and she appeared close to me in age. Maybe a year or two older and about five inches taller. Forest-green eyes reflected an odd combination of confidence and uncertainty. Her gaze flicked over me, then back to Aurora. "I thought it would be a fun way to introduce myself." Her mouth tilted in a smug smile.

My grandmother shook her head and tossed the ruined towel in the sink. "Chalice, this is Rusty, one of the Hatchet knights staying with us."

My heart fluttered. A sister knight, and she stood right in front of me. This was a moment I'd been longing for, but I somehow didn't feel all that pleased to meet her. Rusty's choice of introduction left a bad taste in my mouth, not to mention burned fingers.

"Hello, Rusty." I blew on my hand. "I'd shake your hand if it wasn't for the blisters."

Aurora grabbed my arm to haul me to the sink. She flipped the knob on the faucet and cold water flowed over scorched flesh that was already starting to heal.

"Honestly," my grandmother mumbled. "Rusty can be such a show-off."

"Sorry, Chalice." Sincere regret shone in Rusty's eyes and my irritation waned. She was my sister. I couldn't stay mad at her forever.

I grinned. "No worries. It's already healing. See?" I waved my pink fingers at her.

"No wonder I have so many gray hairs," Aurora said as she tossed me a fresh dish towel to dry my hands.

Another young woman, her small stature and dark

complexion in sharp contrast to Rusty, joined us in the kitchen. She was about my height and had an ethnic cast to her features; her shoulder-length hair was stick-straight and shiny as black glass.

"Hey, Natalie," my grandmother said. "This is Chalice."

"Hello," I said, happy to meet another sister.

She waved a small hand. "Hi."

An awkward silence followed.

"You've witnessed Rusty's ability firsthand," my grandmother said as she tossed a glare at my red-haired sister. "Natalie has a unique talent for finding things."

I was pretty good at finding things, too. I wondered if she shared my freakish anomaly of heightened senses. "That's a handy skill to have."

"I'm a psychometrist," Natalie said.

Oh, yes. I'd met a few psychometrists in my previous line of work. They were clairvoyants with a unique ability to read psychic impressions that people left on objects. There were some who could even recite the history of things that were hundreds of years old. The Vyantara had often used psychometrists for authenticating the cursed and charmed objects I stole for them.

When the phone rang, everyone jumped. I imagined recent bad news to be the cause, though its delivery would have come via angel and not fiber optics. It was obvious that the nerves around here were strung as tight as a hangman's rope.

Rusty snatched the wireless phone from its cradle on the wall. Her expression tense, she nodded and murmured something in the receiver before hanging it up.

"A fire broke out in a farmhouse outside of town." She glanced at each of us, her expression grave. "The snow slowed it down, but flames are playing leapfrog in the treetops and spreading fast."

Aurora put her hand to her chest. "Dear Lord. Was that the fire chief?"

Rusty nodded. "The fire's almost out of control so he's calling all volunteer firefighters."

A firestarter who fights fires? That's a switch. "Is there anything I can do?" I asked before thinking. Fire scared the crap out of me.

"No, Chalice, but thanks anyway." She flashed a smile faster than I could blink. "Natalie, will you drive?"

Natalie nodded.

Rusty trotted to a closed door near the front of the house and yanked it open. Coats and jackets dangled from hangers and she pulled one free.

Aurora had followed her and I was right behind. "I think you should take Chalice with you," my grandmother said.

Rusty blinked in surprise. "There's nothing she can do."

"Yes, there is." Aurora looked at me, her face tight with concern. "We have a room stacked with boxes that contain the curses and charms Quin Dee brought to us."

Quin. I'd never forget the angel whisperer who got killed because of me, though the angels had made sure he didn't stay dead for long. My heart tripped over itself at the memory of his sudden and welcomed resurrection.

"The knights need protection at all costs," my grandmother added in a voice edged with panic. "We can't lose any more. Chalice, will you help them?"

"I'll do what I can," I said, my brain whirring as I tried to remember what all had been in that stash of hexed objects. It was Aydin's pilfered treasure that he had entrusted to Quin. He'd wanted to make sure my sisters would have them someday. My job would be teaching them how to use each one. "I'll grab a charm or two that could be useful."

Rusty huffed out a breath. "We don't have time for this. The chief said the fire is reaching a critical point."

"I'll hurry." I followed my grandmother to a room in the back of the house.

It was all here. Every old rusted trunk, rotted wooden crate, ancient cardboard box, barrel and jar. I felt their power the moment I crossed the threshold into the storage room, but I was immune to their effects. Having endured the gargoyle's curse, I could handle these objects with impunity, as could Aydin. My sister knights could not.

I scanned the stash, remembering what most everything was, and reached for a weathered old ox horn. It had special properties that would be useful in a fire.

I ran outside, where Natalie and Rusty were already sitting inside a battered old red Jeep.

Rafe marched toward me. "Where do you think you're going?"

I scowled. "Since when do I have to check in with you?"

"Since the day I became your guardian."

Which was little over a month ago and I still wasn't used to the idea. "Is that part of the deal?"

"More or less."

I shrugged. "Well, I'm going with my sisters. You do whatever you want."

He raised an eyebrow, looking superior and irritating the crap out of me. "Aren't you forgetting something?"

"Chalice!" Rusty stuck her head out the open window. "Are you coming? Or would you rather wait for the entire town to burn down first?"

I lurched toward the Jeep and Rafe grabbed my arm. He dipped his chin. "You don't want something to accidentally slip from your pocket, do you?"

I blinked. Shit. I still had Shojin's heart. When I started to hand it to Rafe, he backed away. "I can't touch it."

Damn.

"Give me one more sec," I shouted at Rusty, then ran around to the back of the house. A large ponderosa tree stood sentry there, a ring of melting snow at its base. I grabbed a stick to dig in the slightly frozen ground, creating a hole just big enough to conceal the heart. I buried it, then packed a few handfuls of snow on top. That would have to do for now. I'd find a better hiding place when I got back.

five

IT TOOK LESS THAN TEN MINUTES FOR US to reach the burned-out farmhouse at the edge of town. Flames flared orange in the distance, black smoke billowing up to blend with a gloomy sky. The house was just a smoldering mess of charred wood, exposed brick and chunks of blackened plumbing.

Natalie grabbed a toy truck from the ground and clutched it to her chest. "He's still alive."

"What?" I shot a look at Rusty, who appeared equally surprised. "Who are you talking about?"

Natalie swallowed. "The child no one knew was home when the fire started."

Oh, my God. "Where are the parents?" I wondered out loud.

Natalie shook her head. "Not here, that much I know. But the boy is close. I can sense him."

Rusty gave me a disapproving look. "If the boy inhaled too much smoke he may not be alive for much longer."

"Don't you have a fire to put out?" I asked, though I was more annoyed with myself than with Rusty. I shouldn't have taken so much time to hide Shojin's heart. Handing Rusty the ox horn, I told her, "Take this with you."

She pushed it away. "I'm fine on my own. I don't need help from a hex that once belonged to the Vyantara."

I understood how she felt, but seriously? This from someone who whipped up a cloaking spell like a quick cup of coffee? "It can help you. Breathe through it if the smoke gets too thick. It acts as a kind of oxygen mask."

"Thanks, but no thanks." She turned and sprinted toward a line of flames less than a mile away. "I'll send help back for the boy," she shouted over her shoulder.

"I hope she's as good at fighting fires as she is at being stubborn," I said to Natalie.

"She is," Natalie told me. "Though I wish she'd accepted your offer." Her dark eyes shone with concern. "The knights are not invincible. We could use the help."

Help against an unknown, and unnatural, enemy. The kind of help that only something equally unnatural could provide.

I wanted to ask her about the others, what she knew about them and their powers. I wanted details about the knights who had survived. And though it was peaceful here in the deserted yard of a burned-out farmhouse, a clock was ticking. An injured child, possibly a dying one, needed someone to find him.

I watched, breathless, as Natalie's skin paled enough to

rival the whiteness of snow beneath our feet. Her fingers worked over the metal toy, its bright yellow body dented, scratched and rusting on the edges. She gripped the thing as if clinging to life, which its owner might have been doing himself right then. Her knuckles turned bone-white and a drop of blood trickled down the side of her hand that had been cut on the old metal truck.

I knew better than to interrupt a psychometrist's connection to a subject. She was linked to this child and disturbing her now could break the tie, or worse. I'd witnessed a psychic lose his sanity when someone hastily tore him away from the object he clutched. His mind was still attached to his subject and he never recovered. I wasn't about to take that chance with Natalie. A cut hand was nothing compared to a lost mind.

A tear slipped free from Natalie's glazed eyes. "He's hiding."

I'd guessed that already but kept my mouth shut. She was thinking out loud, expressing her vision.

"He's cold," she said, and freed one hand from the toy to hug herself. "And scared."

"Where is he?"

She swiveled to directly face the farmhouse and pointed. "There."

Impossible. The house had burned to the ground. Nothing could have survived that.

"Can you show me?" I asked her.

She shook her head. "That's what I see. The house. And a darkness so black it's as if he's blind."

"Is he?"

"No."

Which meant some part of the house had been protected from the fire. "I'll go look."

"Be careful," Natalie said.

No one needed to tell me that, but I still promised, "I will be."

Seeing the charred remains of furniture and other household stuff tossed here and there reminded me of the Vyantara fatherhouse that had blown up soon after I'd summoned my fallen angel father. But there were no scattered charms and curses here, and thankfully no ghosts, either. Just ruined pieces of a family that had probably lived here for generations.

As I weaved through the smoldering ruins, I visualized the dissolving of walls that guarded my senses. The first sound I heard was a sobbing child. The boy had breath enough to cry and that lightened my heart with relief.

I squinted through the lingering smoke. No auras were visible, and therefore nothing alive that I could see. The boy's crying sounded weak, but I could still feel it through the soles of my boots. He was below ground. I sniffed the air and, although it was heavily scented with the smell of burned wood and plastic, a subtle aroma of soap and shampoo wafted through. The bathrooms above ground had been destroyed, which meant the scent came from the boy.

"What's his name?" I called to Natalie, who stood at a safe distance.

"Timmy."

"Timmy?" I called out. "Can you hear me?"

I heard coughing, then a murmured reply I couldn't make out. He began sobbing quietly again.

"Can you knock on something for me?" I asked, following the trail of muted sound to what must have been the kitchen. A blackened refrigerator lay on its side. "Knock on the wall or the floor. Anything."

No answer.

And no more crying.

I hoped we weren't too late. Where was the boy's family? Why was he left here alone?

My vision could penetrate thin surfaces like paint and paper, even some fabrics. But the solid objects around me were too dense. However, I did manage to see through the black ashes covering the floor and noticed the outline of a door. A cellar door. And the charred refrigerator lay directly on top of it.

I crouched down to try pushing it off, but it was way too heavy for me. Timmy was down there; I could hear him breathing, but only barely.

"Natalie, I found him!" I called out. "He's in the basement, but I can't get to him. There's a refrigerator blocking the door."

"Help should have been here by now!" she yelled back, and I heard the Jeep's door slam shut. "Hang tight, I'll take care of it." The engine started, followed by the sound of tires crunching over snow.

I kept pushing at the fridge, but it hardly budged. Whatever had been inside leaked out onto the blackened linoleum in a dark putrid mess. I closed my eyes to concentrate. Timmy was still breathing.

Then I heard something new. Wings flapped loudly above me and I glanced up at the sky, seeing nothing. Yet a sudden wind swept my hair back and flung ash and charred bits of wood in my face. Still crouched low to the ground, I covered my head with my arms.

I smelled damp fur and animal musk, but also a natural spicy scent I remembered from when he was human. Aydin had found me. Or maybe he'd been following me from the start. Either way, it was a relief to have him here even if I couldn't see him.

His gargoyle form suddenly appeared above me and his talons pierced the appliance like it was made from tin foil. The fridge crumpled when he lifted it off the floor. I watched as it flew a dozen feet to the side, then bounced a couple times before coming to a stop. The cellar door was free. And Aydin was already gone.

Sirens screamed in the distance, meaning help had arrived. I opened the cellar door and a plume of gray smoke puffed out the opening. The dimly lit outline of a child lay at the foot of the stairs. I scuttled down the steps and scooped up the boy, who couldn't have weighed more than forty pounds. His dark hair was powdered with ash, and soot smeared his nose and cheeks. He still breathed, but barely.

I ran up the steps and out of the burned rubble toward the ambulance. "Help!" I called to the two men who hopped out the back. "This boy was in the cellar when the house burned."

They took him from me and got to work. I heard the boy cough and a wave of relief washed over me.

Catching my breath, I scouted the area for Natalie. I saw that a thick wall of smoke had replaced the flames so I hoped that meant the fire was out.

Gasps of heavy weeping came from the back of the

ambulance and I wondered if it held another victim of the fire. I went to see if there was anything I could do to help.

Natalie sat crouched inside, head lowered over a prone figure covered head to toe with a white sheet.

"Natalie?" I climbed up to sit beside her. "What's going on?"

Head still down, she snuffled before saying, "It's Rusty. She's dead."

"What?" I couldn't believe it. An immense sadness welled up inside me, but my fury battered it down. My sister knights were dying and I was helpless to stop it.

Hands shaking, I gently lowered the sheet to find Rusty's pretty, pale face underneath. "How did it happen?"

"Don't know," Natalie said. "I arrived at the front line. Found her by a wall of fire. She was backing it off. Using her will to put it out. Then…" She gulped air before going on. "Then she collapsed."

"Did anyone try to revive her?" I touched my fingers to Rusty's throat. No pulse, but her skin was still warm. I thought about the boy. "She must have suffocated from inhaling too much smoke."

Natalie shook her head. "Smoke has never been a problem for her."

It obviously was now. I lowered my ear to Rusty's face and listened. Not even the slightest breath.

"The EMTs did try to revive her." Natalie wiped her nose on the sleeve of her coat. "But she wouldn't come around."

So that's what had taken so long for them to get here. I

glanced outside the ambulance to see both EMTs caring for the boy, who cried and coughed but appeared to be okay. I didn't want them seeing what I was about to do.

"I'm going to try something." I reached into my coat pocket and tugged out the ox horn charm. "I don't know the extent of its power, but I have to give it a shot."

The ugly black horn, no bigger than the width of my hand, was chipped and blackened with age. I'd never seen one used, but I knew it to be an object of magic the Vikings kept with them as part of their battle armor. It enabled them to breathe through smoke as they pillaged the villages they burned.

I didn't know much about this charm and was hesitant to place the horn between Rusty's blue lips. There was always a price to pay for using dark magic. If it gave her breath back, what would it demand in return?

"Chalice?" Natalie gulped a breath between sobs. "What are you doing?"

"What Rusty should have done when she had the chance." I slipped the horn's tip into Rusty's mouth.

I waited a full minute. Nothing happened.

I started to withdraw the horn when a wisp of smoke trailed out the charm's cone-shaped end.

"I think it's working," I whispered.

Rusty's chest began rising slowly, as if being pumped with air. Now I was afraid she'd burst from a breath too big for her lungs. Instead, color pinked her cheeks and her eyelids squeezed so tight it looked like she was in pain, and I hoped she was. That would mean she was alive.

Rusty coughed and the ox horn flew from her mouth

and landed in the snow outside. She sat up, gasping, clutching her chest and heaving in gulps of air.

Natalie lunged at her and wrapped her in a hug so tight I thought she'd squeeze the breath out of her again. They cried in each other's arms. As much as I wanted to join in, I hung back and tried not to feel left out. I was a knight too, and that knowledge would have to be enough for now.

"You scared me to death," Natalie told her.

Rusty looked confused for a second, then shot me a glance. "Was I dead?"

"Pretty much, yeah," I said.

She touched her lips. "Was that thing in my mouth? That cursed horn?"

I pulled back my shoulders and straightened my spine. "Yes. It gave you back your life."

"If not for Chalice you'd still be dead," Natalie said. "She saved you."

Rusty frowned, not appearing one bit thankful. Then her frown deepened. "Something took my breath away."

Natalie nodded. "The smoke. You suffocated."

Shaking her head, Rusty said, "No, smoke has no effect on me. It was something else."

"Like what?" I asked.

"It felt so…strange." She still clutched her chest, her eyes growing distant as if trying to remember. "Like being inside a vacuum. There was no smoke, no air, no nothing. As if something sucked my breath right out of me."

Natalie and I exchanged looks. She said, "That's impossible, Rusty. It's only happened to knights that are asleep."

"Maybe whatever it was is now desperate enough to prey on us when we're awake," I said. "Rusty, what was the last thing you saw before passing out?"

"Fire."

"You didn't see anyone near you?" I asked.

"Of course there were people near me." Rusty bit off each word. "We were fighting a fire. Four fighters stood beside me, each wearing a protective suit and mask."

"So you couldn't see their faces," Natalie said.

"No, I couldn't."

"I bet one of them did it," I said. "The Hatchet murderer disguised himself to get close to you."

"Hatchet murderer?" Rusty chuckled. "You make it sound like a villain from a bad horror movie."

I glared at her. "I wasn't trying to be funny."

"Don't worry, you weren't," Rusty said, but the corners of her mouth pulled up in a smile. "Thanks for saving my life even if you did use that…thing."

I looked down at the snow where the horn had fallen. It lay there looking dull and ordinary, its power spent. I vaguely wondered if it could be recharged and if so, who could recharge it. Cursed or not, it was a handy gadget to have around, especially for a fire master like Rusty. I hopped down from the ambulance and snatched it up to shove into my coat pocket.

I gazed out at the sky, wondering if Aydin still watched. He was more of a guardian angel than Rafe, who spent too much time being stubborn about accepting Aydin for the good man he was. He wouldn't stop criticizing him for becoming a gargoyle, which wasn't even his fault. Come to think of it, none of our guardian angels had come to the rescue.

"I'm new at all this knight stuff," I told my sisters. "Can I ask you both a question?"

They had guarded looks on their faces, their eyes shifting attention from me to each other and back again. "Sure," Rusty said. "Shoot."

"Where was your guardian angel when you were suffocating to death?" I asked.

The corner of Rusty's mouth slid up in a smug grin. "That's not how it works. It's not like they're on autopilot."

Granted, I still had a lot to learn, but I was confused. "Guardians don't guard?"

"They're more like guides," Natalie said. "Once we're old enough to be knights, our guardians shift roles from protector to partner. They come to our aid only when summoned."

Okay, I could buy that, but I had to admit the partner thing made me squeamish. I was about to say so when the two EMTs came back to the ambulance with the boy on a backboard. They stood statute-still and stared at Rusty, their mouths gaping like howler monkeys.

"Oh!" Rusty scrambled to her feet and wobbled, but Natalie caught her before she could fall. "The boy! Is he okay?"

"Chalice saved him, too." Natalie sounded like a proud sister. It gave me a warm feeling.

Rusty blinked. "Cool," she said as Natalie helped her down from the ambulance.

The EMTs were sputtering something about Rusty being dead, her heart having stopped, blah-blah-blah. I'd been around the supernatural long enough to know death wasn't always a permanent condition, but these guys had no clue.

I infused my voice with amazement when I told them, "It was so strange. Rusty suddenly sat straight up. We about jumped right out of our skins, didn't we, Natalie?"

Natalie trilled a nervous giggle that sounded about as real as a sitcom laugh track. She patted her chest. "Oh, yes. Quite a shock."

The men shook their heads and went on with their work, securing the boy to a gurney. One of them said, "Miss, you need to come with us to the hospital and get checked out. You could be more injured than you think."

"I'm fine," Rusty said, waving them off like flies. "You have a more important patient to worry about."

I tilted my head toward the boy. "Does anyone know where his parents are?"

The EMT who'd expressed concern about Rusty said, "They've been notified. The boy was supposed to be in school, but he snuck out to go home." He frowned at Timmy, who looked no older than six or seven. "We suspect he started the fire."

Someone was in big trouble. "I'm just happy he's okay."

"So are his parents. Thanks for your help." The EMT nodded at me before slipping into the seat behind the wheel. His partner stayed in back and closed the ambulance doors.

We watched them drive off, siren blaring.

Rusty gave my shoulder a friendly yet firm slap. "Welcome to Halo Home."

six

"YOU WERE DEAD?" MY GRANDMOTHER asked, her turquoise eyes intent on Rusty.

Rusty nodded. "Suffocated. And not from inhaling smoke."

"She had the breath sucked out of her," Natalie said. "Sound familiar?"

Aurora's face went pale. "That does it. No one leaves this house until the murderer is found and dealt with. Is that understood?"

"The Hatchet murderer." Rusty waggled her fingers and made a ghostly wailing sound.

My grandmother closed her eyes as if praying for patience. "There's nothing funny about this. Over forty knights have been picked off like flies, leaving only a half dozen left. That's counting the four of us."

Rusty bent her head and mumbled, "Sorry."

"I think Rusty is still suffering from shock. Death will do that to a person." I felt my grandmother looking at me and sensed she didn't appreciate a smart-ass.

Aurora sighed. "Okay, I get it. A little levity in a crisis can be cathartic, but please, let's not forget the knights we have lost."

Damn. Now I felt guilty. I was trying hard not to feel anything at all and being a smart-ass usually worked for that.

Rafe and my grandfather stood by the fireplace in stony silence. They hadn't involved themselves in our discussion, which was probably just as well. I'm sure they grieved in their own way.

"Am I interrupting?" asked a young but strong voice from the foot of the stairs. A teenage girl stood with her arms crossed, her jeans torn in a way that should be fashionable, but I didn't think hers were like that on purpose. Her razor-cut white hair that was too pale to be bleached hung over half her face and the dark liner around her eyes made her look ghoulish. She tugged at her woolen cap as if trying to hide her eyes. Wise choice. She had so much eyeliner on that I couldn't tell what part of her face was real and what was painted.

"Xenia, come in," my grandmother said, making a scooping gesture with her hand. "I want you to meet my granddaughter."

Oh, another knight. Great, but I wondered why she hadn't come with Natalie and Rusty to the kitchen this morning. Had she slept in?

Xenia avoided my eyes, and she didn't venture any

farther into the room. If I thought I was out of place, this one acted like she was in a whole other world.

Aurora smiled. "Xenia is a new recruit for the knighthood," she explained. "She came to us last week."

"A normie," Rusty said under her breath.

"A what?" I asked.

"Normie," Natalie repeated. "Means her father wasn't an angel. She just talks to them."

Exactly like Quin Dee, who was an angel whisperer like his father had been, and his father's father, and so on down the line. Saint Geraldine had been an angel whisperer, too.

"Where do the Arelim find these...normies?" I asked.

"Angel whisperers have a telepathic link with the Arelim," my grandmother said. "The ones selected to train as knights have been screened based on their willingness to devote their entire lives to serving our order.

"Now that we have to practically start the order over from scratch, more young women like Xenia will be joining us." Aurora gave each of us a long look before adding, "And I'll be depending on you three to train them."

I was almost as new as Xenia and still had a lot to learn myself, but I'd do my part. "What kind of powers will the new recruits have?"

"None," Aurora said. "Their only gift is an ability to communicate with all Arelim, not just their guardians. Plus they will only die if the Arelim allow it."

"Normies are immortal?" I asked, stunned by this news.

"Sucks, doesn't it?" Rusty said. "I mean for us. Not for them."

"This only applies to those whisperers who become Hatchet knights. Possible immortality compensates for their lack of supernatural powers," my grandmother explained. "It's their only protection from the evil they will vow to fight."

Of course. Quin had sacrificed himself to the enemy, and the Arelim had given him his life back. It made sense that these new knights would be granted the same gift.

Xenia rolled her eyes. She obviously didn't appreciate her immortal status, or she didn't believe it. If I were her, I'm not sure I'd believe it, either. Pretty far-fetched if you asked me.

"Does this mean they're protected from whatever is killing the knights?" I asked.

"We don't know," my grandfather said. These were the first words I'd heard out of him since this morning. "The angel whisperers, or normies as you girls like to call them, don't have to succumb to natural causes of death. At least not permanently. We're not so sure about the unnatural kind."

"And I suppose guinea pigs for testing this theory are in short supply," Rusty said.

"Let's just say we're not taking any chances," Zeke told her.

Wow, what a day. Too much too fast, and I was starting to fade. I stifled a yawn.

My grandmother cleared her throat. "Chalice, you'll be sharing a room with Xenia."

Xenia rolled her eyes again. If she kept doing that they'd get stuck staring at the back of her own head. The girl jerked her chin in the direction of the stairs before heading that way herself.

"Hold on, Xenia. I need to give Chalice something first." Aurora tugged at a loop of thin chain she wore around her neck and pulled a shiny object out from beneath her sweater. She dragged it up and over her head, then held it out to me. "This belongs to you now."

I glanced at Rafe, who stood still as a mannequin beside the fireplace. He nodded and tilted his head toward my grandmother.

I stepped closer to see what she offered. About the size of my palm, it looked like a talisman in the shape of a shield. An embossed crest was divided in half, with one side the scarlet cross of the Crusades, and the other a silver angel wing. The sight of it brought a lump to my throat. I'd never seen it before, but I knew exactly what it was.

"My mother's shield," I whispered.

Aurora nodded. "I gave this shield to your mother on the day she was old enough for knighthood, just as my mother had given it to me, and her mother to her." She lowered the chain with the shield over my head. "It symbolizes dozens of generations from our bloodline, all the way back to the first Hatchet knights who fought in the Crusades."

Which meant my ancestor was a knight who had fought beside Saint Geraldine. A chill skittered down my spine and made my ears ring. My chest felt tight with so much emotion I was afraid I'd crumble, but it wouldn't do for me to show weakness in front of a recruit who already had doubts.

I inspected the old shield and found deep cracks in the metal and evidence of rust or blood beneath a surface of thick, clear lacquer. "Is this the original?" I asked.

My grandmother tilted her head to one side. "Part of it. The original shield was used in battle, where it was nearly destroyed. After the war ended it was broken down and reshaped into what you hold in your hands."

"Wow." It felt heavy and I couldn't imagine wearing this around my neck 24/7.

"It's a symbol now, Chalice." She smoothed the hair from my forehead, then cupped my face in both her hands to stare into my eyes. "This shield of knighthood is yours to keep. It's who you are and who you'll always be."

I inhaled a shaky breath and pressed the shield to my chest. "I'll take good care of it."

She lightly patted my cheek. "I know you will. Now scoot. You must be exhausted and you have a big day tomorrow."

"I do?"

"A half-dozen squires are expected here before noon."

Squires were knights in training. Oh, my God. So soon? I wasn't ready.

"You're ready," Rafe said, as if he'd heard my thoughts.

I shot him a look and narrowed my eyes. Such a know-it-all. He gave me a crooked grin.

Dazed from my surreal day, I robotically followed Xenia up the stairs to our room. A bed never looked so good. My bag of meager belongings sat on the floor beside it.

I think Xenia was talking to me when I trudged bonelessly to the edge of the bed. She could have been speaking Mandarin Chinese for all I knew. My brain was fried and sleep called to me like a siren's song. I did a face-plant on the mattress, missing the pillow completely, and fell instantly asleep.

I awakened slowly and thought my bladder was about to burst.

Opening my eyes to a deep darkness that only a moonless night could provide, it took me a few seconds to place my surroundings. My night vision kicked in and a bedroom came into focus.

I padded my way down the hall, following the scent of shampoo and soap. By the time I returned to my bed I was no longer sleepy. My brain had already started buzzing with all that had happened the day before and what I'd have going on today. It was exciting and daunting at the same time.

I wandered to the window and glanced outside at a bluish haze, which was how my eyes perceived night. It looked as I expected until my gaze landed on the snow around the giant ponderosa in the yard. The tree glowed with life, which I also expected, but the area where I'd buried Shojin's heart glowed, too. So brightly, in fact, that it could easily be seen by anyone without my superior eyesight.

"Oh no," I murmured. I'd meant to hide the heart, not make it a beacon. If I brought it inside the house, it would glow no matter where I put it. I'd just have to bury it deeper. Then I could cover it with iron to guarantee no one would find it. Iron blocked all magic as well as extrasensory perception.

Since I hadn't bothered to undress before falling into bed, I didn't have to worry about waking my roommate by rummaging through my bag looking for clothes. I glanced over at the twin-size bed on the other side of the room to see Xenia still as death beneath a hill of blankets. I fought the urge to shake her and make sure she was alive. The Hatchet murderer had made me paranoid.

I grabbed my jacket from the floor and scurried down the stairs to the kitchen. It didn't take long for me to find the iron skillet I was looking for. It took a bit longer to find a shovel, which was stashed with a couple of terra-cotta pots and an empty half-barrel planter under the deck outside.

The snow over the buried heart had softened and would probably have been completely melted in a few hours. I scooped away the slush and dug the shovel into the mud underneath. The hole I had made for the heart was even shallower than I thought. Though the stone was probably harder than most rocks, I handled it gently, taking care not to crack or chip its glowing surface. It had to be perfect for Aydin.

I shrugged off my jacket, which had made me too warm anyway, and wrapped it around the heart before getting back to work. The ground became harder the deeper I dug, the frozen mixture of clay and soil solid as a brick. But I hammered at it, swearing under my breath, until I finally pulled away fist-size chunks. Once I got about two feet down, I kneeled to place the heart back in the hole, covered it with the iron skillet, then mounded clods of frozen dirt on top. A generous frosting of snow completed the job. A perfect deep-dish mud pie. And here I thought I couldn't cook.

I stood to survey my work. No more glow. Mission accomplished.

Shaking the bits of snow and dirt from my jacket, I slipped it on over my sweaty shirt and zipped it closed. My boots were covered in mud, the knees of my jeans caked with the stuff, and my face was undoubtedly smudged with evidence of my secret. I'd have to shower and change before anyone saw me and started asking questions. Aurora and Rafe were the only ones beside Aydin who knew about the heart.

No sooner did his name pass through my mind than I caught a faint whiff of damp fur and sandalwood. A bare whisper of Aydin's scent trailed on a chilly breeze, and then it was gone. I'd only imagined it. I couldn't get him out of my mind.

I vaguely wondered what time it was and let my gaze sweep the horizon in search of dawn's faint light. Instead I found the ghostly outline of a figure just beyond the perimeter of Halo Home's warded boundaries. Opening and closing his wings, the hulking form paced slowly back and forth across the road.

I could see that Aydin waited for me. The compulsion to run to him grew like a cresting wave that had nowhere to go but forward. My grandmother had forbidden us to leave the property, but she'd surely make an exception this time. Aydin would protect me. He always had.

I ran through the drifted snow, my boots breaking through a crust of ice that had formed overnight. When

I reached the perimeter of wards, I stopped. Aydin would be invisible to someone with normal vision, but I could see the particles of his life force. His ghostly gargoyle form turned to face me. I breached the wards and walked his way.

He wasn't solid in this state, and I knew he couldn't materialize without the risk of being detected. If I could just get close enough to sense his essence, I could imagine him as he once was and get lost in the fantasy of us being together again. We'd never had a chance to get as close as we had wanted, but it didn't have to stay that way. We could have a future now, but only if he did the one thing that would make him human.

Aydin came to me. His gait was brisk and I realized then that he had no plan of stopping. That's what had happened inside Geraldine's tomb when Aydin's ghostly body had merged with mine, his thoughts blending with my own before putting me to sleep. He'd had to do it to prevent me from accidentally spilling the secrets Geraldine had told us to our Vyantara master. I doubted sleep was Aydin's intention this time and so I welcomed the merge. I needed to feel him close and having him inside my mind was more than okay with me.

I closed my eyes, sensing his presence flow into me like water through a stream. My pulse quickened, my skin flushed with heat, and an electric buzz skimmed down my spine. Aydin and I were now one.

I've missed you, I told him in mind.

I missed you too, he said, and my heart melted because I could hear his voice, his human voice, inside my head.

You're not mad at me anymore? I asked.

I was never mad at you, Chalice. He paused. *I was hurt. You know how much Shojin meant to me.*

Of course I know. His sacrifice was… I couldn't find the words.

He was a selfless creature. I tried to tell you that.

He certainly had and I'd never believed him until it was too late. But even then, I doubt anything could have stopped Shojin from giving up his heart.

I inhaled Aydin's familiar scent and it comforted me. Eyes still closed, it was like being in a lucid dream. I stood, semiconscious, on the snowy road. Scents of fresh pine and new-fallen snow filled my nostrils. Then I imagined him big as life right in front of me.

My head felt suddenly too light and I dreamed of Aydin reaching out with human hands to catch me before I could fall.

You look…human.

It's your imagination. You're seeing me as you remember. His almond-shaped eyes captivated me, and they crinkled in the corners when he smiled. I knew that smile. *I'm inside your head right now. At least this way I can talk to you without snarls and grunts.*

He made a good point. Visualizing him like this was as close as I could get to being with him for real. I reached out to touch him and my fingers grazed the rough cloth of his jean jacket like the one he'd worn when we'd shared our first kiss. That was when we said goodbye at the airport. I never saw him human again after that.

Don't you want to come back? I asked.

He heaved a sigh and closed his eyes. *I've been thinking*

long and hard about that. It wouldn't be right for Shojin to have died in vain. Of course I want to come back. I need you.

Butterflies danced in my belly. He was about to say yes. *So you'll eat the heart?*

He winced. *That sounds so…barbaric.*

I know.

Aydin shook his head. *I can't. Not yet.*

My heartbeat slowed. *Why not?*

You and the few sisters you have left could use a big, ugly immortal gargoyle to your advantage.

Merging with my mind had allowed him to scan my thoughts, which saved me the time of explaining everything about the murders. He now knew as much as I did. Once he became human, he could help me train the squires to use charms for self-protection and lower their risks of getting killed.

I can still help train the squires, he said.

Not if you're on the opposite side of the wards guarding the house. As a gargoyle, you can't cross.

He studied me. *Convince your grandmother to take them down. I'll guard the house. Guarding houses is what gargoyles were originally meant to do before they were turned into assassins.*

I shook my head. *That will never happen. Angels and gargoyles have been enemies since the beginning of time. It will take more than begging to make my grandparents, not to mention the rest of the Arelim, change their minds.*

He shrugged. *Then we'll find another way.*

I felt a pout coming on. *I already know another way. Change back. Be the warrior knight protector you used to be.*

And still am. In this dream we shared, he pulled me

into a hug. *As long as I'm like this, I'm stronger and more intimidating to the bad guys.*

Was it selfish of me to want him the way he used to be? Maybe. I'd been waiting over a month to change him back, so another month wouldn't kill me. But not having his protection could kill my sister knights.

Merging our minds like this was so intimate it made my head spin. I'd never felt this dizzy with him before, but we'd never stayed joined this long, either. That's when I realized I wasn't the giddy, swept-off-my-feet kind of dizzy. I couldn't breathe.

Aydin yanked his spirit out of me so fast that it felt like part of my soul had gone with him. I stood bereft in the icy night without Aydin's warmth. And without oxygen.

My ears rang with a sudden barrage of shouts coming from the house. One shout sounded louder than the others, and I recognized it as Rafe's. I peered through glazed eyes to see Rafe charge at Aydin, who was now in physical gargoyle form. His leathery wings spread wide and a violent hiss spewed from his fanged mouth as Rafe sprouted wings of his own. He shed his human form in one great burst of silver sparks and dived toward Aydin.

I couldn't speak. I couldn't breathe. I lay on the frozen ground like a gasping fish out of water. My eyes watered, but I still had vision enough to see the cloaked figure standing by the side of the road a hundred yards away.

I pointed and struggled to send Rafe a mental message, but he was too busy trying to take down the one person who might save us all.

Hands were holding me, trying to calm me, but desperation had me flailing to signal that the murderer was mere footsteps away. Couldn't they see it? A black cloak fluttered around the shadowed face of whoever was trying to kill me. The strength of this creature's power convinced me I should be dead by now. But it was toying with me, studying me. Clearly it wasn't finished with me yet.

The figure appeared slender, almost skeletal, as a breeze pressed its robes tight against its body. That's when I saw the curves. It was a woman.

I jerked a look at the winged warriors who battled soundlessly in a hovered position above the road. Angel and gargoyle wings beat the snow into blizzardlike flurries. Neither could be killed, so if someone didn't stop them, their pointless fight would last until the end of time.

I saw Aydin try to yank free of Rafe's powerful grasp. Not to escape, but to get at the woman on the road. From the look of intensity in his eyes, I knew he'd seen her, too.

Air suddenly whooshed into my lungs. I gulped it in, the dry cold making me cough as the top of my head felt ready to explode. I blinked in the woman's direction. She was gone.

My grandfather wrapped his arms around me in a fierce embrace. "Thank God we have you back," he said into my hair. I felt his tears wet on my face. He'd thought I was dying.

My grandmother was already on her feet and stomping across the road to where Aydin and Rafe still hovered in battle.

"Kill it!" Aurora shouted to Rafe, her hand stabbing the air in Aydin's direction.

Nothing but another gargoyle could kill Aydin. However, a knife made from the body of one would do the trick. Rafe pulled something sharp, purple and shiny from the belt around his white tunic.

"No!" I shouted, or tried to. It came out as a squeak no one could hear. But Aydin had. With a powerful flap of wings tough enough to ride a tornado, he shot up into the air and vanished from sight.

seven

I DON'T REMEMBER GOING BACK TO BED,
but I wakened there, my head pounding while sunlight
stabbed into my corneas like ice picks. Closing my eyes
to block it out didn't help. I buried my head beneath
the blankets, where I noticed someone had removed my
muddy clothes and left me wearing nothing but panties
and a T-shirt.

"Xenia, I told you the light hurts her eyes," my grandmother said from somewhere in the room. "Close those
drapes right now."

"It's almost noon," Xenia said. "None of the rest of us
is allowed to sleep in."

"The rest of you didn't almost die last night," Aurora
scolded as she stepped into the room.

When I heard the sound of the drapes being closed I
peeked outside my cave of bedcovers.

"How are you feeling, Chalice?" Aurora asked, her voice not as warm as I would have liked. "Can I get you anything?"

You can get me my gargoyle boyfriend. But of course I didn't actually say that. So I asked for water instead. My throat felt like I'd gargled with sandpaper.

After downing the full glass, I said hoarsely, "About last night…"

Aurora sat on the edge of the bed. "You're lucky to be alive."

I leaned forward and forced out a wheezy breath. "I know. But it's not what you think."

"It's exactly what I think. That gargoyle tried to kill you."

"Aydin? That's ridiculous," I said. The stern look in Aurora's eyes told me she thought otherwise. "He'd have no reason to kill me."

"Then how do you explain what happened?" She stood and stepped to the window, and I was suddenly afraid she knew where I had buried the heart. But its glow was hidden, I'd made sure of it. "A gargoyle is a creature of darkness, a trained assassin. Its nature is to kill people like us. I realize it was only doing what came natural, but that's no excuse. It has to be destroyed."

"Grandmother, you're not listening to me." I gritted my teeth to stop myself from saying something bitchy. "Aydin cares about me, about all of us. Being our knight's protector has been his calling since the day he helped Saint Geraldine birth her child nearly a thousand years ago."

She nodded. "He also made a deal with one of the

Fallen, who just happened to be that child's father. I've heard the story. But let me remind you that Aydin is a monster now. He can't help what he is."

"He isn't a monster!" I bit my lip a split second after I shouted the words. I glanced at my grandmother, who looked neither astonished or hurt. Her expression was apathetic.

"Sorry," I said.

"Don't be." She patted my knee. "You're having a hard time letting go. I understand. In a few weeks you'll be over this crush you had on a man you hardly knew who no longer exists."

I buried my head in my hands. How could I get through to her? Maybe I shouldn't even try. There had to be a better way to convince her how wrong she was.

So I offered her an objective observation. "Did you see the cloaked figure by the side of the road?"

She scowled. "I was too preoccupied with watching you die and Rafael battle a gargoyle. No, I didn't see anyone else on the road."

"It was a woman wearing a black cloak with a hood that hid her face. She was the one stealing my breath."

Aurora stared at me, then sat down on the bed again. "You were delirious from lack of oxygen, honey. Seeing things. Who knows what kind of strange visions that gargoyle planted inside your head."

Good grief. "Aydin saw her, too."

My grandmother huffed. "What he saw was his own ass getting kicked by an angel."

"Chalice wasn't seeing things." Xenia, who I'd forgotten was still there, stepped out of a shadowed corner. She apparently had a gift for fading into the background. "I saw it from my bedroom window after I told you and Zeke that Chalice was gone from her bed."

I was starting to like this girl.

Aurora crossed her arms and tilted her head while looking up at Xenia. She wasn't easily convinced.

Xenia shrugged. "I saw what I saw."

"I'm sure Rafe saw it, too," I said, hearing the defensive edge in my voice. But I was more than defensive. I was determined to put an end to a threat I'd seen with my own eyes. Until my grandparents realized the danger was real they'd continue to lay blame where it didn't belong, which put Aydin and the entire order at risk.

Aurora stood. "Let's go downstairs and ask him."

"I need to shower and change first," I told her while digging through my bag for something clean to wear.

She nodded. "We'll put off the squires' training until tomorrow. All five of them are here at the house now and settling into their dorms."

"There are dorms?" I asked, having thought the upstairs of this house had the only living quarters.

"We added a new building to the property last month." She offered me a quick smile. "When the Arelim found out you had contacted Quin Dee, I had a feeling you'd be coming to us soon. The time to organize the Hatchet ranks was long overdue."

A twinge of grief touched my heart. Our ranks had dwindled to hardly enough players for a game of poker, and the stakes were higher than ever.

I fiddled with the zipper on my bag. "And here I am, late to the party."

"No, dear." She smoothed her hand over my bed-head hair. "I'd say you were just in time."

I emerged from the bathroom and nearly ran over Xenia.

"Do you always pop out of nowhere?" I asked her.

She smiled, her Cupid's bow lips curling up in the corners and making her look sweeter than I think she was. But I didn't know her yet.

"Sorry," she said. "I grew up in a family where I had to hide a lot."

At least she had a family, but it would be rude to actually say that. "I bet you miss them. Do they know you're here?"

She shook her head. "I'm all that's left, which is kind of why I'm here. My father isn't around and my mom died soon after I was born. I was raised in foster care."

Good to know we had some things in common. "Shouldn't you be in school?"

Frowning, she said, "College?"

"No, high school."

Xenia barked a laugh. "I graduated high school four years ago. You thought I was a kid?"

I tapped my chin and tried to look serious, but I had to laugh myself. "Guilty."

"I know I look young for my age, but so do you."

I topped out at a mere five foot two, but at least I had boobs. "I never thought much about it."

"I turn twenty-one this summer so I'll finally get to meet my guardian."

"You mean you haven't known him all your life?" I asked, surprised with this new tidbit of info.

She gave me a quizzical look. "Are you saying you've known yours?"

"Hell no," I told her. "I only met him a month ago."

Her eyes widened.

"It's a long story. I was sure you'd heard it by now."

Xenia shook her head. "I knew you had one, but Aurora said you'd tell us all at the same time."

"By all you mean…?"

"The squires."

"I see," I said, nodding. That made sense. No point in anyone having to tell it more than once.

"So I take it you're new to all this knight stuff, too."

"Yep." Yet I was to be her teacher. I think in this case we'd be teaching each other and that's what my grandmother had in mind all along. "You talk to angels?"

"Well, I mostly listen." She glanced behind her as if to make sure no one else listened in. "My foster family thought I was crazy and pretty much convinced me of it, too. The social worker assigned to my case had me diagnosed as schizophrenic. I was institutionalized, fed a bunch of drugs, but I eventually ran away. Once the crap cleaned out of my system, I could hear the angels again."

"And they told you to come here," I prompted.

"Something like that."

"Chalice?" my grandmother called from downstairs. "We're waiting for you."

By *we* I'm sure she meant Rafe was with her.

"Good luck," Xenia told me.

As I turned to go she gently tapped my arm and said,

"I know what it's like when no one believes you. I saw what you saw."

I smiled. "Thanks."

"Anytime."

Wrapped in a thick wool sweater and wearing a clean pair of Levi's, I padded my way down the stairs and into the great room. Rafe and my grandparents stood stoically beside the fireplace, all eyes on me.

I glanced down at my jeans to make sure they weren't stained. There was an old bloodstain on one cuff but I was the only one who could see it. "What's wrong?" I asked them.

Rafe, now back in his GQ human form, asked, "What's this about a mysterious cloaked stranger?"

He had to be kidding me. "Come on, Rafe. You must have seen her, too. Your eyesight is almost as good as mine."

"I had something else on my mind at the time," he said, and rubbed one of his shoulders like it was sore. I didn't think angels could get hurt. "Your BF kept me busy."

I crossed my arms. "You started it."

He scowled at me. "He was trying to kill you."

"No, he wasn't."

Aurora held up her hands in the shape of a T. "Time out. You two should talk. Right now."

She was right. The only way to convince them that Aydin wasn't a threat was to get Rafe on my side.

I needed to show him where I'd seen this woman. It might jog his recollection of events. Even if he hadn't seen her I felt certain his sharp angel senses had picked up her presence.

Rafe followed me outside, but when I got close to the warded entrance to the property, he ran ahead of me and blocked my path.

"What do you think you're doing?" I asked.

"Stopping you from leaving the safety of this home," he said.

"There's nothing dangerous out there. I'll prove it." I stood very still, opening my senses to the wilderness. The graceful soaring of a hawk drew my attention upward and I scanned the skies for anything out of the ordinary. Too cold for insects, I heard no buzzing but detected the scraping of deer or elk antlers against a tree about a quarter mile away. Leafless branches of aspen trees rattled against each other in a mild winter breeze. A nearby brook bubbled beneath a thin crust of ice. The air smelled crisp and untainted by the stench of the black veil. There was no safer place on earth at that moment than this very spot.

"Such a peaceful setting could change in a flash," Rafe said, his voice low and calm. He appeared nothing like the fiery angel that had attacked Aydin in the early-morning darkness. He was as serene as the babbling brook that echoed in the distance. "It happened once and can happen again. I'm prepared for the deluge. Are you?"

"More than you are," I told him.

He smirked at me. "Does that mean you'd kill your gargoyle if he attacked you again?"

I gritted my teeth. "How many times do I have to tell you there was no attack, at least not by him. Let me show you where I saw the woman." I shouldered past him and he grabbed my arm. I yanked away. "What are you going to do, ground me?"

His jaw tightened and his eyes went cold. "As your guardian, it's my duty to protect you."

"I know that." I folded my arms. "But you can't protect me by letting a murderer go free."

"I have no intention of letting him go free."

"You mean *her*." I stepped backward toward the boundary, my gaze glued to his stubborn face. "It wasn't Aydin. Xenia saw the woman, too. Let's both go look at the spot where we saw her. It might jog your memory."

"I can help." Natalie trotted down the front steps toward us. "If the woman left something behind, I may be able to learn who or what she is."

My grandmother came out of the house behind her, but she didn't venture beyond the porch. If her hearing was anything like mine, which I knew it was, she wouldn't need to. I wondered why she didn't protest Natalie's offer to help. Maybe she was giving us enough rope to hang ourselves, or to hang someone else, depending on what we discovered. The knights weren't children and she knew that. Must be some kind of test that I had every intention of passing.

Rafe appeared slightly unhinged. "Natalie, it's not safe for you or Chalice. Your guardian wouldn't approve."

"Camael is my guide, not my boss," Natalie told him in a steely tone that surprised me. "I listen to his suggestions, but I'm the judge of what I can and cannot do. If I need his help, I'll let him know."

Rafe squinted at her. "You've been a knight longer than Chalice has. She still has much to learn."

Natalie shook her head. "Not about something like this. She's encountered more dark forces than any of us, and I'd say she handled herself just fine. Wouldn't you?"

"Of course," Rafe admitted. "But this is different. She was almost killed today."

"Rafe, I can count on both hands the number of times I've almost been killed," I told him. "Today wasn't all that different." I jerked a quick look at my grandmother, who grinned before turning to go back inside the house.

"Come on, Natalie," I said, and led the way to the road. "I'll show you where she was."

Natalie followed me, and Rafe trailed behind her, his eyes narrowed as he scanned both sides of the road. He popped out of human form like an exploding firecracker and spread his impressive wings. Rafe wasn't the type to flaunt his angelic beauty. What he did flaunt was far more lethal to any baddie who might be lurking nearby. I had no doubt his show was also for Aydin's benefit, just in case.

When we arrived at the spot where I'd seen the woman, I scrutinized the disturbed snow. There was the indentation of footprints, but none leading to that area. It was as if she landed there from out of the blue. Maybe she had.

I sniffed and smelled nothing but pine and a well-used squirrel's nest that had me wrinkling my nose at the stench. Ammonia tended to wipe out other scents, at least it did for me. I detected no other odors. But I did see something.

"A crow's feather?" I said, bending down to pluck the black plume from the snow. "A damn big one, too."

"Not a crow." Rafe stood rigid, his broad chest expanding before a deep sigh escaped his lips. "That feather belongs to one of the Fallen."

eight

"WHAT DOES THE FALLEN WANT WITH US?" I asked, though I doubted either Rafe or Natalie could give me that answer. The angels who fell had no ties with the Hatchet knights, not once they chose the darker road. The Arelim and the Fallen kept to opposite sides of the fence and their paths rarely crossed.

"I wish I knew," Rafe said, his voice lowered to a whisper. He appeared deep in thought and I imagined he was speaking telepathically to the Arelim about our curious find.

I clamped my jaw to keep from saying *I told you so.*

Natalie held her hand out to me. "Can I see?"

I frowned. Though spells could affect me, I was immune to cursed objects and charms. But I wasn't so sure Natalie could escape whatever nastiness the feather might contain. However, it could just as easily be harmless as a feather duster. "I don't know, Natalie. It might be dangerous if you touched—"

She snatched it away from me. "Too late."

Her tenacity surprised me, yet I admired her for it. I didn't think she had it in her.

Rafe looked ready to pounce. "Don't hold it too tight," he warned, though Natalie had already gone into her psychometric trance.

An entire minute passed in silence.

"She should have said something by now about what she senses," I said, concern tying a knot in my stomach.

Natalie groaned and whispered, "No. It can't be."

"What can't be?" The fine hairs on my skin bristled.

She swayed slightly, then gasped as her eyes popped open with only their whites showing. Her lips were turning blue.

"Oh, my God," I said. "She's suffocating."

Rafe lurched toward her and I shouted, "No! Don't touch her. Break the connection and you could destroy her mind."

"She's dying," he said, his eyes shining as he pierced me with a pleading look. "We have to make her stop."

Whatever she had connected to was using the feather to steal her breath. Nothing I knew of had such power, but whatever this was obviously did. And it was killing Natalie.

The veins at her temples swelled like slender blue worms just beneath her pale skin. Her mouth opened wide as she struggled to breathe. I knew how she felt. I'd experienced the same thing just hours ago. I had survived and I was determined she would, too.

Broken mind or certain death, I didn't know which was worse. We had already lost too many knights. I refused to count Natalie among the fatalities.

I nodded at Rafe and he grabbed the feather from her. Natalie gulped in air like a drowning person and just before she crumpled to the ground, she whispered, "Maria."

I sat beside Natalie's bed as she slept. She'd lost consciousness right after saying the name Maria. It sounded so familiar, but I couldn't recall anyone I knew by that name. It nagged at me like a fly buzzing in my ear. I should know what it meant, but the harder I tried to remember, the more evasive it became. As if the name itself was a spell created to halt any memory of it.

Natalie's room was next to the one I shared with Xenia. Rusty slept in a bed at the other end and was oblivious to everything around her after crying herself to sleep. With the exception of Camael, she worried more about Natalie than anyone. I hadn't seen her guardian, but I'd sensed his presence. Unlike Rafe, who enjoyed slipping into a human guise, Camael seemed shy and unassuming. I wondered if Natalie might consider a trade, but I knew better. Big brother Rafe and I were stuck with each other.

How could I have let this happen? I'd wanted to protect my sister knights, not endanger them more than they already were. But my plan to prove Aydin's innocence as a way to enlist his help had backfired. He might be clear of any wrongdoing, but wrong had still been done and I was the one responsible.

"Chalice." My grandmother rested her hand on my shoulder. "It's late. You need to eat and get some rest."

I covered her hand with my own. "I can't. There's something I need to remember, but…" I shook my head in frustration.

"You'll think more clearly in the morning," she told me.

I looked up at her and asked, "Now do you believe that Aydin wasn't responsible for any of this?"

She sat in the ladder-back chair beside me and leaned forward, her elbows resting on both knees. "Yes."

Relief flooded me in a waterfall of tingles from head to toe. "Then you must lower the wards so he can enter Halo Home. Aydin can help take down the murderer."

"That may be," Aurora said slowly. "But we have to think about all the squires here, not to mention Rusty and Natalie. Removing the wards would leave them vulnerable to attack."

She made an excellent point. Spirits crushed, I sought a different solution and an idea came to me. "What if the wards were reset to allow ghosts inside? That way Aydin could enter in his invisible form."

My grandmother winced. "I hate ghosts."

"So do I." That confirmed she had the same talent for seeing ghosts that I did. "But they're lesser evils than demons and other black veil entities, including the Fallen."

She hesitated before saying, "True. But ghosts aren't entirely harmless. There's an old Indian burial ground about a half mile from here." She shuddered. "It's loaded with the things."

I lit up with another idea. "How about a charm?"

Looking dubious, she asked, "What kind of charm?"

"A ghost-repelling charm. And I know just who can make it, too. Quin Dee." Quin had a talent for creating pendants out of Celestine, a crystal with the power to connect to the realm of angels. Quin used to make them for the people he did angel readings for. "The Arelim can invoke a protection spell in the crystals and everyone can wear one." Everyone but me, of course. Though I could still wear a pretty piece of jewelry around my neck even if it didn't keep the ghosts away.

Aurora smiled. "I like that idea, Chalice." She stood and grabbed my hand to pull me to my feet. "I'll call Quin now so he can get started. I'm sure the squires will enjoy a pretty new bauble as part of their initiation into the knighthood."

I still held the blighted black feather by its quill and absently ran my fingers over the silky vein, then the downy fluff at the feather's base. How could something so beautiful be so deadly? I gazed down at Natalie's serene face, her eyes closed in sleep. "Hang in there, Nat. We'll get you out of this." I prayed I was right.

The following day there was still no change in Natalie's condition. We took turns sitting vigil at her bedside and I'm sure Camael never left her for a moment. I felt his presence every time I was with her.

Rusty had begun preparing the squires for their continuing education in the ways of the knighthood. Aurora had me sit in on her first session since I was about as green as the normies who had yet to receive their shields.

It was also a good way for me to get to know them

a bit before I began their instruction on the fine art of charms. I still hadn't decided which ones to use. I needed to go through Aydin's collection to determine the most useful and least dangerous of the bunch. Some charms also went dormant after fulfilling their designated task and would require recharging before they could be used again. Who would recharge them? Yet another obstacle I had to overcome.

Rusty gazed down at her small gathering of eager young faces, all of whom sat in a circle on the floor of the great room inside the main house. "And that's how the Hatchet Knighthood of Medieval Times continued on with daughters born of human women like you. We inherited our supernatural powers from our guardian angel fathers."

"Will we have superpowers, too?" one of the women asked. She sat Indian-style with her arms wrapped around a pillow, her freckled face as innocent as a cherub on a Christmas card. I studied the others. They all had that wholesome look about them, the kind that made me think of gingham dresses and bobby socks. All but Xenia. Her innocence hid beneath a ton of kohl eyeliner and a bad haircut. Now I understood why she covered herself with that junk—she really was trying to hide. Why had the Arelim chosen these pristine little ladies? I'd expect them to recruit Amazons, not Rebecca of Sunnybrook Farm clones.

Rusty smiled. "No, Lisa, you won't have powers. But your daughter will."

Disappointment flickered across their faces.

"That doesn't mean you won't have supernatural ways

of protecting yourselves in dangerous situations," Rusty told them, and tilted her head at me. "Chalice has some tricks to share with you."

Six heads turned in my direction.

"Um…" I shrugged. "Yes, I do. They're not really tricks, they're charms. Magic invoked in objects to make them do special things."

"Like what?" a blond ponytailed girl asked me.

I glanced at the paper name tag she wore on her chest. "Well, Dale, there are a variety of charms that can be helpful. There are some that make you invisible, fly, run faster than a speeding car, deflect bullets, block someone from reading your mind. I could go on and on, but I'll save it for later. This is Rusty's time with you right now."

The little group erupted with questions.

"What charm do I get?"

"Can I be as strong as a super hero?"

"Is there one that can make me shrink to the size of a mouse?"

I held out my hands. "Whoa! Hey, I said we'd go over all this later." Not to mention I wasn't prepared. I needed to know something about each squire before assigning them a charm suited for their individual needs. Baby steps.

Rusty glared at me and I understood why. I'd stolen her thunder.

"Look," I said to them, wearing my patient face that felt tight since I hadn't donned it in a while. "Our attentions are divided right now. As you all know, one of our sister knights is in a coma caused by whatever took the lives of so many in our order. You'll just have to be patient."

They bowed their heads and tossed ashamed looks at one another.

"No worries, okay?" I melted the chill from my smile as I said, "I'm almost as new to this as the rest of you."

"We heard," said a pixie of a girl with black hair in a Peter Pan haircut. "Aurora told us you have a story to tell."

Murmurs fluttered between them and they looked at me expectantly.

"That's true," I said. "And I promise you'll get the full scoop on my sordid life and the curse that nearly killed me. Just not today."

They groaned, looking dejected.

This session was as much for my education as theirs, so I had a question of my own. "You six are the chosen few, and I'm curious what you have in common." They stared at me as if I'd just told them their panties were showing. "You're all lovely young women with a unique talent for speaking with angels. But what makes you more special than other girls with the same gift?"

"I think I know," Xenia said. "Without having talked to the others I'm betting they're all orphans like me. Am I right?"

Each of them nodded. Okay, that made sense. No family ties, meaning no awkward questions from loved ones about how they lived their lives, and it lessened the chance for a division of loyalties. I sensed these girls' need to belong. It takes one to know one.

"It's not like we joined a cult," the blonde Dale said.

"We've had a telepathic connection to the Arelim since birth. No one understands us like they do."

I nodded. "True enough. How old are you?"

They all said at same time, "Twenty."

And less than a year away from meeting their guardians. Interesting.

"How do you feel about having a child destined for knighthood?" I asked.

"I feel honored," said the girl with the Peter Pan haircut. "It's my destiny."

I frowned, but quickly sobered. No sense in giving away my personal opinions on the matter. Battling gargoyles and dealing with neurotic sorcerers is not a destiny I'd have chosen for myself. As far as feeling honored to carry a halfling child fathered by an angel I didn't love? I'd just as soon be sterile. However, my life had been different from these girls'. My cynicism was justified. I slid a sideways glance at Xenia, who looked sad beyond reason, and I wondered at the source of her grief. Perhaps I wasn't the only one with reservations about Hatchet knight traditions. Misery loved company.

A girl with bouncing red curls who could put Shirley Temple to shame said, "Let's see a demonstration."

Rusty scowled. "A demonstration of what?"

"Your superpowers," she said.

The others applauded and nodded with enthusiasm.

"Mine's a bit hard to demonstrate," I told them.

"You're Aurora's granddaughter, right?" one of them asked. "So you have her powers. Super senses are awesome."

And sometimes annoying, I thought. They had no idea

how intrusive it could be and the amount of concentration required to keep it in check. "Okay, I'll bite.

"Dale, you need to eat something. Breakfast is the most important meal of the day," I told her.

"You can tell what I had for breakfast?"

"Or what you didn't have, as the case may be," I said. "Your dental hygiene is excellent, by the way."

My nostrils flared as I caught a whiff of Xenia's breath. "Xenia! Lay off the booze, especially before five. Alcohol blunts the senses and you need to be sharp at all times."

Xenia flushed and her jaw dropped. "Chalice, please don't tell Aurora."

"I won't if you promise not to sneak whiskey from Zeke's liquor cabinet again."

Her head bobbed as if perched on a spring.

"Rusty?" Dale asked. "Will you show us your ability?"

Rusty stood, her eyes revealing her pride for what she could do. And she should be proud. Controlling fire was a powerful talent she put to good use. There was no doubt she'd saved thousands of lives not to mention forests and buildings from going up in flames.

She stared hard at the candle on a coffee table. Seconds passed and nothing happened. Scowling, she cupped her hands in front of her, then clapped. Still nothing.

"Rusty, what's wrong?" Xenia asked.

Eyes glazed, Rusty glared at me and said, "My ability. It's gone."

I felt my heart lodge in my throat. Some charms and cursed objects were known to exact payment for the help they offered. In this case, I believed the Viking horn of breath had taken Rusty's ability in exchange for giving back her life. "Are you sure it's completely gone?" I asked her.

"You're the one who stuck that disgusting horn in my mouth," Rusty said, her tone close to a growl. "You tell me."

"It could be temporary." At least I hoped so.

"I thought you knew all there was to know about charms and curses." Rusty gazed down at her students, eyebrows raised. "That's why you're here, right? To teach these girls how to defend themselves with magical objects?"

Of course, that's why I was here. I didn't appreciate Rusty's sarcasm, but I understood her shock at the sudden loss of something so important. I imagined it felt the same as losing an arm or a leg. A vital piece of yourself suddenly gone.

Dale's eyes widened. "What happened? What's going on?"

"Nothing much." Rusty's eyes hardened to marbles. "I died the other day and Chalice brought me back to life."

There was a collective gasp from the little group.

I didn't defend, object or deny. Rusty needed to vent, and if that involved mocking me, I could take it. Up to a point. I was big enough to accept responsibility, but I didn't want these squires to get the wrong idea. Not about me, necessarily, but about the charms they'd be using to protect themselves.

"Apparently there's a price for resurrection, huh, Chalice? Kind of too late for buyer's remorse though," Rusty said.

Xenia shook her head and the rest of the girls blinked, looking confused.

"I didn't know the horn of breath had strings attached. I'll fix it."

"Fix it?" Rusty asked, her forehead puckered with an ugly frown.

"There has to be a way to return your powers." All the girls stared at me and I threw up my hands. "I still have the horn that gave you your breath back. The key must be there somewhere." Or so I wanted to believe.

Rusty struggled to compose herself, but I saw her hands were shaking. "You've been nothing but trouble since the day you got here, Chalice."

I stood from the chair I'd been sitting in, my muscles bunched with tension. "Prescribing charms is still new for me. Give me a break."

"You don't deserve a break." Rusty stepped closer to me. She stood at least a head taller and I had to crane my neck to meet her glare. "You're a menace to the order. You'd have made a much better gargoyle than you do a knight."

I was starting to get angry. "I've vowed to do right by the order. I'm here to help, and I'm here to fulfill my mother's legacy."

Rusty's smile didn't reach her eyes. "By letting your family's bloodline die after nine centuries?"

To say that barb didn't hurt would be a lie. "I honor my mother and the knighthood with my life."

"There's no honor in destroying a lineage." Rusty put her hands on her hips. "You'd rather bear disgusting baby gargoyles than be the blessed vessel for a future Hatchet knight."

Heat engulfed my neck and I knew my tattoo would have been on fire by now had I not broken the curse it symbolized. I gulped air to try cooling off. "I know you're upset, Rusty. You don't mean what you're saying."

She snorted. "Like hell I don't."

We glowered at each other and from the corner of my eye I saw Xenia hop to her feet and rush from the room.

Rusty's eyes narrowed. "Maybe what I heard about your mother was true."

If she said one bad thing about my mother I'd make sure she lost more than just her powers. I felt the weight of the knife sheathed between my shoulder blades.

"What was that sorcerer's name?" Rusty's eyes rolled as if she tried to think of the answer. "Oh, yeah. Gavin. The Vyantara's head honcho and your mother's lover."

I sprang at her.

It was totally impulsive and completely driven by some primal part of my brain. Anything having to do with my mother was a sensitive issue. To hear the name of that sociopathic sorcerer and my mother in the same breath sent me over the edge. I couldn't stop myself.

The knife was in my hands so fast I barely registered my fingers wrapping around the hilt and my thumb springing the latch to pop the blade.

Lucky for me Rusty was just as fast. She kicked my hand so hard the knife went flying, the blade lodging firmly into the wall behind me. A good thing no one was standing there or they'd be shish kebab right now.

Her hands fisted my short hair and I did the same to

hers. I wrapped her long tresses around my fingers and yanked her down to floor, where we rolled around like a couple of TV wrestlers. I focused on holding her head away from me so she couldn't bite my ear off. She came pretty close a couple of times.

"What the hell is going on in here?" my grandmother yelled as she stormed into the room and grabbed me by the arms. She tried pulling me away from Rusty, who had no intention of letting go.

Now it was three of us on the floor with my grandmother on top trying desperately to pull us apart. I was expecting the water hose at any second. But instead it was my grandfather who broke up the brawl and sent both Rusty and I sprawling to opposite sides of the room.

"Enough!" he shouted. "What's wrong with you two? Now's not the time for fighting." He glowered down at the two of us as we lay gasping and bleeding and literally growling in rage. "Stop it, both of you."

A sudden bright light flared in the middle of the room and the silver veil rippled like a lake disturbed by skipping stones. An enormous angel emerged, his white hair floating around him in graceful waves that looked peaceful and terrifying at the same time.

I glanced over at Rusty, whose eyes had gone wide and her face drained of color. She looked scared, and I knew for a fact it wasn't me she was afraid of. This angel frightened her.

"No," she said quietly. "Please, Harachel, I promise to be good. I won't fight anymore." She tried to scoot backward on the slick wooden floor, but the angel easily reached down and grabbed both her arms to haul her to her feet.

He wasn't exactly gentle about it and despite my rage a few minutes earlier, the instinct to protect my sister made a sudden and unexpected appearance. "Leave her alone," I said. "Can't you see she doesn't want you touching her?"

"What she wants does not matter," the angel said, his deep voice strong enough to make the pictures on the wall shudder in their frames. "She needs to calm herself. I am her guardian and I will help her do that."

I just bet you will. I wasn't sure why I didn't trust him. He was supposed to be one of the good guys, but then again, Aydin was assumed to be a bad one. It's best not to judge a book, or an angel or gargoyle, by its cover.

I prepared to stand and felt a firm but gentle hand clutch my elbow and guide me to my feet. Rafe gave me a stern look, though his eyes held a deeper understanding of what I sensed. He felt it, too. My skin went cold. He jerked a warning nod and I held my tongue.

The angel Harachel pulled Rusty into his arms and lifted her like she weighed no more than a rag doll. If he ever dared treat her like one he'd be hearing from me. Turning to face the veil, he slipped through it and the shimmering surface vanished as if it had never been there.

The room became quiet as a tomb.

My grandmother sighed and pressed her hand against her forehead. "You girls gave me a migraine."

"Sorry," I said, aware that I'd been apologizing a lot lately.

Aurora shook her head. "It's fine, Chalice. That fight was bound to happen sooner or later. Rusty has been jealous of you since the day she heard how you broke your curse and killed that gargoyle."

"Can we hear the story now?" one of the squires asked.

I'd totally forgotten about the squires. I could only imagine what they must be thinking.

"Honey, I don't think Chalice is up to it right now," Aurora told her. "Class is over. You're all dismissed for the day."

While watching the women disperse, I touched my lip and winced, then saw the blood on my fingers. I didn't remember Rusty hitting me. It all happened so fast.

"Let me see." Aurora leaned over me to study the top of my head. She whistled. "Oh, dear. I'll have to remind Rusty to cut her nails. She raked you pretty good."

As soon as she said it my head began to hurt. I'd be healed by morning, but that did nothing for me now. I wanted aspirin. And a shower. And a nap.

"You're not off the hook, young lady," Aurora said as she released my head and backed up a step. "You must learn to control yourself. You're dangerous with a knife."

I stared down at my feet. "I know I need to work on my self-control. Rusty pushed my buttons and I pushed back. It won't happen again."

"I know you mean well, dear, but if you're anything like your mother, it *will* happen again." She held me by the chin and gazed into my eyes. "Work harder than your mother did to restrain yourself. Her impulses were what got her killed. I don't want the same to happen to you."

I started to say something, but she abruptly turned and walked away, her steps solid and determined. She meant what she said. And so did I.

nine

I COULDN'T GET RUSTY OFF MY MIND. AN entire day had passed and she had yet to return from her trip through the silver veil. She wouldn't be in trouble if I had kept my temper. Maybe Rafe had some pointers on how I could do that.

Natalie continued to sleep, but my grandmother had managed to spoon some soup and high-protein milk shakes into her. She'd also taken on the unpleasant duties of diaper and linen changing. The woman was a saint. A pang of pride made my eyes sting and I blinked. I'd become far too emotional lately, which was out of character for me. Six months ago I could block my feelings, but my world was different now. I finally had something, and several someones, to feel deeply about.

"You need to talk to me?" Rafe asked as he walked into my room.

He had heard my thoughts and that shouldn't have surprised me, but it always did. I should be grateful. But I appreciated him more when my resentment toward his attitude about Aydin didn't irritate the hell out of me.

I sat on my bed with my back slouched against the wall, knees pulled to my chest and arms hugging my shins. I gazed up at him and said, "What's going on with Rusty?"

He glanced at the foot of the bed. "May I?"

I nodded.

He sat and turned slightly to face me. "She's being counseled by her guardian."

I frowned. "I don't trust that guy."

"It's none of your business."

"I'm worried he'll hurt her."

Rafe shook his head, a lock of perfect blond hair falling over one eyebrow. "He will not. But Harachel is strict and demands stellar behavior. Maybe I should be more demanding of you as well."

I suppressed a growl and sat up straighter. "Don't even think about it."

A small smile tilted up the corners of his mouth. "I wouldn't dare."

Smart man. "So why are you so different?"

"I'm not."

Rafe stood and stepped to the window to gaze out at the night, which was finally clear of snow flurries. Stars glittered against the inky darkness, which made Rafe's silhouette even more pronounced. "Angels of the Arelim are as different from each other as you humans are. We have our good points and our bad ones."

"You're angels," I said. "You're supposed to be the epitome of goodness."

He chuckled. "Says who?"

"Says Christmas."

He laughed harder. "You watch too much television."

"I know." I laughed, too. "So bad angels become fallen ones?"

"Sometimes." He turned toward me so the window was at his back. "Those who father children for the Hatchet knights definitely do, unless they choose to have their wings clipped so that they can become human. All angels have a choice."

"And the fallen ones? What choices do they have?"

He hesitated before saying, "I don't know much about them."

I wished he did, because I wanted to know more about my father. Barachiel had helped me escape the Vyantara fatherhouse, and I considered that a good deed. If all the Fallen were evil, my father never would have done what he did.

"I think it's fair to say the Fallen serve their own interests, whatever those may be." Rafe approached my bed again. "Is that all you wanted to know?"

"Yes," I said, then leaned forward. "I mean no. I'd like you to teach me self-control."

He raised an eyebrow.

"Like how to stop myself from acting out my anger," I explained. "You helped me learn to balance my senses so they won't take me over and I was hoping you could do the same for my temper."

He rubbed his chin and studied me. "Perhaps. But only on one condition."

Conditions made me nervous. "Depends on what it is."

"Fair enough." He crossed his arms over his chest. "Chalice, all I ask is that you never shut me out again."

"Even when you insult the man I love?" Though I had to admit I'd acted childish. My emotions were balanced on a knife's edge and Rafe had pushed me over. I'd meant to teach him a lesson, but he was supposed to be *my* teacher. I could learn a lot from him.

His jaw muscles tightened and his eyes narrowed, but he expressed the same self-control that I wanted for myself. "Yes, even then."

I sighed and said, "I'll do my best."

"Quin!" I shouted when I greeted him at the door.

"Hey, you." He gathered me in his arms for a hug. "Long time no see."

It had only been a few weeks, but he was right. It felt like ages. "I know. I've missed you."

Quin grinned, his bespectacled eyes bright with optimism and his sandy hair sticking up in a stylish cowlick. That was new. He was a couple years older than me and quite British. I'd first met him on a kidnapping assignment when I was still working for the Vyantara. He was the one I'd been assigned to kidnap but, when I'd wound up saving his life instead, we'd become allies.

"I missed you, too." He gave me a quick squeeze and let me go. "So are you all settled in?"

I rolled my eyes. "Yes and no. I think I've already

worn out my welcome." I told him everything that had happened over the past few days, from the burned-down farmhouse and forest fire to Natalie's brush with death and then the awful fight I'd had with Rusty. "Now I need to redeem myself."

"Let's see if there's anything I can do to help." He led the way to the storage room that held Aydin's collection of charms. He dug into his jacket pocket and came out with a key, which he deftly plugged into the hole beneath the doorknob. But he didn't have to turn it. The door swung open by itself. "That's odd."

"I must have forgotten to lock it when I was here last." I fiddled with the knob and tested the lock. "Because it's working fine now."

Quin shrugged and glanced at the stacks of boxes and crates. "I catalogued every one of these before bringing them here."

"Quite a project."

"You're telling me."

"What can you tell me about the Viking horn of breath?"

He grimaced. "No more than you already know. You're the one who stole the bugger."

I sighed. "Unfortunately, its history is vague. I need to know if there's a way to make it give back Rusty's power."

His brow furrowed in thought. "You'll have to find a shaman with a background in old Nordic magic."

"Do you think Elmo would know of someone like that?" Elmo was a mutual friend who owned a coffee shop in Denver favored by the fae. He was an elf with ties to the land of Faerie beyond the green veil. It was another realm beyond the human one, just as the black veil harbored demons, and the silver veil was home to the Arelim and the innocents who needed sanctuary.

"I don't know if he does, but it can't hurt to ask."

I added that to my to-do list. Though I wasn't sure when I'd get the chance to ask him since Halo Home was my virtual prison for a while. Elmo didn't have a phone so I couldn't call him. I supposed I could write him a letter if I had to.

I scanned Aydin's charm collection, remembering the day I'd hastily grabbed that stupid horn. Though I didn't totally regret it. After all, Rusty would be dead right now if I hadn't used it on her. There might even be something here that could counteract what the horn had done, but I felt pretty sure Rusty would refuse whatever I found. I now knew that charms worked differently on knights than they did on full-blooded humans.

I heard a scraping sound in the far corner of the room. "Damn. We have mice?"

"I didn't hear anything," Quin said.

I smirked. "Of course not. Your ears aren't as sensitive as mine." I thinned the mental barrier around all my senses so I could pinpoint the whereabouts of the rodent, and that's when I smelled it. Alcohol.

Hands on hips, I said firmly, "Xenia? Get your ass out from behind those boxes right now."

Silence.

My nose twitched with another scent that confirmed the intruder's identity: Xenia's pungent perfume that smelled like rotting gardenias.

"Give it up, Xenia," I said.

Some of the crates and boxes shifted as a figure on hands and knees emerged from behind them. Xenia stood and brushed at the dust bunnies clinging to her sweater, though they blended naturally with the matted yarn that twisted through quarter-size holes from neck to hem. "Hi," she said with the flash of a grin.

She gazed up at Quin and her eyes suddenly brightened, as did her smile. "Hello."

Frowning, Quin crossed his arms and didn't return her greeting.

"What are you doing in here?" I asked.

"Looking around." She started backing her way to the door. "Sorry to intrude. I'll leave you two alone."

My nose twitched again as the scent of old wood drifted out from the pocket of Xenia's jeans.

"Hold it right there," I said. "Hand it over."

She blinked. "Hand what over?"

I made a *gimme* gesture with my hand and she sighed. Her small, pale fingers slid into her pocket and pulled out a bracelet made with oak tiles linked together by tiny, tarnished silver roses.

It was a Celtic bracelet and each of the seven tiles was marked with a rune. Together the runes predicted a day's events from dawn until dusk. The rune symbols changed every day. It was a very powerful charm that could easily be abused in the wrong hands.

Xenia dropped it in my outstretched hand.

"Do you know what this is?" I asked her.

"Pretty?"

I rolled my eyes. "Yes, it's very pretty. But it's not simply a piece of jewelry. It's a very powerful charm."

"I...I uh..." she stammered, and shoved her hands in her pockets. "I didn't realize. I just thought it was some old stuff in storage."

I nodded. "It's old stuff and it's being stored, but each object here has a special purpose. Some of these things can protect you, or help you. But if used the wrong way they can hurt you."

"Like the one that hurt Rusty."

"Exactly." I stepped behind the boxes and crouched down to retrieve the rusted metal box that had held the bracelet. "This is nothing to fool around with. Understand?"

She nodded. "Can I go now?"

My eyes spotted movement from underneath Xenia's sweater. She quickly covered the spot with her hand and coughed. "Wow, the dust in here is bad."

I held out my hand again. "What's under your shirt?"

"Nothing," she said, taking her hand away. "I swear."

Whatever it was jumped again. I lunged at her and reached my hand down the front of her sweater.

"Hey!" she said, trying to push me away.

My fingers wrapped around the object I suspected and my heart jerked with dismay. Xenia had tried to steal my pet. She'd almost taken Ruby.

I opened my hand. The jewel-encrusted frog gazed up at me with shining ruby eyes and chirped. I petted her head with the tip of my finger. "Hello, Ruby."

"That's its name?" Xenia asked, excitement in her voice.

"Yes, it's Ruby and it belongs to Chalice," Quin said in a steely tone that sounded nothing like him. "How dare you try to steal from someone who's here to help you."

I imagined Xenia had done this kind of thing before. I was like her at that age, only I hadn't stolen things for myself. I'd stolen them for a sorcerer who'd sworn to have me killed by the creature bonded to me if I didn't do what I was told. Xenia was under no such pressure. She stole for the hell of it.

Xenia's expression made a sudden transformation from awe to rage in under ten seconds.

"You think you're better than me?" she asked.

What the hell? Dealing with these women the past few days made it clear why I had so few girlfriends. They made no sense. "No," I said firmly. "Do you think you're better than *me?*"

"Yeah, I sure do." She stalked to the door and Quin stepped ahead of her to lean against it, barring her way out. "I was called here. I'm special. And I'm not like you or Rusty or any of those other bitches pretending to be squires."

"Aren't you a cheeky little thing," Quin said, his lip curled in distaste. This was a side of him I hadn't seen before. He'd never been so outspoken in front of me.

"You're not helping," I told him.

He grunted and glowered at Xenia. Was there some history there I didn't know about?

"I'm not like you or anyone else here," Xenia went on.

"Good to know," I said calmly, feeling proud of myself for not losing my cool. "Care to share your divine purpose with the rest of us?"

"No." She glared at me, reminding me of yesterday's confrontation with Rusty. I wasn't about to go through that again. "It's none of your damn business."

Okay, so she'd gotten caught and was obviously used to getting away with the stuff she stole. I should expect her to be defensive. But there was something else here, something I couldn't quite put my finger on. And it worried me.

"Maybe we should discuss this with Aurora," I said.

Her face suddenly changed to that of a scared little girl. "Chalice, I'm so sorry. I don't know what got into me." She caught her bottom lip between her teeth and looked remorseful. "I never should have picked that lock. When I was a kid I had to steal to survive, sell what I could to buy food. That's the only life I knew and old habits die hard. I didn't mean to—" She broke out in tears, the gasping kind that caused hiccups.

Looking pained, Quin carefully placed a fatherly arm around her shoulders. "Chalice won't tell on you. Will you, Chalice?"

He changed his tune awful fast.

"Xenia, we really need to talk to Aurora about what you said." Warning bells clanged inside my head, but I couldn't explain why.

Xenia nodded. "You're right. I need to tell her what I was doing in here. I have to apologize."

"I mean we need to tell her what you said about being more special than the others. What did you mean by that?"

She laughed and waved me off. "I didn't mean anything. I was just trying to save my own ass by making up shit. Forget about it. It was nothing."

It wasn't nothing, but I'd let it go for now. We could explore it further after I decided what charms to assign the squires, and after we had Natalie back to her old self again. The first order of business was getting Aydin in here to guide Natalie's mind back from wherever it had drifted. Whatever mystery Xenia had cooked up would have to sit on the back burner for now.

"What are you doing?" I asked Quin once we were alone. We sat at the kitchen table drinking tea and eating the last of my grandmother's peanut butter cookies.

"I'm untangling the chains for these charms," he said, his fingers nimbly working at a tangle of fine silver. He spread the necklace out on a black velvet cloth and began working on the next one.

"That's not what I meant." I took a bite of a cookie as I watched him work. "What's up with you and Xenia?"

His hands remained steady as his nails tweezed a stubborn knot. "I don't know what you mean."

"There's something about her that bugs you." It bothered me, too, but I couldn't wrap my mind around exactly what. I was hoping he had more insight.

Quin stopped messing with the chains to lean back in his chair. "What I know is that the Arelim have been having trouble communicating with her over the past few days."

I frowned. "Do you all have some kind of mental chat room where you converse telepathically?"

"Something like that, yeah." He took a sip of tea.

"While the three of us were in the storage room, they buzzed me about this. That's why I came off so...gruff."

I recalled the night I first met him, when he'd been "told" telepathically that I was cursed. Within minutes his attitude had changed from charming to trying to get as far away from me as possible. News travels fast between the Arelim and their whisperers.

"By trouble communicating, what exactly do you mean?"

He brushed away some cookie crumbs before leaning forward to rest his elbows on the table. "I mean she ignores them completely."

"Then why was she even recruited?"

"The angel who recruited her claims she's the perfect choice. He never explained why, but he's highly respected among the Arelim and no one questioned his decision."

"What's the angel's name?"

"He's Rusty's guardian, Harachel."

I knew there was something about that guy I didn't like. It made me wonder if he had an ulterior motive. "What do you make of Xenia's claim to be extra 'special.'"

He shrugged. "No idea, but I'm certain she's hiding something she doesn't want the Arelim to know."

"So what happens now?"

He licked his lips and swallowed. "They've selected her guardian to present to her on her twenty-first birthday, but now they're rethinking their decision."

"Their decision about the guardian? Or about her becoming a knight?"

"Both."

"Is she aware of any of this?" Xenia was a confused kid and I was worried. It must be difficult giving up the life she'd always known in order to live a new one filled with danger and magic. I could relate, only I'd never had a choice. Maybe she wasn't up to it. "If not, she needs to know."

Quin shook his head. "It's not my place to tell her, and it's not yours, either. Nothing changes, at least for the time being. The Arelim are more concerned about Natalie."

"What do they think of my idea to have Aydin merge with her to bring her mind back?" I asked.

He visibly shuddered. "Oh, dear. That brings back some unpleasant memories."

Poor Quin knew firsthand what that was like. "It couldn't have been that bad," I said.

"No, not really. It only hurt when he squeezed my lungs from the inside and made me pass out."

I tilted my head down and looked up at him through my lashes, trying to look ashamed. He smiled. I failed.

"That was then and this is now," he said. "I know Aydin. He's an honorable man and I'm sure he'll do all he can to help Natalie."

My shoulders lifted and dropped with an exaggerated sigh. "I'm so glad to hear you say that. As soon as everyone has their ghost-repellent charm, the wards around the property can be changed and Aydin will finally be allowed inside."

He handed me a necklace. "What do you think?"

I held the shimmering blue Celestine crystal and let my sensitive gaze pierce the multifaceted surface. The stone sat in a silver filigree setting, the intricate threads wound into an elegant design. I found Celestine to be more beautiful than any diamond. A miniature galaxy of stars appeared to pulse at the crystal's core and it gave me goose bumps.

A gentle touch on my shoulder broke me out of my trance.

"Thought I'd lost you there for a second," Quin said.

I smiled. "Only for a second. And I felt more found than lost." I handed him back the necklace. "You do beautiful work."

He beamed at me. "Thanks." He continued his job of untangling the chains. "As soon as I'm done Rafael can take them through the silver veil so the Arelim can invoke the ghost-repelling charm."

In the meantime, I'd decide which charms from Aydin's collection would best suit each squire. Not all charms were created equal, and though each squire would eventually use more than one, their first time was meaningful. Charm virgins should be handled with care.

ten

I HAD QUIN'S DETAILED LIST OF EVERY CHARM in the storage room. Ruby perched on my shoulder, chirping softly to let me know she'd rather not go back inside her box. But it didn't feel safe leaving her out in the open. Ruby was enchanted, but she wasn't a charm. She couldn't really *do* anything, though she did have an uncanny skill for detecting lies. That could come in handy.

Ruby hooked her metal toes into my sweater and disguised herself as a pin.

"What a brilliant idea, Ruby," I told her. "If you keep that up, I'll let you stay out. I'm only thinking of your safety."

The emeralds on her back blinked, which I took to mean she understood.

It comforted me to have her around. Despite all the people in the house, my grandparents included, I felt lonely. I missed Aydin. I could talk to Rafe, but his presence was often intimidating and he wasn't the friendliest guy in the world. I needed a little fun in my life and Ruby made me smile.

I picked up a charmed pen and held it up to the light. Before I'd broken the bond with my gargoyle, this had been my last acquisition and it was a powerful find. It held invisible ink that affected the person using it instead of the surface it was applied to.

I had intended the pen for Xenia because of her uncanny skill for hiding. But in light of what I now knew about her, I wasn't so sure it was a good idea. Then again, I'd see her regardless of any magical ink, and so would my grandmother. Aurora and I shared the same gift for seeing the unseen. And if Xenia tried to hide from us, we would find her.

I watched the girls' faces as I entered the great room. They looked bored and listless, and who could blame them. We'd all been stuck inside this house too long and needed a change of scenery. Rusty still hadn't returned from her sojourn with Harachel beyond the veil, and Natalie slept on. Something had to break soon or we'd all go stir-crazy.

They perked up when I lifted my canvas bag of goodies. "Are you ready to be charmed?"

Judging from their gasps of enthusiasm, they were ready.

They'd heard my tale of having been kidnapped as a child and bonded to a homicidal maniac for half my life, so they knew enough about my past to trust me. Wariness was to be expected, but at least now they had some context of who I was and where I came from. Credibility carries a lot of weight when you put your life on the line for people you hardly know. It's true that we were sisters in knighthood, but the bond between us had yet to be forged.

I gazed down at a freckle-faced girl, her red hair springy with curls and her eyes round with wonder. I chose for her the Forget-Me-Not charm so that she might regain a few extra minutes when faced with a villain intent on doing her harm. What better way to escape a situation than to make the perpetrator forget why they were coming after you in the first place?

I held up the delicate ring. "This ring is for you." I handed it to her. "Go ahead and put it on. It's perfectly safe."

She looked doubtful and kept her hands in her lap. "What does it do?"

"It causes short-term memory loss for whoever you want to make forgetful." I smiled and put the ring on my own finger. "I'm immune to charms, but I can still show you how to make it work. All you need to do is shake the person's hand. The tiny blue flowers on the ring scratch the person's skin and the spell is invoked." I pointed at the forget-me-not flowers surrounding the band. "Be careful not to scratch yourself. If you do, you'll become the forgetful one."

She blinked. "It's not going to make me pay with my soul to use it, is it?"

I shook my head. "Only a charm or curse that returns a

vital part of yourself will take something similar in value. The charms I'm giving you aren't that powerful. They'll just offer you an edge."

Lisa accepted the ring. "How far back will the person forget?"

"Not long, so you won't have much time to do whatever you need to do." I winked at her. "They'll forget anything that happened up to two hours earlier. So if you're trying to make someone forget the day they met you, it ain't gonna happen."

She giggled. "Cool. Thanks."

"You're very welcome." I turned my attention to Dale, the blonde with blue eyes so pale that I worried how well she could see. "You strike me as a happy person."

She brightened. "Oh, I am. My glass is always half full."

"Great." I smiled. "Then you'll love this charm." I held up a small book the size of my palm. It had a cartoon drawing of a laughing mouth on the cover and the title *World's Best Jokes*. I held it out to her.

She frowned. "That thing's older than I am," she said.

I nodded. "It was published in the fifties and is one of thousands just like it, but don't let the cover fool you." I flipped through the pages. "It was once owned by a comedian who dabbled in magic. He used it in nightclubs whenever his stand-up routine bombed. Kept him in the circuit for years."

Dale glanced sideways and gave the girl with the ring an envious look. "It doesn't turn into a pretty ring, does it?"

I chuckled. "Sorry. No."

She shrugged and accepted the book. She thumbed to the middle and recited, "What do you get when you cross a shark with a snowman?"

One of the girls smiled and said, "No idea, but I think you're about to tell us."

Dale chuckled. "Frostbite."

That had to be the lamest joke I'd ever heard. But every girl in the room, except for Dale and me, burst out laughing so hard they were crying. They couldn't even talk.

"I think you can guess what this charm is for," I told her.

She scowled at the hysterical girls. "Distraction?"

"Exactly."

Another minute passed before the girls sobered.

"Again, this charm doesn't last long so you need to act quickly. Make sure you're prepared before you leave 'em laughing."

Dale nodded and continued flipping through the book.

I handed a box of tissues to one of the girls, who took one to blot her eyes before passing it on. "Remember that if you tell one of the jokes without the book in your hands it won't do anything. You have to hold the charm for it to work."

"Got it," Dale said.

Now it was Xenia's turn. She gazed up at me eagerly, her crazy hair more disheveled than usual. I was surprised to see she'd cleaned the gunk off her eyes, which were the color of storm clouds. I hadn't realized her eyes were so big, and the dark circles beneath them made them appear even bigger.

"Xenia, I have a special pen for you," I said, studying her expression. She appeared excited, and that was no surprise. Who wouldn't be excited to get a magic charm of their very own? "It holds invisible ink."

"So I can write secret messages?" she asked.

"Not exactly." I gave her the pen. "Your messages won't be invisible, you will."

He mouth gaped open. "I sure could have used this as a kid."

I smirked. "I bet you could. But it's not meant to help you get away with stealing. It's meant to help you get away if you're attacked, or to hide you if you're acting on behalf of the order. Understand?"

"Oh, yes." She uncapped the pen. "I can write on anything?"

Nodding, I said, "Sure, but paper is probably best."

Xenia jumped up from the floor and trotted to the kitchen. She returned with the small notepad Aurora kept by the phone and scribbled something on a page. Right away her body began to fade.

"Wow!" Dale peered at the space where Xenia had stood a few seconds before. "She's gone."

I removed the mental shield from my eyes and stared hard at the spot where Xenia had disappeared. I saw her as a misty ghost, the particles of her essence shimmering like tiny, incandescent moths.

"Yep," I said. "Totally gone. And to come back all she has to do is destroy whatever she wrote."

I waited for her to do that, but she didn't. At least not right away.

"Can I have the same charm?" one of the other women asked.

"Sorry, there's only one." I sighed with relief when Xenia reappeared again.

"That's the coolest thing ever," Xenia said, her eyes sparkling with wonder. "I love this!" She scribbled something again and disappeared again. Only this time she didn't come back.

I'd admit to having made a mistake if I didn't see her, but I did. Yet I pretended not to.

"Uh-oh," I said, infusing my voice with concern. "Xenia? Are you there?"

I saw her misty form, but it stood still, waiting. I guessed she waited to see how far her little trick would go. That was her style. And I played along.

"Is something wrong?" one of the girls asked, her freckled face pinched with worry.

I turned my back on Xenia's misty form so she wouldn't see me mouth the words, *Everything's fine. Xenia is right behind me.*

I hoped the girl would take the hint. A twinge of surprise flashed across her face before she recovered her worried expression. "Can I do anything to help?"

I shook my head. "I'm sure Xenia's okay. You and the others can take a break and we'll resume class tomorrow."

Her smile was so frozen I could have chiseled it with an ice pick.

As the young women dispersed, I kept my eye on Xenia's "ghost." She didn't move for a couple of minutes and then crept to the front door. She couldn't open it without revealing herself so she must have been hoping someone would open it for her.

I walked purposely toward the door and lifted the drape from one of the windows to peer outside, pretending to look for something. Then I opened the door and called, "Xenia? Are you out here?"

That's when she whooshed past me to get outside. She stood on the front porch and lifted her vaporous arms to the sky in triumph. I wanted to laugh, but I couldn't let on that I knew. This game wasn't over yet. I had to see what she planned next.

She walked down the steps and headed for the road.

Aurora came to stand beside me in the doorway. "You better do something."

"I know." And I should do it fast before Xenia got beyond the protection of the wards.

I stepped off the porch and trotted toward Xenia's retreating form. "Xenia! You can stop now. I've been able to see you all along and so has Aurora."

She stopped and turned around to face me, hands on hips. "Can you hear me, too?" she asked.

I nodded. "The charm only makes your appearance vanish along with whatever you're wearing. Anyone could hear you."

She popped from invisibility into full view. "Wow, that was a kick in the ass."

Though I felt tempted to *really* kick her in the ass, I swallowed my irritation and heaved a relieved breath. "I doubt the wards would have allowed a ghost to come or go on either side."

Xenia frowned. "What would have happened if they stopped me?"

"Death, more than likely." My grandmother stood beside me and raised one eyebrow, staring down at Xenia.

A tentative smile played at Xenia's lips. She laughed. "Then it's a good thing I was only pretending." She pointed at my sweater and said, "Is that the same little frog from the storage room?"

"Yeah. Why?"

"Wow. It even lights up," she said.

I gazed down at the tiny jeweled frog clinging to my sweater. Ruby most definitely was twinkling, and that meant only one thing. Someone was lying and it sure wasn't me.

"How did you know?" Xenia asked. "I thought my acting skills were pretty good."

"They were," I told her. We each sat on one of the beds in our room and my grandmother had taken the chair by the window. "But Ruby has an uncanny sense for the truth. When someone lies, she twinkles."

"Will I get the pen charm back?" she asked.

"Maybe." I glanced at my grandmother, who dipped her chin in a quick nod. "You're not entirely on board yet, Xenia," I added. "If this behavior keeps up, we can't trust you."

She lowered her head to stare at her lap. "I understand."

"You need more time to adjust," I told her.

"The knighthood isn't for everyone," Aurora said. "It's

not unusual to question a calling as demanding as this one. We've turned away squires in the past."

"Good to know I'm not the first to be on the chopping block." She stared anxiously at my grandmother. "You're not turning me away, are you?"

Aurora shook her head. "No. At least not yet."

"Xenia, why have you been ignoring the Arelim?" I asked.

Her eyes rounded with surprise. "How did you know that? My relationship with the Arelim is private."

I tilted my head to one side, then the other. "It's private unless something you're saying, or not saying, affects the knighthood."

She frowned, a spark of the rebellious girl from yesterday flashing in her eyes.

"We all have a relationship with the Arelim in some way," I said. "When you hide something from them, you may as well be hiding it from your sister knights, too."

"It's none of your business," Xenia muttered, the volume of her voice barely loud enough for anyone but my grandmother and me to hear.

"Is there something you need to talk about?" Aurora asked. "I'm a good listener and I'm always here for you girls. I promise whatever you say will stay between us."

"What's the drama this time?" asked a tired voice from the hallway.

I jerked around to see Rusty standing there, her red hair a matted mess, her eyes puffy from either lack of sleep or crying. What had Harachel done to her? "Rusty, are you okay?"

She yawned. "I'm fine. Just sleepy."

She didn't act hostile toward me or anyone else and I hoped she wasn't carrying a grudge.

"Welcome home," Xenia said, her tone not a bit welcoming.

"Thanks, normie," Rusty said in a voice equally chilly. "Hey, Aurora. How's Natalie?"

"No change," Aurora said. "Not for a couple more hours, anyway."

"Oh? What happens in a couple hours?" Rusty asked.

Aurora looked at me, then back at Rusty. She stood up from her chair and said, "Come help me in the kitchen and I'll tell you what we have planned."

"Sure," Rusty said, her eyes a little dazed. I wondered if hypnosis was part of Harachel's method for calming her down. Her reaction time was slow and her movements appeared sluggish. From the look my grandmother gave me, she was thinking the same thing. I hoped that meant Harachel had a reprimand coming, and not just for his treatment of Rusty. He also had some explaining to do about his role in Xenia's recruitment.

I was about to ask Xenia for her thoughts when I noticed she was gone. I rushed out into the hall to see her emerge from the bathroom. I hadn't even seen her leave.

I must have looked panicked because she said, "Chill out, Chalice. I had to use the bathroom. Sheesh."

"After the stunt you pulled today, can you blame me for being cautious?"

"Yeah, as a matter of fact, I can."

I had really hoped to develop a rapport with Xenia, but it hadn't happened yet. I thought that because our backgrounds were similar—growing up without family and struggling to survive under adverse conditions—we'd have a lot in common. We did, but it wasn't enough. Her heart was more callused than mine. Even so, I had no intention of giving up.

eleven

I'D GET TO SEE AYDIN TONIGHT, AND I wouldn't have to sneak around to do it. My heart did a little flip against my ribs at the thought. He'd be welcome at Halo Home with a chance to become a real hero. He already was a hero as far as I was concerned, but a few others still needed convincing. I doubted Rafe would ever be won over. Aydin could save a bus full of children from a raging fire while rescuing a litter of kittens from a tree and Rafe would still call him a winged devil.

Quin passed out the ghost-repellent charms after dinner. The squires were ecstatic with their new treasures, as well they should be. The pendants were gorgeous, but their ability to ward off questionable specters was even better. I just wished one would work on me.

"Look at the center of this crystal," a squire said, her

face lit with wonder. "It's like tiny stars are floating around inside."

"Don't look too closely," I warned. "Unless you want to go into a trance."

She quickly released the Celestine to let it dangle against her chest. The others did the same.

"So what happens next?" Dale asked.

"We wait a few minutes for the wards to be switched," my grandmother said. "That will allow the ghost form of the gargoyle Aydin to get through and help Natalie escape the mental fog that's holding her prisoner."

"Aren't gargoyles evil?" Xenia asked.

I rolled my eyes. "As a general rule, yes. But remember the story I told you? Aydin saved my life by letting his curse change him into a gargoyle like the kind he and I were bonded to. He's a good man."

"So what?" Xenia's brows knitted in confusion. "It doesn't change the fact that he's a monster now."

Holy crap, was everyone's head as thick as Rafe's? "Yeah, it does, Xenia, because Aydin pledged his allegiance to the knighthood nearly a thousand years ago. His physical appearance doesn't change the man he is. He's devoted to us and our cause."

"And what exactly is our cause?" Xenia asked.

She should know the answer by now. "To protect humanity from evil, supernatural and otherwise."

She shrugged. "How about saving hungry kids who live on the streets?"

"That goes without saying," I said, shocked she would ask such a thing.

"I used to be one of those kids." She crossed her arms with such force I heard her shirt rip at the seam.

I knew what Xenia's problem was: she was scared. Scared of Ayden, scared of ghosts and demons and intimidating angels that could kill you as easily as look at you. I'd felt that way once, but I had to suck it up to survive. Xenia would have to do the same.

The squires, Rusty, Xenia, Quin, my grandparents and myself stood facing the window in Natalie's bedroom. Natalie slept so deeply we often had to check to make sure she was breathing. We had a clear view of the road and the perimeter of Halo Home's property, so when the angels gathered there it was easy to see who was in attendance. I recognized Rafe, of course, so I assumed the others must be knight guardians as well. Harachel swaggered while pacing back and forth like a caged animal and I wondered if he didn't feel comfortable in the human realm. I had a fair idea what he would become after fathering Rusty's child.

The angels spread out along the property's boundaries and extended their wings until the tips of their feathers touched to create an unbroken circle. I counted at least a dozen angels, yet there had to be more I couldn't see. The Arelim had a natural glow to begin with, but now they pulsed with such brilliance it turned night into day within a ring of linked suns.

I glanced at the Celestine charms worn around the necks of everyone in the room, including Natalie. They started glowing with pale blue light and tiny sparks flew out from the crystals. The ghost-repellent spell must be reacting to the new wards.

The luminous circle dialed down a few watts and I blinked. Bright light would normally hurt my eyes, but angel light didn't affect me in the slightest. I could even see through it to the road beyond, where a handful of misty figures gathered.

"Oh, shit," I said to no one in particular, but my grandmother responded with a nod.

"I see them, too," she said.

They were ghosts looking for a new haunt and had probably been hanging around for a while. We'd never noticed them before due to the wards that kept them out. There was nothing stopping them now. Or so they thought.

"You see who, too?" one of the squires asked as she narrowed her eyes while gazing out the window. "The angels? They're beautiful and they're everywhere."

"Mmm-hmm, yes, the angels, that's exactly it," I told her, not wanting her to panic. There was no sense getting the girls worked up over something that couldn't bother them. As long as they wore their charms, they'd be fine.

"Can you ladies do me a favor?" Aurora asked. "Keep your ghost-repellent charms on at all times, even when you go to bed at night."

"Why?" Xenia asked, her tone wary. "What's out there?"

"Nothing for you to worry about," Aurora said.

Xenia stared down at her charm. "If you say so."

I saw one extra large, winged ghost in the middle of the others and it was all I could do to stop myself from hopping around like a lovesick teenager. Aydin was on his way here.

"Okay, here he comes," Aurora said as she followed my gaze.

His presence didn't go unnoticed by the angels, who stepped back to create more distance between them. They knew who he was and *what* he was. For them not to react would be like asking a lion to ignore a tiger. They were natural enemies with an instinct to fight if provoked.

I ran out of the room and down the stairs as fast as my short legs would take me, which was pretty fast. I sprinted out the door and practically ran right through Aydin, whose transparent gargoyle body stood waiting. He expected me to come. I doubt he expected what I was about to ask.

I nodded and said, "It's okay. They want you here. We have an important favor to ask."

Aydin hesitated and turned to look at the ghosts wandering onto the property. The angels had seen them, too, and didn't appear to care. Aydin did. He spread his wings as if preparing to attack any specter that came too close.

I waved them off. "Ignore them, Aydin. They're not important, but the woman inside is. We need your help."

Aydin had witnessed the attack on me, but he hadn't seen the episode with Natalie. I quickly explained what had happened and that she had been in a coma for almost a week.

"I know you can reach her, Aydin. You're the only one who can bring her back. Plus she's our key to learning who's murdering the knights."

Though he couldn't speak in his current state, his body language let me know he was eager to help. He waved a beastly paw toward the house. I preceded him inside and he followed me up the stairs.

The others were waiting for us and when they saw me, their eyes jerked in their sockets as they looked around for what they couldn't see. But my grandmother saw him. She blinked and placed her hand flat against her chest.

"Is it here?" Xenia asked, appearing more eager than fearful. So she wasn't as repulsed as she'd led us to believe.

"Aydin is with us, yes," I said in a strained voice.

She retreated toward the window and pressed her back against the wall, feigning disgust.

I rolled my eyes at Xenia, then looked at my grand-mother. "Can he try now?" I asked her, and she nodded, eyes closed as if in prayer, which she might have been.

Aydin's misty bulk lowered to Natalie's bed and seemed to melt inside her. Her body shifted and her closed eyelids twitched. Something was happening but it was impossible to know exactly what. Her lips moved and I leaned in to hear her if she spoke. I opened my auditory senses and tuned out the breathing and heartbeats of everyone else in the room so I could focus just on her.

"She... But that's impossible," Natalie muttered.

Her head moved side to side and she moaned.

"Maybe he should stop," Aurora said. "Natalie is be-having like she's in pain."

"She probably is if her conscious mind is buried some-where. It won't stop hurting until she comes out." I leaned in closer. "She's trying to talk."

"What's she saying?" Aurora asked.

"That it's impossible."

"What is?"

I shook my head. "I don't know."

Natalie's eyelids squeezed so tight it looked like it hurt. She muttered, "One of us."

I repeated to my grandmother what she said.

"She lives on the blood of the dark ones." Natalie gasped. "She's so old. How did she live so long?"

Again I repeated Natalie's muttered words and watched my grandmother go pale.

"What is it?" I asked her. "What's wrong?"

Aurora fanned herself with her hand. "Hot flash."

I doubted menopause was her problem. Something Natalie just said upset her. "Who do you think she's talking about?"

"Let's wait until Natalie is out of the woods, okay?" Aurora began wringing her hands, something I'd never seen her do before.

Though her eyes were still closed, a small smile formed on Natalie's lips as she whispered, "I don't know how to thank you. I can't believe I made it back."

I heaved a lung-collapsing sigh. "She'll be okay," I said to everyone in the room. They all murmured to one another and I made a down motion with my hands to lower their voices.

"She's back, but I don't know if she's fully recovered. We'll know more after we talk," I said.

Natalie rolled onto her side and fluttered her eyelids, but didn't open them. She hugged the blanket close around her shoulders and seemed to nestle deeper into the pillow. And then she was asleep again. I prayed she could wake up on her own.

I watched Aydin's ghost lift from Natalie's body. He

pointed to himself and then to me before clasping his hands together. He wanted us to merge so he could explain what had happened with Natalie.

Still standing, I closed my eyes and welcomed Aydin in. I felt a rush of warmth and a wave of calmness that made me feel safe, protected. This intimate connection caused my yearning for him to grow even stronger. I struggled not to collapse in a whimpering puddle right in front of everyone in the room.

Her mind is back, but she needs rest, he told me. *She's been through a severe trauma.*

So you knocked her out? I asked.

I saw Aydin's face in my mind and he looked just as handsome as he had before he changed.

In a sense, yes, I knocked her out. She didn't know what hit her. She's sleeping normally now and without dreams.

What a relief. *So what did she mean about the woman being one of us?*

His image appeared troubled. He rubbed his chin and stared as if deep in thought. *She didn't give me a name, which was probably kept from her on purpose. But she managed to see how this creature survived for so long.*

How long? I asked.

He paused. *Close to a millennium.*

And it being one of us means that it, or she, is a Hatchet knight?

He nodded.

Are there many knights left who are that old?

None that I'm aware of, he said. *Unless you count Saint Geraldine.*

Oh, yes, Geraldine, the one with enchanted remains.

But I didn't really count that as living. Quin and I had rescued her disembodied head from the Vyantara and it was now with the Arelim. Once her body parts were reunited she could become a whole woman again. Finding them was another item on my to-do list.

The old one responsible for the murders was alive and completely whole. I'd seen her standing on two legs, but I supposed anything could have been under the cloak she was wearing.

Did Natalie see her?

Aydin shook his head. *If she did, she's blocked the image from her mind, because all I picked up from her was a dark crystal cave shrouded in fog. That must be the woman's lair. And I saw the dark ones she shared it with.*

I imagined some horrible kind of monster, possibly even the gargoyle assassins the Vyantara used for their dirty work. Or maybe Maågan demons. Natalie had said the woman drank their blood so that gave me a better of idea of what these dark ones could be. The only creatures I knew of that drank blood and lived forever were vampires.

Is she a vampire? I asked Aydin.

He tilted his chin down and gazed at me, eyebrows raised. *The blood she drinks doesn't come from humans. She survives on the blood of the Fallen.*

Oh, my God. A good knight turned bad with the help of the Arelim's estranged dark brothers. *Why? And why did she wait until now to reveal herself?*

Both good questions, Chalice. I only wish I had the answers. Natalie doesn't know, either.

A hand shook me gently by the shoulder. I wasn't ready

to leave Aydin. Who knew when I'd get to see him again? He'd done what my grandparents and the Arelim wanted, so now they could shun him. I wouldn't let that happen.

My trance broken, I popped open my eyes to see my grandmother standing in front of me, her hands grasping me by the shoulders. Getting jerked from my connection to Aydin had given me a pounding headache and I stomped backward to break my grandmother's hold.

"What?" I barked.

"It's Xenia," she said, her eyes holding a mixture of anger and panic. "She's gone."

I looked at Aydin's ghost and watched him shake his large, gargoyle head.

"She was standing right by the window," I said. "How could she suddenly vanish in a room filled with people?"

"It wasn't that sudden," my grandmother said. "You've been in a trance for nearly an hour."

I blinked. It hadn't felt that long. I glanced around the room and found everyone gone but a sleeping Natalie and my grandmother. "Have you looked everywhere?" I asked.

"Of course." She sounded annoyed. "And so have the Arelim."

I thought about the pen charm, but I'd taken it away from Xenia. It was back in the bag where I had stored the charms reserved for the squires.

I ran to the room Xenia and I shared and lifted the mattress from the box spring on my bed. The bag I'd hidden there was gone. Damn it!

"She has the pen charm back," I told my grandmother

through gritted teeth. "And you and I are the only ones who can see her if she uses it."

"I've been watching for a visible Xenia, not an invisible one." Her mouth turned down at the corners when she added, "Now that the wards are set to allow ghosts through, she could leave without anyone knowing."

And that, apparently, was my fault. "You know as well as I do that Aydin had to be allowed in so he could help Natalie."

Her shoulders lifted and fell with a deep sigh. She rubbed her temples. "Of course I know. I'm not blaming you, I'm just worried about Xenia. She could be the murderer's next victim."

I should have felt more concern than I did, but at that moment I was too pissed off. The little thief had lied and stolen from me. She'd reneged on a promise to her sister knights and to the Arelim. I wasn't sure I'd ever forgive her.

"She can't have gone very far," I said. "It's after midnight and freezing outside. How could she leave without a car?" My heart gave a shudder as I remembered one of the items in the charm bag she'd taken. I slapped a hand against my forehead. "Crap!"

My grandmother frowned. "Zeke and I were just about to head out in Natalie's Jeep to look for her."

"I doubt that will do any good," I said. "Xenia has the flying charm. I'm sure that's how she got away."

Aurora nodded as if flying was a perfectly acceptable mode of transportation. I doubt anything surprised her anymore. "I think I know where she went."

"Home?"

"Yep, back to the city. I bet she's in Denver by now."

At least it was a city nearby and not in another state. And if she were in Denver, we had eyes and ears there who could scope out any magical dealings if she tried to sell the charms. Knowing what I knew of Xenia, I believed that's what she was up to.

My stomach made a little jump as I thought about returning to Denver. I felt a mix of good and bad vibes about that city and some of my memories terrified me. Didn't matter, I had to go back eventually and now was better than later.

"I'll find Xenia," I told my grandmother. And when I did I'd spank her to within an inch of her bratty emo life. "I need to go to Denver anyway. I have to search the Vyantara fatherhouse ruins." Namely to find whatever charms and curses had survived the fire.

My grandmother shook her head so fast I was afraid she'd knock something loose. "Chalice, you can't leave."

"Why not?"

"You know why not." She began wringing her hands again and started to pace, her steps hard and fast. "It's too dangerous. The murderer is still out there."

"I know that, which is why I'm going. Someone has to stop her."

"That someone doesn't have to be you." She stopped moving to give me such a tender, pleading look I was at a loss for words. She took my hand and clasped it between both of hers. "It's taken so long to finally have you with us," she said, her eyes brimming. "I lost your mother to violence. I can't lose you, too."

My eyes stung and I found it suddenly hard to swallow.

"You know the risks to living as we do. I'm sure your mother worried about you the same way."

"I wouldn't know," she said, her voice soft as a whisper. "I never knew her. I was adopted into another Hatchet knight family after she was killed."

I didn't know my grandmother had been an orphan. "How old were you?"

She thought for a second. "Four, I think. Maybe five. But I don't remember anything about my mother. I don't think she stuck around much when she was alive."

I had no desire to have children and my grandmother just provided a good reason for that decision. So what if the order needed more knights? The Arelim could collect them from among the whisperers. That's how the order had begun in the first place.

I pulled my hand from my grandmother's firm grip. "I realize how hard this is for you, but it's the only way. We can't send the squires to Denver, we can't ask for Rusty's help while her powers are gone, and Natalie is too weak."

"I can go," she said. "I'll find Xenia myself and take down that bitch who's murdering our knights."

I had no doubt she could pull it off, but her job at Halo Home was more important. "Rusty and Natalie need you. So do the squires. And I have connections in the city that you don't. It's best that I go." I let my lips soften into an almost-smile. "You know I'm right."

A tear slipped free and she hastily swiped at it with the back of her hand. She nodded.

"Quin can take me back with him to Elmo's," I said. "I'll be safe there. And Aydin will come, too."

I searched the room for Aydin and saw his ghost filling the doorway. My grandmother saw him too because she offered him a grateful smile. "What were you able to learn from Natalie's memories?" she asked him, though the question was really meant for me since Aydin couldn't talk. So I told her everything he'd told me. Her face drained of color.

"You know something else, don't you?" I asked her. "Something Natalie didn't say."

"It's only a suspicion," she said, the worry lines on her forehead going even deeper. "Natalie never gave a name?"

I looked at Aydin, who shook his head. "No. Aydin thinks it was kept from her on purpose." But I remembered a name. A name I heard Natalie whisper just after she'd almost suffocated to death. "Does the name Maria ring any bells?" I asked.

My grandmother took a step back and her knees wobbled. Aydin rushed up behind her as if to catch her in case she fell, but she'd just fall through him. He was about as solid as a cloud of fog.

I guided her to my bed and she sat down, her fingers clutching at the neck of her sweater. Her breathing picked up speed and the dark circles beneath her eyes stood out against her pale skin. "I do know of someone named Maria." Her voice came out ragged, as if she'd run out of breath. "Maria was Saint Geraldine's daughter."

Now I remembered where I had heard the name before hearing it from Natalie. Aydin once told me he had helped deliver Geraldine's baby on the battlefield. That the child's fallen angel father had tried to force Geraldine into giving her baby to him. When Geraldine was drawn and quartered by the church, it was assumed the village midwife had kept Maria to raise as her own.

"You don't know that it's the same Maria," I said.

"When I was young I heard a rumor that Maria was still alive and living with her father behind the black veil, but I never believed it." My grandmother hugged herself. "Perhaps I should have."

If Maria's father had tried to take her, he probably succeeded after Geraldine's execution. After getting hacked to pieces there'd have been nothing Geraldine could have done to stop him.

"I need to contact Saint Geraldine," I said. "It's possible she can help us find her daughter."

"I've heard of knights going bad before, but nothing like this. Living on the blood of the Fallen?" My grandmother visibly shuddered.

Creepy. And probably dangerous as hell.

If I was to stay in Denver a while, I wasn't about to leave Shojin's heart behind. Hidden or not, I needed it for Aydin when he was ready to become human again. As soon as the Hatchet murderer was caught, I would have my man back.

I left my mother's shield with my grandmother for safekeeping, and I asked her to take care of Ruby for me while I was gone. If anything were to happen to me I wanted to make sure they didn't fall into the wrong hands. I tossed all my belongings into the canvas bag I'd arrived with and tucked the black fallen angel feather into the side pocket of my coat. What a relief Xenia hadn't stolen it, too. I wasn't sure how valuable it was, but it could have hidden properties I had yet to discover.

I shrugged on my coat, headed downstairs, and once out in the yard I found the same shovel I'd used to bury the heart. I began digging around the giant roots of the ponderosa tree.

"Need some help?"

I glanced up to see Rafe standing there, his human guise expertly back in place. He'd changed his look from Mr. GQ to stylish mountain man complete with plaid flannel shirt, denim jeans and heavy Sorel boots. He'd completely bought into the whole manly man thing.

"Thanks, Rafe, but I'm almost done." I dug the spade in for another scoop of dirt. It was easier than I thought it would be, even after a fresh snowfall.

"Does this mean Aydin has made up his mind?" Rafe asked.

Not that it was any of his business. "Yes, but he's planning to wait until after we've caught the murderer. In the meantime, he thinks he'll be more helpful as a gargoyle than a human."

Rafe knelt down to watch me dig. "I understand you'll stay in Denver awhile."

Of course he would know my plans already. The Arelim's network was like a grapevine.

"I will be, yes," I said.

"Is Aydin coming with you?"

"He'll help me while I'm there, but I don't know where he'll stay." I dug the spade in deeper and heard it clang against the iron skillet. Jackpot. "The Vyantara may still be looking for him so he's doing his best to stay out of sight."

"The fatherhouse is gone," Rafe said. "There are no Vyantara left in the city."

"Are you sure about that?"

He huffed. "No."

"We're not taking any chances."

"You could use my help, too, don't you think?"

I looked up at his face and saw the sincere question in his eyes. He really wanted to be a part of this.

"We can use all the help we can get," I told him. "I'll let you know when. But for now we'll be going places where angels fear to tread." I grabbed the skillet's handle and yanked it up out of the hole. And gazed down into empty space.

twelve

"IS SOMETHING WRONG?" RAFE ASKED.

I couldn't believe it. "Shojin's heart. It's gone!"

"Are you sure that's where you buried it?" he asked, sounding like his usual calm and collected self.

"Of course I'm sure." I grabbed the skillet and flung it out into the snow. "That little thief took it."

"What thief?"

"Xenia!" I glared at him. "You do know she's missing, right?"

"Yes, but we stopped looking when we realized she used the pen charm to hide herself. She's beyond our capacity to see."

Unfair as it was, I knew that to be true. The Arelim were powerful and possessed some magical abilities, but it was their fallen brothers who topped the charts on spells, charms and curses. The knights took mostly after their

Fallen fathers and not the Arelim angels their fathers used to be.

"How can you be sure it was Xenia?" He sounded genuinely curious.

"Because I reburied the heart the night the Hatchet murderer almost killed me and Natalie." It made perfect sense now. Xenia had watched me from our bedroom window and she'd run to tattle on me to my grandparents. I could have done without the drama. "She must have seen exactly where I buried it. Maybe you saw, too." I narrowed my eyes at him.

He cocked a hip and met my glare. "Are you accusing *me* now?"

Rafe would prefer Aydin be out of my life completely and keeping Shojin's heart would just about guarantee it. He couldn't lie to me. It was against Arelim law.

He gave me a smug grin and wiggled his fingers in the air. "You know very well I can't touch anything associated with a gargoyle."

I frowned, realizing he was right. He couldn't have taken it.

Looking bored, he asked, "What will you do now?"

"Now I find Xenia and take it back."

Quin drove Elmo's Studebaker along the dark city streets of downtown Denver. My heart stuttered when we rounded a corner and headed toward the same street the Vyantara fatherhouse had been on.

He must have seen me stiffen because he asked, "Are you okay?"

I breathed out a shuddering sigh. "Fantastic. This is good for me, really."

"There's a lot to be said for facing your fears."

"I'm not afraid." At least I didn't think I was. All the things I feared were either dead or gone. "If I fear anything, it's my past, which is ridiculous because it's over."

Quin nodded. "I know it's over, but I think you're afraid of losing what you finally have now."

How did he get to be so smart? "You're a wise man, Mr. Dee." I had no problem facing a dozen gargoyles or a dozen nasty sorcerers, but threaten to take my family away from me and I'm shaking in my boots.

"I'm here for you, Chalice," he said. "And so is Elmo and Aydin and…" He stopped for a theatrical pause. "So is Geraldine."

I turned in my seat to stare at him. "You're in touch with her? Through the veil?"

He grinned. "Almost every day."

I should have known. I'd sensed something between those two, even if one of them was a mummified head. She wasn't dead, just altered in a nonliving sort of way. Besides, I'd be the first to admit that physical looks meant next to nothing when you cared deeply about someone. "You're in love with her," I said.

The dark of night wasn't enough to hide his blush. "It's still too soon to say. We have a few obstacles to overcome."

If anyone could relate to obstacles in a relationship it was I. "I know what you mean."

"I believe in my soul that Geraldine will be whole one

day," he said, his tone wistful. "But I often find it hard to be patient."

I was both happy and sad for them. I knew firsthand how painful it was to love someone you couldn't have. "Does Geraldine feel the same about you?"

He shrugged. "Possibly. We're staying good friends for now."

That was the sensible thing to do, at least for the time being.

"I figured you would want to talk to her as soon as possible," he said.

He was right about that. Though it was after three in the morning and I'd had no sleep in over twenty-four hours, we couldn't afford more delays. I needed to change my sleep schedule back to days anyway. Operating under the cover of darkness was safer for everyone, especially innocent bystanders. I preferred being out and about when the rest of the city was asleep.

Quin steered the car to the curb in front of a magnificent church with spires tall enough to pierce the sky. It still looked like a great white dragon crouched in a city of asphalt and concrete, but the sight of it didn't induce a feeling of awe this time. I had nearly died here, murdered a gargoyle here, and watched my adoptive sorcerer father bleed to death at the foot of the altar. The Cathedral Basilica had become a beautiful horror for me. And seeing as how Quin had parked the car here, I assumed it's also where I'd be having my chat with Geraldine.

"I realize this church makes you uncomfortable," he said, looking sheepish. "But it's the only place Geraldine can come through."

I heaved in a breath. "Don't worry, it's fine." When I opened the car door to step out, my feet felt weighted and I had trouble standing. I didn't suspect any supernatural forces at work, just my own mind playing tricks.

Forcing one foot in front of the other, I followed Quin to the back door and waited for him to pick the lock. He used a key instead.

"Wait a minute," I said. "How the hell did you get a key?"

"I forgot to tell you," he said, while opening the door. "The church is no longer owned by the Vyantara."

That was good news, but it didn't answer my question. "So who owns it?"

"The Arelim."

I chuckled. "Very funny. Angels can't own things."

"Says who?" He preceded me inside and I hesitated at the threshold. "There are no ghosts in here," he assured me.

Maybe not the woo-woo kind, but my mental ghosts were almost as bad. I followed him to the stairs leading down to the basement, where Geraldine's tomb used to be. I stopped to gaze toward the front of the church, where mayhem had ruled less than two months ago.

"All traces are gone," he said, as if reading my mind. "Go see for yourself."

I sniffed the air and smelled dust, remnants of stale sweat from the occasional transient, and furniture polish on the pews. All blood scents were gone, as was the dead-animal stench that attached to Shui like a second skin. The church smelled clean, but I had to see it to believe it.

I headed down the aisle between rows of pews and ap-

proached the altar. I cued up my super vision and scanned
every corner. Not a stray piece of shattered gargoyle in
sight. Gazing upward, I marveled at the stained glass
windows that shimmered in the moonlight. It had to
have cost a fortune to replace what Shui had broken. If
the Arelim now owned this church, it wouldn't surprise
me if the angels themselves had created the windows.

Feeling cleansed of concern, I turned to head back to
the stairs. Shadows in the corners appeared more menacing in the dark than they should have. I chalked it up
to a heightened state of paranoia and tried to look away,
but my eyes refused. My vision pierced the gloom and
I discovered the outline of a figure. At first I thought
the murderous Maria had found me, but the body belonged to a man. He was impeccably dressed, his silver
hair combed stylishly, and his black eyes stared at me with
such intensity I thought they'd burrow a hole straight
through my skin.

"Quin!" I shouted. I froze in place, unable to move.
Nothing physical held me, but my own shock was par-
alyzing enough. I couldn't believe what I was seeing.
"Quin!"

He ran up to stand beside me and I pointed at the
shadowy figure in the corner.

"Chalice, what's wrong?" He gazed in the direction of
my pointing finger. "What do you see?"

My mouth was so dry I almost couldn't speak. I managed to croak, "Gavin. It's Gavin!"

Quin touched my arm and I yanked away.

"You told me there were no ghosts here." My anger

and terror twined around each other to make my voice shake. "Gavin's dead. His ghost is haunting the church!"

Quin shook his head. "I promise you there are no ghosts here. The Arelim made sure of it."

I jabbed my finger toward the menacing figure of Gavin, who continued to glare. "Then what the hell is that?"

"I don't know. I can't see anything." He started to walk toward the shadowed corner and I screamed at him to stop. He did. "Okay, I'll have the Arelim sweep the church again. I'm sure it's just a bad memory rearing its ugly head."

"It's not moving, but its eyes are glaring at me."

"I bet it's only a soul-stain," Quin said. "Gavin's death was so tragic and sudden that his dark soul must have stained the air inside the church. Nothing a little spectral bleach won't wipe clean."

I'd heard of soul-stains, but had never actually seen one until now. Ghosts were shells of those who passed on, and soul-stains were imprints of souls that died in rage. They were supposedly harmless, but a soul-stain of Gavin Heinrich could never be harmless. He'd been my master far too long and if anything could force his soul to cling to this plane, it would be his hatred of me.

I shuddered and headed for the stairs, rushing down them so fast I nearly tripped over my feet. Not even Gavin could make me run away from this church and stop me from talking to Geraldine.

An ornate tapestry used to hang over the vault door to Geraldine's tomb. It was gone now, as was the door. The tomb with black walls and a rickety old table in the center now looked like a room out of *Better Homes and Gardens*. A wood laminate floor covered the twentieth-century tiles and the brick walls had been painted pale sage. Floor-to-ceiling curtains in a garden print hung on one side, and the other walls held ornate light sconces along with several framed photographs of lush flower gardens. A cream-colored chair and love seat were artfully arranged around a green braided rug. All that was missing were flowering shrubs and potted plants.

The room helped lessen my shock at having seen Gavin's soul-stain. The colors and light were so lifelike I could have sworn it was spring.

"Wow, Quin, did you do all this?" I asked him.

"Mmm-hmm." He straightened a pillow on the love seat and ran his hand along a bookshelf. He blew on his finger. "Time for the feather duster."

"It's lovely." I lowered myself to the chair and surveyed Geraldine's shrine. A pity she couldn't enjoy it for herself. "Very peaceful. A perfect place to meditate."

"It's even better than that, Chalice." He closed his eyes and within seconds the shimmering surface of the silver veil appeared on the curtained wall. It rippled in rings of undulating sparkles before parting to allow a woman through.

Not just any woman. It was Saint Geraldine, in the flesh.

I stood up so fast I almost lost my balance. Geraldine looked elegant in a long white toga-style dress with her golden hair cascading in soft waves over her shoulders. Her crystal blue eyes were pinched nearly closed by a broad smile that stretched from one ear to the other. "Chalice!" she said, arms open wide.

I leaned forward to embrace her, and only then noticed the transparency of her body. I could see through her to the rippled veil and delicate floral curtain behind it. When I reached out to touch her, my fingers contacted nothing but air.

"I honestly wish I was able to hug you," she said, and lowered her arms. "The gesture was sincere."

"You're a ghost?" I asked, not liking that idea at all.

She held out one hand and tilted it like the wings of an airplane. "Sort of, but not really. I'm not dead."

"Does this mean all your body parts have been re-united?"

Quin shook his head. "No. That's why she isn't solid."

"As long as my head is with the Arelim I can take physical form even if I only appear wispy as a cloud."

I didn't mind. I preferred this to the shrunken mummified head I'd had to talk to before. This seemed more...natural. I twirled around slowly. "I love what you've done to the place."

"Isn't it incredible?" she asked, beaming at Quin, who colored with the compliment. "Quin knows exactly what I like."

"It's the least I could do for you," he said.

The two of them held each other's gaze for several long seconds and I suddenly felt like a third wheel.

"I wish this was just a reunion visit, Geraldine," I said. "But I'm here because I need your help."

"Already back to work?" she asked. "I'm sorry that I wasn't able to speak with you while you recuperated on this side of the veil. The Arelim have a strict policy regarding the knights who visit. No mingling allowed."

How could I forget? When Rafe wasn't training me to control my senses, I'd been bored out of my mind. Yet the peace and tranquility behind the veil is seductive enough to block most yearnings. I must have been a special case because I got antsy to leave on my first day.

"It's about your daughter," I said slowly, gauging her reaction by watching her face.

Her brows made a little twitch and her perfect peach-colored skin maintained its healthy glow. She wasn't real flesh and blood so her complexion couldn't actually tell me anything. But her eyes grew round and filled with ghostly tears.

"Maria," she said, as if tasting the word. She moved slowly over to the love seat and sat down. I marveled that her insubstantial body didn't fade right through it. "I haven't spoken her name in centuries."

"We believe she's still alive," I said.

She stared at me then, her forehead wrinkling. "That's absurd. It would make her over nine hundred years old."

I sat back down in the chair. "My grandmother said that as a child she heard rumors about Maria still being alive."

Geraldine pressed her lips together in a bitter line. "Dark fairy tales. Cruel stories about a motherless child who didn't know how to deal with whatever powers she was born with."

The chair felt suddenly too hard and I shifted forward to the edge of the seat. "It's possible she found a way to survive all these years."

"How?"

"By feeding off the blood of the Fallen," Quin said.

Geraldine gasped and her ghostly fingers fanned out against her throat. "My baby, my Maria."

"If she's who we think she is, Maria's not a baby anymore," I said. "She may be the one responsible for murdering the knights."

Geraldine shook her head slowly. "A Hatchet knight would never knowingly kill her own sisters, especially not without cause."

"She's not a knight," I told her, and Geraldine snapped her head around to stare at me. "I mean, she was never admitted into the knighthood. She's never been trained or mentored by her guardian."

She blinked. "When Maria disappeared after my death, I assumed she had died and her soul taken to hell because of who her father is."

"We think her father is the one who took her, and she might be living with him now." I watched as Geraldine stared off into the distance, possibly replaying ancient memories inside her head. "What we don't understand is why she waited until now to begin her killing spree."

"I wouldn't know," Geraldine said softly. "I never thought a child of mine would be capable of such cruelty."

"I've seen her," I said.

"You have?" she asked. "When?"

"When she tried to kill me." I licked my lips and scooted so far forward on the chair that my butt balanced on the edge. "I couldn't see her face because it was hidden under the hood of her cloak. She stole the breath from my lungs and I almost suffocated."

"Dear God." Geraldine leaned back on the cushions, grabbing a pillow to hold close to her chest. I saw through her arms to the patchwork fabric underneath. "Her father could steal breath. It's how he vanquished his enemies."

I was fairly certain that confirmed the identity of our killer, but now came the question of where, and how, to find her.

thirteen

"WE NEED TO FIND MARIA'S FATHER," I SAID. "What's his name?"

Geraldine sucked in her lips as if trying to stop herself from talking. Names were powerful magic and saying someone's name could potentially give them power over you. I guessed that's why she hesitated.

"The Arelim will protect you," I told her. "Tell me his name and I promise not to speak it aloud unless I have to."

She seemed to summon her courage by closing her eyes, but they flashed open with the whispered name "Pharzuph."

The sound of it fluttered through my ears and shuddered down my spine. It made me feel dirty. "His name sounds wicked."

She nodded. "Pharzuph is the fallen angel of fornication and lust."

I didn't consider sex bad, but associating it with this creature made it seem filthy. My heart went out to Maria for having been raised by this fiend. I knew what it was like to be kidnapped by a sociopath, so it wasn't a stretch to imagine her having to live with a sex maniac all her life. I'd managed to escape my kidnapper with limited damage. Maria, on the other hand, had been adversely affected. Something had driven her to murder and she enjoyed killing.

"Where do you think he is?" I asked Geraldine.

"He's probably where all fallen angels go. Beyond the black veil."

According to Barachiel, the black veil didn't appeal to all Fallen. He wanted nothing to do with it.

"How do I get there?"

Quin took a step closer to me. "You don't want to go there, Chalice. I doubt you could even if you wanted to."

"We know very little about the Fallen's domain," Geraldine added.

I'd thought the Arelim would glean all the intel they could about their enemy, though come to think of it, no one ever said they were enemies. Estranged brothers with opposing interests, yes, but one had never directly threatened the other. They each kept to their own side of the fence. I had a strong feeling that whatever was going on with Maria was about to tip a precarious balance.

I remembered the black feather that had sent Natalie's mind down a dark and dangerous rabbit hole. I slipped it out of my coat pocket. "Maybe this will help me."

Quin stepped in front of Geraldine as if to protect her. "Put that away."

"Why?" I asked. "It's only a feather."

"It could be more than just a feather," he said. "What if it's enchanted? It might even be like one of those bugs you see on the telly."

"You mean for tracking?" I asked.

"You never know. The last thing I want is for the Fallen to come after Geraldine."

Geraldine stood. "Quin, even if they did, I'm not actually here anyway. This form is only a projection of my physical self and not the real me." She tried to rub his back but her hand passed straight through him.

The thought of a creature like Pharzuph tainting these hallowed halls made my skin crawl. I put the feather away. "If the feather is a conduit of some sort, maybe it can be used like a homing device. It could lead me to wherever Maria is hiding."

"That's a really bad idea," Quin said. "Your grandmother would have a fit if she knew."

"My grandmother doesn't have to know." I gave him a pointed look and raised an eyebrow. "Right?"

He narrowed his eyes at me. "Right."

I yawned and checked my watch. It would be light soon, which meant bedtime for me. My brain would be as useful as oatmeal if I didn't get some sleep.

"I can take a hint," he told me, and turned to face Geraldine. They shared a meaningful look. Oh, yes, those two had something going on. The look of longing in Quin's eyes made me think of Aydin. At least now Aydin and I could be together without having to sneak around.

Elmo would welcome Aydin, in any shape or form, into his home.

"Geraldine, did you know Gavin's soul-stain is inside the church?" I asked.

Her eyes flashed alarm and she blinked. "What?"

"I'm sure it's nothing, but Chalice is the only one able to see it," Quin said. "The Arelim should be able to easily get rid of it."

Geraldine scowled. "That shouldn't have happened. The church was thoroughly cleansed."

Quin shrugged. "It's harmless. It's like a painting on the wall."

A painting that induces nightmares. Sharp tingles pierced the back of my neck to remind me of Gavin's bony-fingered grip. Quin had forgotten the extent of Gavin's cruelty because he didn't know the half of it. The fact that the man's soul-stain existed here did not bode well at all. I wasn't the only one who thought so. Geraldine felt it, too.

The mattress I lay on in Elmo's third bedroom was so soft it felt like lying on a pile of marshmallows, and just as lumpy. The old elf had bought this house, along with all his possessions, in the late thirties and never saw the point in upgrading because he was rarely home. He spent the majority of his time either in his basement coffee shop or with friends beyond the green veil. His house and everything in it was as preserved as a museum.

I liked the nostalgic mood here. It made me feel as if I'd been transported to a different time, before my mother's death and my hellish life of bondage to a gargoyle, and before the murders of my sister knights. It offered me a sense of being outside of things for a change, like a barrier of time that insulated me from what troubles lay ahead.

The heavy drapes were closed against the day's sunlight, but I still had trouble falling asleep. Elmo was already asleep by the time Quin and I arrived so I never got a chance to say hello. I'd been tossing and turning for nearly two hours, despite being only half conscious when I fell into bed. Turns out I was overtired. My brain refused to stop its troubled musing.

Xenia. Damn. Where the hell was that girl? I hoped not literally in hell, because I'd feel responsible if so. If I hadn't introduced her to the pen charm, she would never have run away. On second thought, she was so good at disappearing in full view that she might have pulled it off anyway. The question of why she'd leave the security of the order still nagged at me. She was bitter about her past and felt like an outcast, but she hadn't given the knighthood a chance. She hadn't given *me* a chance. I should have tried harder to break through her armor of false bravado. At least she had removed her war paint. That had to be a good sign, right?

Then there were Natalie and Rusty. Rusty hated me, and reparations on my part were desperately needed to get her powers back. Natalie had been imprisoned in mental limbo because I had given her the fallen angel feather that sent her there. I should have followed my instincts. I craved my sisters' acceptance so much that I had made some bad choices. Natalie was hopefully on the road to recovery. Rusty? Her recovery wouldn't be so easy.

Rafe. I shouldn't even be thinking about him or he might appear right in front of me. I couldn't dwell too long on thoughts about him, but he at least deserved some pondering. Poor angel. He was so enamored with humans and their ways that he sometimes forgot who and what he was. He clung to my now-human grandfather like his new best friend, and the longer Rafe remained in the realm of humans, the more he seemed to take after them. He was possessive and judgmental and moody. I'd been under the impression angels were above petty human flaws, but what did I know? I was half angel and certainly didn't act any better myself.

I drowsed in a state of near sleep, drifting in and out of consciousness. A fuzzy sort of warmth enveloped me and I became suddenly aware that I wasn't the only one in the bed. A man lay beside me and he looked exactly like Aydin.

"Aydin?" I whispered, his image fading in and out of sight. Just a dream, but I felt the heat of his skin, heard his soft breathing, his heartbeat... No, not a human heartbeat. It was the rapid bass drum beat of a gargoyle.

He rolled over to face me. "I never want you to forget what I used to look like."

"I never will." I cupped the side of his face and smoothed my thumb over his cheekbone. His eyes gazed into mine and I saw his desire reflected there. The smoldering look he gave me sent a missile of heat down my body, over my breasts, across my stomach and between my legs. I gasped.

His hand covered mine. He gently pulled my fingers from his face to plant a slow, hot kiss in the center of my palm. "I've missed you."

When Aydin was human, most of our time together had been spent following Gavin's orders and doing our best not to let the curse we shared change us into monsters. The lingering attraction between us grew and our desire intensified when the tattoos on our necks throbbed with need for our gargoyles. I regretted that we had never given in to our carnal hunger.

Aydin's gargoyle form was the only thing keeping us physically apart. I wanted *him,* the flesh-and-blood man I'd fallen for, but I'd settle for the mental equivalent if that was all I had.

His body appeared hazy, like a blurred rendition of his former self. Yet I could sense every part of him, smell his skin, taste his lips when he kissed me. I pressed against him and felt the hardness of his body as sensations thrilled my every cell. Dream or not, my body was consumed by passion that melted into me like hot lava.

Aydin filled my mind, which enabled me to get inside his. I found love there, and concern, and hesitation. His need overwhelmed me, yet knowing his feelings were as strong as mine put me at peace.

His arms held me close, his chin pressed against my neck as we lay spooned on the bed. I snuggled against his naked chest and his hold on me tightened as he gently nibbled my ear.

"I wish this was real," I told him.

He kissed my hair. "It *is* real."

I smiled. "I know, but I mean physically real."

"Felt pretty real to me." He rolled me over onto my back and ran a finger from the hollow of my throat down to my navel.

I held his hand to keep it still. "I need to get some sleep."

"You *are* asleep."

I sighed. "You know what I mean. Dream sex is confusing."

"But you enjoyed it."

I reached up to pull his head down close so I could kiss him. "Yes, I did. Very much."

He grinned. His features turned fuzzy before sharpening into a more sober expression. "I do want to be a man again. For you. For myself."

I kissed him long and deep. "I know you do."

"I should have taken Shojin's heart when I had the chance."

I agreed. Now it was gone and who knew when, or if, we'd get it back. I cringed at my mental admission of doubt.

"It's okay, Chalice," he said. "I have my doubts, too."

I turned onto my side to face him. The dream lost its surreal edge and my focus sharpened. This is how I wanted him all the time, even if I had to knock myself out to have it.

A knock sounded at the door and the room instantly popped into crystal clarity. Aydin vanished.

A few more knocks and then "Chalice? Better get up."

I blinked the sleep from my eyes. "Quin? Is that you?"

He opened the door a crack and said, "It's about Xenia. She's been spotted."

★ ★ ★

"She sold it to who?" I asked Elmo, as he placed a cup of espresso in front of me. I blew away the steam and touched my lips to the brim. Too hot to sip.

"One of the sewer rats." Elmo set a teacup on the table by Quin, sloshing some over the sides.

Quin flinched when a drop of tea splashed out of the cup to land by his hand. "Hey!"

"Pardon me, your royal sir," Elmo said, his mouth set in a crooked grin. "Can I get you a crumpet to go with your tea?"

"You don't serve crumpets." Quin mopped at the spill with his napkin. "I prefer tea to coffee. Get used to it."

"Tea." Elmo harrumphed and waddled his short legs back to the coffee bar.

I chuckled to myself. It was fun seeing Elmo rib the proper Quin. I knew he missed Aydin, who'd been Elmo's best friend, but Aydin had to be careful while in the city. His visit with me today could have been danger-ous if the Vyantara were still looking for him. Both Rafe and Quin had said the nefarious group had left town, but I didn't think all of them were gone. After seeing Gavin's soul-stain inside the church I felt doubly sure that a member or two had stayed behind.

There was a good crowd at Elmo's tonight. The green veil had rippled open three times since Quin and I got here, and a variety of fae had emerged. Faeries, elves, and a handful of my personal favorites, chimeras.

I looked at Quin and made a gimme gesture with my hand. "So what's a sewer rat?"

"In this case it's not a disease-carrying rodent," Quin

said. "Elmo is talking about a tribe of adolescents who dabble in the dark arts."

I nearly choked on my espresso. "Teenage sorcerers in training?"

"It would seem so."

Children and magic were a bad combination. Especially teens, whose hormones already made them an emotional wreck. Add unstable elements of unknown origin from the black veil and you were guaranteed a tragic outcome. During my years as a thief I'd seen too many kids meet an early end. A few I'd managed to save in time, but the others were already lost to whatever cursed object they had in their possession.

"The head rat, so to speak, fancies himself a real sorcerer and when he heard about Xenia's flying charm, he couldn't get his hands on it fast enough."

"How did Elmo find this out?" I asked.

"I have friends in high places." Elmo joined us at the ancient spool table that had more scars than I did. "A winged faerie I know almost had a midair collision with him in LoDo's warehouse district."

Uh-oh. That was bad news. This guy's open use of the charm could easily attract the Vyantara's attention. After all, I'd stolen it from the Canadian fatherhouse. It didn't take a genius to figure out how the charm got here.

"We have to get it back and fast," I told them. "Where can I find this guy?"

"Their nest is in an abandoned theater on the north side of town," Elmo said before biting into one of the honey rolls that he baked himself. My mouth began to water. I hadn't eaten since we left Halo Home. "If it's still there."

"Why?" It alarmed me that I might be too late. Again.

"The building is condemned." He washed down the roll with a swig of coffee. "The sewer rats are lucky no one but a few of us from the green veil knows they're using it."

"What about the Vyantara?" I asked. "Do they know?"

"Haven't caught wind of any around," Elmo said. "If they're here, they've managed to keep it secret."

Oh, great. More confirmation of my suspicions. They'd probably already picked through the old father-house ruins so there wouldn't be anything left for me to scavenge.

I drank down the dregs of my espresso and winced at the aftertaste. "Where can I find this theater? And who's going to take me there?"

fourteen

QUIN PARKED THE CAR ON A SIDE STREET about a block away from the old theater. No wonder it was condemned. A six-foot chain-link fence surrounded the building, which didn't appear too bad from the front. A dilapidated roof, peeling paint and some loose boards made it look trashy but not unfixable. On closer inspection, however, the structure was a demolition waiting to happen.

"It's not safe," Quin said, his lip curled in disgust. "Even if the roof doesn't cave in, the asbestos will kill you."

I tapped my chin in thought as I studied the building. No lights on inside, which didn't mean no one was there. I heard voices, five distinct ones. Three male, two female, and all were young.

"I'm going in," I said, and took a step forward.

"Wait." Quin touched my arm and I turned to face him. "You don't know what those kids are capable of. You shouldn't go in alone."

"You think I should take Aydin with me?" I offered him a crooked grin.

"Very funny." He brushed imaginary dirt from the sleeves of his coat. "It would be great if you could, but if they saw him—"

"There'd be panic and mayhem." Making Aydin public would be a really bad idea. Most of the world thought monsters and magic were only found in movies and video games. They didn't know there was a chance their next-door neighbor was a witch and little Johnny down the street could start howling at the moon on his thirteenth birthday. People believed what they wanted to believe, even if it meant denying the truth. It was human nature.

"Quin, I'm used to going it alone," I told him. "It's how I was trained. Not a big deal."

His brows tilted in a worried frown. "Chalice…"

I held up my hand. "I have a plan." I slid out the bal-isong from the sheath on my back. "And I have a knife."

I peeled back the loosened chain link in the fence where dozens before me had done the same thing. My plan wasn't to boldly march through the front door. I'd assess the situation first.

Stealth had always been one of my stronger skills so I had no trouble creeping soundlessly around the side of the building in search of a back entrance. A foot of snow helped muffle any sound I might have made. I listened to what the kids were saying.

"The spell book I found in my grandfather's attic is awesome," said a male voice.

"You don't know how to get half those ingredients," said one of the girls.

"Can't be too hard. I can order 'em off the internet." Laughter.

"Like dried goat brains are going to pass inspection through the mail." This from a guy whose adolescent voice cracked on every other syllable. I was guessing sixteen, seventeen tops.

I found the back entrance with a door slightly ajar. I guessed it's how the kids got in. Lifting the door slightly as I eased it open kept it from creaking on its hinges. I slipped inside and pushed the door back in place, then walked down a narrow dark hall to get closer to where the voices were coming from.

I found myself backstage behind a heavy curtain, where I peeked through an opening to see all five teens lounging on a pile of torn sofa cushions, pillows and stained mattresses with piles of dirty blankets all around them. It really was a nest. A couple of gas lanterns flickered on either side of the stage.

At first glance I saw the kids were bundled up in layers of sweaters, coats and scarves, which was a good thing because it was freezing in here. I wondered if their parents knew where they were and if they cared.

It wasn't hard to identify the leader in this motley crew. He wore a long, red velvet coat that appeared to have been pilfered from a wardrobe of theater costumes. He sat slightly higher than the others, his stack of cushions molded into something like a throne. How cute. Boys and girls playing make-believe.

What wasn't so cute was the way he waved the gray dove's feather over his head, creating tiny white sparks that drifted down around him before lifting him up in the air.

The girl with the braces said, "Enough with the stupid feather, Evan. We know you can fly. Stop showing off."

"Yeah," said the boy wrapped so tightly around her that at first I'd thought they were one person. "Listen to Lilly. She knows what she's talking about."

Lilly gave him a peck on the cheek. "Thanks, Duster."

Lilly and Duster were a mismatched pair. Lovely Lilly wasn't so lovely with her pasty, pimply complexion and greasy brown hair that hadn't seen a shampoo bottle in a while. Duster, on the other hand, was a teen's dream, the prom king, and a rock 'n' roll idol all rolled into one. I sensed something amiss. Looks weren't everything, but seriously?

I sniffed the air and caught a whiff of musk and amber. A lot of musk. And I knew exactly where it was coming from: the seduction charm I'd intended to give one of the squires. This Lilly girl must have bought it off Xenia.

That left one charm still unaccounted for: a powerful wind charm that would literally blow someone away. The charm was a scarf that fluttered whether there was wind or not, and considering the layers these kids wore, it could be worn by any one of them.

The other couple hadn't said a word because they were too busy sucking face. It was the longest kiss I'd ever seen. I hoped it didn't progress to something more than a kiss, at least not while I was watching.

Evan floated down to his throne of cushions. "I'm bored."

I did a mental eye-roll. He had a flying charm and a spell book and he was bored? Maybe I could add a little excitement to his dull life.

Stepping away from the curtain, I pivoted to head for a short set of steps that I assumed led beyond the stage to the seating area. Sure enough, several rows of folded wooden seats spread out in an incline beyond the stage. I popped the lever on my balisong to release the blade and walked out into the open.

I kept my eyes on the little group as I strode in front of the stage, making sure they could see me. My swagger displayed a cool confidence I needed them to believe. Being short gave me the advantage of looking younger than my age and I had no trouble passing for a teen among adults. Passing among other teens could be more challenging.

Everyone but the snogging couple had their gazes locked on me, their expressions surprised and annoyed.

"Who the hell are you?" Evan asked.

"Who the hell are *you?*" I asked back.

"This is our place," Lilly said, her tone indignant. "You're trespassing."

I motioned toward the front of the theater with my blade. "According to the sign outside, you're the ones trespassing."

The three looked at each other.

I jabbed my blade in the direction of the lip-locked pair. "Don't they ever come up for air?"

"Mind your own business." Lilly pressed closer to Duster and he nuzzled her neck.

I shrugged. "Whatever."

Lowering one of the seats, I plopped onto it and leaned back with my ankles propped up on the seat in front of me. I began cleaning under my fingernails with my knife.

"Leave," Evan said, though he didn't sound convincing.

"Make me." I looked up at him through my lashes and sneered.

"Bitch," he said, and smiled. I smiled back. One point for me.

I stood and closed my blade, sticking the knife in my front pocket instead of my sheath so they all could see it. If I needed to use it, none of them would have a chance to finish a breath by the time I snapped it open.

Sauntering down the aisle toward the stage, I swayed my hips and kept my gaze locked on Evan. He stared at me, his mouth slightly open.

"Evan, do something," Lilly complained. "Get her out of here."

Duster blinked and said, "Yeah, Ev, get rid of her."

Evan stood and flashed an angry look at the two. "Shut up."

I kicked a pillow out of the way so I could get closer to him. "Evan? That's your name?"

"You can call me master," he said with a snide smile.

"I don't call anyone master." At least not anymore.

"What do you want?" Lilly asked.

"Magic," I said.

The group went silent. Even the spit-swapping couple stopped long enough to look up at me.

"I have some magic." I reached out to run my index finger down the front of Evan's coat. "I'll show you mine if you show me yours."

Lilly chuckled. "Yeah, right."

I glared down at her and focused my senses on what I could scope out. An edge of the seduction charm—a bronze brooch in the shape of a rose—peaked out from the collar of her coat. Through her sweater I saw a coin-size birthmark on her stomach. Listening hard, I detected a fluttering little heartbeat in addition to hers. She was pregnant.

My heart gave a jolt, but I couldn't let my surprise or my pity show. "Is the baby his or someone else's?"

Lilly gasped. "How did you know?"

I grinned. "Magic." I cocked a hip and added, "Cute birthmark. Wish I had one shaped like a butterfly wing."

Lilly scowled and clasped her hands over her belly. "Stop it."

"Awesome," Evan said with an approving nod. "What do you know about me?"

Scanning him up and down I let my gaze linger on his face. "What did you do to the guy who stabbed you in the cheek with a pencil?" I saw pieces of lead still embedded in the scar.

His smile wavered. "No one knows about that."

"I do." I studied the healed puncture wounds on his neck and sought out the scent for where it came from.

"If you're going to be someone's blood doll, you better make sure they're a real vampire first."

He fingered the scar. Staring vacantly, he whispered, "He promised to make me one of them."

"You got bit by a dude?" Duster asked.

Evan scowled. "He told me he was vamp, promised to turn me."

Duster laughed. "That's so lame, man."

"As for you," I said, turning my attention to Duster and staring at his crotch. It took a few seconds to see what I was looking for, but well worth the wait. I smiled. "Your swimmers ain't swimmin'."

He frowned and stared down at himself. "What?"

"They're DOA." I looked at Lilly, then back at him. "At least now we know for sure whose baby it isn't."

Duster snorted. "Lilly and I haven't been together long enough. Besides, it doesn't matter. I love her no matter whose baby it is."

"Oh?" I stared down at the rose brooch Lilly wore and swiftly crouched beside her to snatch it out from under her coat. "How about now?"

Lilly screamed. "Hey! That's mine! You have no right—"

"Pretty." I held the charm close to my face as if studying the petals. "I think I'll keep it."

Lilly tossed Evan a pleading look. "I paid for that with my own money, Evan. It's not fair! Make her give it back."

"You want it back?" he said to her. "Take it yourself."

She was starting to stand up when Duster abruptly pushed her away from him. "What the hell are you doing so close to me?" A look of disgust distorted his handsome face. "Ugh. Get away." He scrambled on hands and knees until he was on the other side of the stage. "I need to gargle with bleach now."

Evan laughed. "Wow, that's some powerful charm."

I tucked it inside my coat pocket.

"Babe?" Lilly pleaded. She stepped toward Duster and he held his arms over his face as if to ward her off. "You told me you loved me."

"I must have been drunk." Duster stood and stomped his way to the edge of the stage. "I'm outta here." He hopped down and trotted down the aisle toward the exit.

"Wait!" Lilly ran after him.

The other couple had soundlessly watched the unfolding drama and looked uncomfortable. They stood and walked arm in arm down the stage steps.

"Bye!" I called to them with a wave of my hand.

They said nothing.

"So…" Evan took a step closer to me. "You're psychic?"

"Something like that." *Not even close.*

"Can you tell the future?"

"Mmm-hmm. I think you and me might have one. Together." I leaned forward so my breasts pressed against his chest. Desire flashed in his eyes and I knew my distraction was working. I slipped my hand beneath his coat as I rose on tiptoe to bring my lips closer to his. My fingers crawled lightly over his chest to his pocket, where I felt the feather.

I pinched it between thumb and forefinger and gently lifted it out.

He grabbed my wrist. "They warned me you'd try something."

Evan squeezed so hard I had to let the feather go.

"Who told you?" I asked, alarm squeezing the pit of my stomach. I felt sick.

"The people I want to impress." He put more pressure on my wrist as he crouched down to retrieve the dropped feather. "They came looking for this, said you'd stolen it from them. Told me I could keep it if I caught you and turned you over to them."

The Vyantara. Just what I was afraid of. My free hand grabbed for the blade I'd tucked in my pocket, but it was gone. Evan dangled it in front of me. "Looking for this? You're not the only thief here."

"The last thing you want is to become one of them." I tried to tug myself free, but it was no use. "They'll bond you to a gargoyle to ensure your loyalty. You'll be their slave."

He laughed in my face. "Gargoyle? Wow. You'll say anything to try getting away."

"You don't believe me?"

He shook his head.

"Fine. Don't say I didn't warn you." I twisted around and donkey kicked him hard in the stomach. He doubled over, releasing my wrist, but didn't stay down long. He whipped out a fireball, balanced on his palm.

I turned and jumped off the stage, somersaulting in midair to evade the ball of fire aimed straight for me. It burst in the air behind me, sprinkling sparks that faded into nothing. When I landed on my feet, I spun around to face Evan in time to see another fireball speeding at my head. I reflexively thrust out my hand and the fiery missile stopped in place.

What the hell?

"Hey!" Evan looked angry. "No one told me you could do that."

That's because I couldn't. At least not until now. I made a pushing motion and the fireball rolled back through the air away from me. I swung my hand to the side and it flew off toward the curtain, which immediately burst into flame.

Shit. Did I do that?

Evan cooked up another ball of fire and drew back his arm to throw it. I stared at my own hand and concentrated on the flame that spewed from my fingers. It rolled itself into a neat ball the size of a grapefruit.

I saw the fiery curtain from the corner of my eye. Flames climbed the brittle old fabric like monkeys running up a rope. I had to do something. I hoped Quin saw the smoke and called the fire department, but I didn't hear any sirens.

Evan released his ball and I volleyed mine toward his. The two collided, exploding in a spray of sparks that danced across the floor and joined their siblings on the curtains.

If I could make fire and move fire, could I stop it as well? I focused my will on the flames and watched them dwindle as if dowsed with water.

It was hard to believe I now had Rusty's power over fire.

A woman's throaty laugh reverberated against the walls of the theater. At first I thought it belonged to one of the sewer rat girls, but it sounded too mature for a child. I glanced in the direction from which it came. A woman wearing a cloak with the hood hiding her face stared down at us from the balcony.

I expected my breath to get sucked from my lungs, but when it didn't happen, I guessed she was toying with me again. Was she waiting for me to beg? I wouldn't give her the satisfaction. A new fireball rolled onto my fingertips.

Evan had the same idea, because he let his fireball fly before mine had a chance to completely form. Instinct to protect a sister knight, albeit a bad one, redirected my aim so that I could protect Maria. The two balls exploded when they collided, raining a spray of fire above the rows of wooden seats.

Evan paused as if to refuel whatever energy he needed to create his blazing ammo. I noticed his hesitation wasn't on purpose. He'd given up his fireballs to concentrate on catching his breath. He dropped to his knees, eyes bulging and mouth agape. He was dying.

"Stop!" I screamed.

Maria didn't stop completely, but she did allow Evan to take in enough air not to pass out. He appeared frozen but for his blinking eyes, and I saw the subtle rise and fall of his chest and heard his wheeze of shallow breaths. Judging from the strained cords on his neck, he wouldn't last much longer.

"Why are you doing this?" I shouted up at the balcony.

"I'm saving you from him." Maria had a deep voice, but its inflections sounded like a taunting child. There was something familiar about it and I waited for her to say more.

I searched the shadowed cowl covering her face, but not even my extrastrength vision could penetrate the black fabric it was made with. "That's not what I mean. Why are you killing us, your sisters?"

"I have my reasons."

"And I'm asking you what they are."

"You're not privileged to know," she said, sounding petulant. "But the squire you lost is perfect for my needs. You could be, too."

My blood turned cold. "What are you talking about?"

"You call her Xenia."

Oh, my God. She had Xenia? "You kidnapped her?"

"She came to me willingly."

My mind spun around this new information. I couldn't imagine what Maria had planned, but there was no time to ponder. The sewer rat boy was dying and I couldn't save him. Or could I?

Flickers of flame formed on my fingertips.

Maria laughed again. "I don't have to read your mind to know what you're thinking, and you can forget it. Fire? Please. I'm older than dirt. I can't die."

I didn't want to kill her, I only wanted her to stop killing. If I could distract her long enough...

An icy wind whooshed down the aisle toward the stage, followed by a light bright enough to illuminate every dark corner of the theater. Within seconds the source of both the wind and light hovered above me, blocking me from Maria.

Rafael.

The power of his flapping wings blew Maria off her feet and she tumbled sideways to fall from the balcony.

The wooden chairs below rattled from the impact of her landing.

Rafe hardly seemed to notice. His focus was on the kid, who'd been released from Maria's death grip. Evan crumpled onto the pile of blankets on the stage and lay still.

I ran to him. Leaning toward his face, I listened to his shallow breathing and slow heartbeat. He was still alive.

Rafe hovered wordlessly where he was. His expression looked pained, not triumphant. He'd saved a boy but possibly killed a knight. Sirens screamed in the distance and I realized I didn't have much time. I grabbed the flying charm from underneath Evan, then rushed over to where I'd seen Maria fall. But she was gone. Left in her place was a single black feather.

fifteen

AN HOUR LATER I STARED AT THE SURFACE of my espresso as I absently fanned myself with the feather Maria had left behind.

"That thing gives me the creeps," Elmo said.

I ran the feather through my fingers. "It could be the key to finding Maria's lair. And to finding Xenia."

"If the girl is really with her," Quin said.

True, since Maria could be lying. Taunting me into a trap, though I had no clue what she'd want with me. Unless, of course, her motives were the same as Evan's. If she turned me over to the Vyantara, she would get something of equal value in return.

"Could Xenia still be in the city then?" I asked them.

"I'll check my sources," Elmo said. "You get back all the missing charms?"

I shook my head. "There's still one left."

"Let me guess." Elmo scratched his temple and scowled, then snapped his fingers. "The wind charm."

"Elmo, you're a terrible actor," Quin said. "You knew which one it was all along."

"Guilty," Elmo said, and shrugged. "Just trying to make Chalice smile."

It didn't work. "What have you heard?"

"I caught wind of a wind blowing where it shouldn't blow," he said. "Inside a building."

Like that's not going to raise a few eyebrows? I had to wonder about some people and the logic they used.

The reasons to recover the charm didn't matter at this point. I had no choice but to either retrieve it or render it useless. Putting the charm out of commission would be a shame, but it would be more damaging to let it fall into the wrong hands.

"Thanks, Quin, for contacting Rafe. He couldn't have arrived at a better time."

"You should have called him yourself," Quin said. "Why didn't you?"

I bit my bottom lip. "Because I didn't think of it." And Rafe had made it a point to give me shit about it, too. He was mad at me for putting myself in a dangerous situation, saying I should have consulted with him first. But I don't consult, I *do*. Which had become a problem for me lately. Teamwork was still a foreign concept, though I'd get it eventually. I had to. It was supposed to be my job.

I yawned. "I'll need the address for that building, Elmo." I blinked and my eyelids struggled to open again. "After I get a few hours' sleep."

"Make them count," Quin said as he dipped his chin and gave me an intense look. "Rest up quick before the DPD intervenes and the press joins them. It wouldn't take much for Denver to become a hot spot for ghost chasers and witch hunters."

"No worries," Elmo said. "We have people watching the place. They'll misdirect anyone who comes too close."

Now that I felt reassured, I needed sleep, but what I really *wanted* was to dream. That was my only chance to see Aydin.

This time there was no tossing and turning in bed. My head hit the pillow and it seemed like only seconds passed before I was awake again. I felt rested and alert, but also alarmed. This wasn't the same bed I'd fallen asleep in.

Two thoughts hit me at once: I'd missed my time with Aydin, and someone had traded beds with me while I was sleeping. But I turned out to be wrong on both counts.

Aydin lay right beside me. He turned to me and said, "Welcome home."

Now I was really confused. "I'm dreaming?"

"Mmm-hmm." He reached out a very human hand, thick-fingered and strong, to smooth a wisp of bangs from my forehead. "It's my own design. Do you like it?"

I liked it too much. It was easy to see how some people could get so caught up in a fantasy they confused it with reality, or preferred it to real life. Dreams were becoming my virtual reality and I doubted that was healthy.

"Don't worry." Aydin lifted himself on one elbow to look down at me. "I'm in control. I've had centuries of experience with dreamscaping. You couldn't be in safer hands."

"Dreamscaping? Never heard of it."

He smiled. "It's like landscaping, only with dreams instead of land. I've become quite good at it, though this is the first time I've ever brought someone along." He leaned down to kiss me, letting his lips linger on mine. "I'm happy to share it with you."

If only I could relax and enjoy the experience. I wasn't sure I could.

"If it makes you uncomfortable, you can wake up." He lifted his hand as if to snap his fingers and I stopped him.

"No." I curled my fingers around his. He felt so warm, his callused flesh so real. There were no blurred edges this time, no sense of the surreal like before. The sheets were silk, the pillow beneath my head filled with down, and the air freshened by rain. I even heard the twitter of birds outside the window.

"You called this home. Where are we?" I asked.

"My oldest and favorite dreamscape. I allow my mind to drift here after I fall asleep." He tossed back the covers and stood naked from the bed. I marveled at his sculpted backside, the way his muscles rippled when he walked to the window. Sunlight streamed in when he pulled back the sheer drape and sprinkles of dust glittered against the glare.

Not surreal, but superreal. His human silhouette outlined against the spring meadow outside took my breath away. Though in reality we were sleeping, his mind wrapped around mine in a semiwakened state and I felt his sweetness seep into me like steam. Peering through his mind's eye at his creation enhanced every emotion I felt. I loved him more at that moment than I ever had.

Not surprisingly, I was also naked when I joined him at the window, my feet sinking into the plush carpet and sending goose bumps up my legs. The colors around us were vivid and the scents sharp enough to tickle my sensitive nose.

He draped an arm over my shoulder, then turned me to face him so he could pull me close. The erotic touch of his skin against mine filled me with need. His hands trailed over my back and cupped my ass, pressing me even closer, and I felt his own need hot and hard against me.

Gently holding the back of my head with one hand, he explored my neck with his lips, his tongue sweeping down to the hollow of my neck. His head dropped lower and he captured a nipple in his mouth.

I gasped and moved my hips against his. He lifted one of my legs and wrapped it around him, then eased himself inside me to make us one. With amazing tenderness he leaned me against the wall beside the window, his kisses hot and urgent. We swayed together, our bodies so in tune that our pleasure mounted and peaked at the same time. Our minds were linked so we experienced each other's feelings simultaneously. The intensity of it was almost too much.

My knees buckled and Aydin lifted me up and carried me to the bed. We lay snuggled close, our hearts pounding in perfect rhythm with each other.

Dream or no dream, I knew my breaths came hard and fast, even in sleep. I never realized making love could be so powerful without physical touch.

We lay quietly for a time, and I trailed a fingernail lazily up and down his arm, thrilling to his shivers.

We had a lot to talk about, but not much time since nightfall was closing in.

"Aydin?"

"Hmm?" He sounded as drowsy as I felt.

"The Vyantara know I'm here."

"I know."

How could he possibly know? He wasn't anywhere near the old theater last night. "I don't understand."

"Chalice, I was there. Up on the balcony on the other side of the theater, but you were busy. I saw everything."

I felt a twinge of anger. "You saw and you didn't try to help me?"

"You were doing quite well on your own until Maria showed up."

"Bitch," I said under my breath. "She took Xenia."

Aydin hugged me gently. "We'll find Xenia." He petted my hair and it immediately calmed me. "Two reasons why I didn't jump into the middle of your chaos—I didn't want the kid to see a gargoyle, and I didn't want to distract Rafe from doing his job."

He made good points. Rafe would have focused entirely on fighting Aydin, which wouldn't have done us any good. Aydin was getting to know the angel as well as I did. "I worry about Rafe," I told him.

"Me too," Aydin said.

"He's such a traditionalist, yet he's losing himself in his desire to be human."

"And part of that desire is to bed you."

I abruptly sat up. "What?"

He tenderly pulled me down into his arms and pressed his lips against my ear. "Having a child with you is his only hope of becoming human."

"That's not what I want," I said, feeling panicked.

"Shh." Aydin planted a light kiss on my temple. "I know that."

"I think of Rafe like an uncle, not a…" I couldn't even say it.

"Let's not worry about that now. I'm more concerned about your safety, and Rafe will do whatever he can to keep you out of harm's way. I'm also concerned about Shojin's heart."

"If Xenia sold it to someone in the city, we'll find it."

"That's the problem," Aydin said, his voice deep with meaning. "It's not in Denver."

"How do you know?"

"Shojin and I had a connection. If his heart were here, I'd know."

Of course he would know. But if not here, where could it be? My only guess was still with Xenia, and if she's with Maria…

Aydin sighed. "It's possible that it's on the other side of the black veil."

Our problems were mounting into a stack harder than hell to climb. But not impossible. I couldn't let worries interfere with my plans.

"I noticed an addition to your abilities last night," Aydin said. "I always knew you were hot, but wow."

I nudged him with my elbow. "Very funny."

"Isn't that Rusty's power?"

"It was." I explained what had happened the day of

the forest fire, after Aydin had helped me rescue the boy from the cellar. "I didn't mean to take her power from her, and I especially didn't mean to have it for myself."

"This is the first I've heard of an object transferring power from one knight to another." He looked pensive while staring off into the distance. "You say it was the Viking horn of breath?"

I nodded. "It saved Rusty's life."

"Where is it now?"

"I have it with me."

"Maybe you should destroy it," he told me. "If it has the power to steal a knight's abilities, it's a danger to the order."

From a different perspective, fewer knights in the order meant fewer abilities at risk of being stolen. However, I'd rather not destroy the horn if I didn't have to. What if it could give Rusty her ability back? If so, I needed to learn how.

sixteen

I FACED THE BUILDING PEPPERED WITH broken windows and crumbling bricks. Could Xenia have chosen a more scummy part of town to sell the wind charm? I heard the whistle of wind through cracks in the door and focused my eyes through a hole in one of the windows.

Yep, there it was. The scarf wrapped around a cement block in the middle of the room, the silken fabric fluttering like a sail in a storm.

The charm had often been used as a defense against attack, but it could come in handy in other ways, too. Like blowing away toxic fumes or hazardous smoke, or filling a sail on a calm sea to propel a boat. It even helped with air travel as a source of lift for gliders. But inside an empty building? For what purpose?

I squinted and searched deeper, but there really wasn't

much inside. The building was part of an old elementary school awaiting demolition. The auditorium had been cleared of all bleachers and only an American flag had been left behind on a pole. It flapped in the wind made by the charm.

I took a few steps forward and a ghost slithered out from between the cracks in the door. Oh, great. A wispy distraction was just what I needed to confound my situation.

I tried not to look at it, but the thing wasn't backing down. It had a message to deliver and it would be damned if I'd ignore what it had to say. Not that it could say anything. It was just a pesky shade of its previous owner. It had no voice, but it had plenty of hand gestures and used every single one of them. There's nothing like having a ghost flip you the bird.

This one was super pissed off, and the only ghost I'd ever come across this mad had been Zee, the housemother for the fatherhouse. She'd gotten blown up with the house and somehow blamed me for her death. This ghost wasn't Zee's, but it was definitely familiar. It belonged to Lilly, one of the teenage sewer rats from last night. She had apparently met an untimely end and was trying to tell me about it. However, my understanding of ghost lingo was sorely lacking.

She motioned me to follow her into the building. Her being here and so close to the charm made it obvious the two were connected. I guessed she had bought this charm from Xenia and somehow managed to kill herself with it, though I couldn't imagine how. Either that, or this staged event was a trap.

I had to think for second. Trap or no trap, that charm must be dealt with now, or the incident it could create would make Denver the center of too much attention. I'd take my chances.

If the charm was responsible for killing Lilly, it had to go. I reached into my coat pocket for the bottle of salt water I'd mixed up at Elmo's. A good splash of this and the charm would be rendered useless.

Lilly's ghost jumped in front of me and grabbed her neck as if choking herself. She stuck her tongue out the side of her mouth, closed her eyes and fell to the ground. Had the scarf done that to her? Or was her murderer someone, or something, else? Did it matter?

I passed through her to reach the door. She moved in front of me again and shook her head this time. She didn't want me to go in. I peered in through a different broken window and it still looked the same inside: a blowing scarf pinned to the middle of the floor by a cinder block. I neither heard nor saw anyone else around. Midnight was near and darkness permeated every corner, yet I saw clear as day. No obstacle prevented me from going inside to dispatch the scarf.

I tried the door handle and found it unlocked. Or it could have been broken. The scarred wooden floor was covered with broken boards. I stepped over the threshold and paused. Nothing.

I sprinted to the center of the auditorium and tossed the salt water on the scarf. It steamed and smoked, and purple sparks glittered around it like a dying Roman candle. The charm was dead and the wind inside the building abruptly stopped.

But the wind below me didn't.

I glanced down at the boards beneath my feet and saw an energy spiral through the gaps in the floor. The spinning caused something like a vacuum that sucked at my feet and I fell to the floor. My hands clasped the cinder block that had anchored the scarf in place, but I was a few pounds heavier than that scarf. It wouldn't hold for long. In fact, it was already starting to slide in the direction of the growing hole trying to eat me.

I gazed down into the vortex and saw the body of a man twirling around as if circling a drain with a black hole at its center. He appeared calm, lying on his back, legs crossed at the ankles and arms cradling his head. I knew this man and the sight of him had me choking on the breath I'd been holding. I gasped and sputtered as I scrambled for a better hold on the block. I managed to make it onto my elbows, but the block slid the same number of inches I'd gained.

"Gavin!" I screamed with what I hoped wasn't my last breath. "Stop! Our battle is over. Let me go."

He laughed. "You think it's that easy?"

"I'm not your slave anymore."

"The hell you say."

He was more than a ghost. His soul-stain in the church wasn't harmless as a painting—it was real, and Gavin had been watching for me. Now he had me. His tie to the Vyantara continued even in death.

I had asked Aydin to stay clear of me for this very reason. Better they get only one of us than both. I didn't come in here without an escape plan, but I hadn't expected a hole to open up in the floor with a dead sorcerer trying to take me again.

The sigil on my palm pulsed with my will to open the veil. But I couldn't without my blood on it first. I'd need both hands to grab my knife and cut myself, and if I let go of the block, I'd be a goner.

I brought my palm to my mouth and bit hard into my scar. The pain nearly jolted the fingers of my gripping hand loose, but I dug harder into the brick, feeling my nails splinter.

Gavin laughed.

The sadistic son of a bitch was enjoying himself at my expense. Some things never changed.

"We'll meet again, my dear," he said, his voice a loud reverberation inside my head. "Bet on it."

I swung my bleeding hand up to slap empty air, and the shimmering silver veil rippled where I touched. Gavin's cruel laughter echoed from the depths of the vortex still sucking at me. Maybe I wasn't strong enough to pull myself out.

A pale hand thrust through the silver curtain and grabbed my arm to hoist me up and out of the pit that surely led to hell.

"What were you thinking?" Rafe shouted as he paced in front of me. The silver walls around us were blanketed in pale fog that swept up the sides and undulated across the floor. Serene, calm, empty, safe. The silver veil was the sanctuary that could drive me out of my mind.

"I was thinking about *us,*" I said. "About everyone who

has anything to do with the order. If left where it was, that charm would have only caused trouble."

He nodded. "You did what the Vyantara wanted you to do. You fell right into their trap."

Nice pun, but I knew what I was doing. "So?"

He glowered at me. "You're not taking this seriously."

"Oh, this is very serious, Rafe. Trap or not, I did what had to be done."

"Without discussing it with me first." A twinge of hurt flickered in his eyes. "I'm your guardian, Chalice. We're supposed to be a team."

"You're my guide, not my guard," I said.

"Who told you that?"

Was this something I wasn't supposed to know? "Rusty and Natalie. They said it's why their guardians don't come rushing to their rescue."

Rafe shook his head. "Such modern sensibilities. The Arelim forget their vow to protect their knights. It shames us."

I frowned and shook my head. "Don't be ridiculous. We're not in the Middle Ages anymore, Rafe. The knighthood is made up of strong women with the power to protect."

"And look what's happened to them." Rafe stood looking down on me with his arms crossed. His posture degraded me. He saw me as weak, someone he had to protect, and that pissed me off. "Nothing like this ever would have been tolerated eight centuries ago."

"The knights have evolved," I said.

"You've become arrogant and foolish."

"Look who's talking?" I stepped up to him and jabbed

a finger into his rock-hard chest. "You think you're all that and a bag of chips, but you can't even stop the knight who's killing us." I folded my arms to match his stance. "Think about that, Mr. Save The World Angel."

His eyes softened and his shoulders lost some of their starch. "I promise you that our daughter—"

"Our what?" I backed up and held out my hands, palms out. "You and I are not—" I swallowed and bit my bottom lip when I saw the anguished look on his face. "It's not happening, Rafe. I'm sorry, but get over it."

I turned around and walked blindly into a white fog that never seemed to end.

An hour later I opened the veil inside Geraldine's shrine at the cathedral. I knew it would be peaceful and safe there. Some alone time to calm myself was exactly what I needed.

I stepped out into the little garden room and heaved in a breath of sweet, sanctified air. The veil closed behind me and I stepped over to the plush sofa to drop bodily onto it, the cushions enveloping me in softness. I could easily drift off to sleep right here and now.

Surprised to see the veil suddenly reappear, I watched its rippling surface and braced myself for another confrontation with Rafe. I couldn't talk to him right now. He'd put a strain on our friendship and I wasn't sure I could ever feel comfortable with him again.

It wasn't Rafe who emerged, but my grandmother followed by Natalie.

I shrilled a happy hello and ran into my grandmother's arms. I'd never been one for hugging before, but I was learning that a warm and comforting embrace from someone I cared about felt pretty darn good. I really needed that right now.

"Natalie! I'm so happy to see you," I said, throwing my arms around her neck. She hugged me back. "You look great."

"Thanks." A slow and gentle smile played at the corners of her mouth. "I'm totally back to normal. Thanks to Aydin."

"And you still have your abilities?"

She nodded and my grandmother said, "We know you have Rusty's powers now."

Damn the tell-an-angel newswire.

"The Arelim have a hive-mind, dear," my grandmother said. "What one sees or hears, the others do as well. Unless one of them makes a conscious effort to block it."

"And Rusty knows, too?" I asked.

Natalie winced. "I'm afraid so. Harachel told her."

Big mouth. Oh, well. It was bound to get back to her sooner or later, but it bothered me that it came from Rusty's angel. He was a jerk who treated her like crap. He probably got a kick out of her reaction, which I guessed involved some very angry words.

"I'm so happy to see you. I need girl company in the worst way right now." I waved them over to the love seat and chair. "How did you know I was here?"

"Rafael told us," my grandmother said. "He mentioned you two had a fight and that you might need someone to talk to."

Who did he think he was to assume what I did or

didn't need? I wanted to get mad at him for it, but I couldn't. He knew me too well. I sighed and said, "He presumes too much sometimes."

"He wants a future with you, Chalice," my grandmother said.

"You have no idea how uncomfortable that makes me," I told her. "Rafe is my friend and my mentor…when I want him to be. But that's as far as it's ever going to go."

"Your grandfather and I have been happily married for over fifty years," she said.

"Yeah, but the two of you love each other—"

"And Camael and I are starting our wedding plans," Natalie said with pride. She glowed like I imagined any bride-to-be would. Or was that glow something else?

I pointed at her flat belly. "You're not, you know…"

She giggled. "Not yet, but I plan to be. Right after the wedding."

I narrowed my eyes and rubbed my chin. "Um…I don't think it works that way. I'm no expert, but as I understand it, conception isn't a wham–bam–thank-you-ma'am kind of thing."

Natalie and my grandmother passed each other knowing looks.

I stared at one and then the other. "What am I missing?"

"The facts of life," my grandmother said.

I blew a raspberry at her. "Please. I'm a grown-up. I know all about the birds and the bees."

"Not when the birds are angels and the bees are Hatchet knights," she said.

I braced myself. "Do tell."

Natalie scooted to the edge of the love seat and leaned forward. "I was promised to an Arelim angel the day I became a woman."

I coughed into my hand. "The day you first started your period is the same day your union was arranged?"

She nodded.

"But you didn't even know Camael yet."

She shook her head. "We didn't meet until my twenty-first birthday."

"I see." I studied her face. "How old are you now?"

"Twenty-two."

They'd known each other for at least a year so that had to count for something, though I wasn't sure what.

"Do you love him?" I asked.

Her eyebrows raised in a quizzical arch. "No, but we care about each other. Love isn't important."

"I beg to differ," I said.

My grandmother patted my knee. "Chalice, dear, we grow to love our Arelim mates if they choose to lose their wings. If they don't, we take their seed and they go the way of the Fallen."

I gasped. "Just like that?"

"It's how it's always been. Our guardians have had centuries to think about their choices," my grandmother said, as if it were as natural as choosing what college to attend.

"And the abandoned knight who's left to care for a baby all alone? What happens to her?" I immediately thought of my mother.

"The Arelim make sure she's well cared for," Natalie

said. "And there are other Hatchet knight families to help if needed."

"That's right," my grandmother said. "I rarely saw my own mother. I was fostered by another family."

An awkward silence followed as I digested all this information. I didn't like what I was hearing. It sounded so...archaic. "So why are the facts of life so different for us?" I finally asked.

"A knight will conceive immediately after intercourse with her guardian," my grandmother said.

Unbelievable. "How very clinical and unromantic."

Natalie shrugged. "Camael and I will stay together as husband and wife after he becomes human."

Yet Barachiel, my own father, had chosen to keep his wings and join the ranks of the Fallen. What was up with that?

"As for you, my darling granddaughter," my grandmother said. "Rafael doesn't have to love you to want a life with you after you conceive."

Oh, my God. "I'm not conceiving anything with Rafe unless it's to conceive our next fight."

"Then you won't conceive at all," Natalie said with a note of sadness.

"What?" I didn't think I heard her right.

"I thought you understood," my grandmother said slowly. She took my hand in hers. "Chalice, it's not physically possible for you to bear a child without an Arelim mate."

I must have subconsciously chosen a dreamless sleep because I didn't see Aydin at all that day. I'd slept deeply and wakened with the moonlight, feeling alone and depressed. My conversation with my grandmother and Natalie kept replaying in my mind. Arranged couplings, not even a real marriage. And I had to accept the fact that I was barren.

I never wanted children anyway. I wasn't the mom type. I'd never spent more than ten minutes with a child my entire life, so what would I miss? It was a relief to know I wouldn't become saddled with maternal responsibilities. I should be thrilled to death with this news. So why was I feeling so down?

I knew just the ticket to lift my spirits: get back to work. The first order of business would be to scavenge the fatherhouse leftovers, if there were any.

I met with Elmo and Quin in the coffee shop, which had become our unofficial headquarters. After relaying the previous day's experience with the wind charm, I tolerated their scolding and advice until we could get to the good part.

Trying very hard not to roll my eyes, I said, "You guys make some really good points. I appreciate the warnings."

They both looked at me with narrowed eyes, their lips tight against what I imagined were gritted teeth. "I mean it," I said with a nod. "I'd be lost without you two."

"No, you'd be dead," Quin said before taking a sip of tea. He pointed at his cup. "I'll take another one of these, thanks, Elmo."

"Your legs broken?" Elmo peered at him from beneath a wad of wiry white eyebrows. "You know where the tea bags are. Help yourself."

Quin shrugged and scooted back his chair to stand.

I watched him meander toward the counter and stop along the way to have a quick chat with a young chimera couple. They'd brought their baby along. Or was it a cub? Hard to tell with all the hair. Or fur.

Elmo snapped his fingers, making me jump.

"What?" I tore a piece off one of his excellent honey rolls and popped it in my mouth. While chewing I said, "Don't snap at me."

He grinned. "I need your attention. Fast, before Quin comes back."

What could he not want the angel whisperer to hear? "I'm listening."

He leaned forward and whispered, "All this sleuthing has uncovered some mysteries I didn't know about. Like a changing charm I had no idea existed until now."

I'd never heard of it, either. "What does it do? And why don't you want Quin to know?"

"It's kind of evil for a charm so it's probably not a good idea for the Arelim to know about it. However, I do believe it can help Aydin."

I stopped chewing. "Because…?"

"Because it could make him human again."

I scowled and swallowed the lump of dough in my throat. "Shojin's heart will do that."

"What if you never get it back?"

I took a deep breath as I considered that possibility. "What makes this charm evil?"

"It needs angel blood to work."

That could be a problem. Now I understood why he didn't want Quin to know. "How can I get my hands on it?"

"I don't know."

Feeling defeated, I slouched in my seat. "You're no help."

"I mean, I know where it might be if it wasn't destroyed by the explosion that took the fatherhouse."

I was about to head there anyway so I added this changing charm to my task list. If it were there, I'd find it. "What does it look like?"

Elmo glanced toward the kitchen and we watched Quin standing over a kettle, apparently waiting for it to boil. "I've never seen it myself so I can only tell you how it was described to me," he said.

I wished I had a photo, or at least a drawing. "Quick, tell me."

"It's very old and made of metal that rusts. Could be iron."

"That's impossible, Elmo. Iron repels magic."

"Not if it's strong enough," he said. "And this charm is reported to be very powerful. I'm thinking that if it was in the fatherhouse at all it would have been secured in a safe place."

Gavin had mentioned a safe to me once. In the basement. But he'd never said anything about a changing charm, not that I'd expect him to. He got a kick out of keeping secrets from me. "I know where to start searching. Describe it for me."

"It's shaped like a key."

"A skeleton key?"

He nodded. "A fancy one with scrollwork around the image of an animal's head."

"What kind of an animal?"

Elmo paused before saying, "Wolf."

I stood up straighter in the chair. "This isn't a were-wolf's transformation charm, is it?"

He shrugged. "It may have been at one time, but my sources tell me it can change anyone into anything." He peered at the nonhuman crowd in his coffee shop. "Anything."

Quin returned with his tea. He glanced between us and said, "Did I miss something?"

"I was just telling Chalice about a way to make it easier for her to search the fatherhouse ruins," Elmo said.

I scowled at him and asked, "You were?"

Elmo grinned. "It's called ash eating."

"Sounds delicious," I said with a grimace. "And how will eating ashes help me find anything?"

"It's common knowledge that if you consume the ashes of the dead, you can see them. At least for a little while."

I squinted at him. It might have been common knowledge where he came from, but not on this side of the veil. "I don't need to eat ashes to see dead people, Elmo. They show up just fine on their own."

"You once told me the fatherhouse was alive," Elmo said. "If you eat its ashes, you might see the house as it looked while it was still standing. Then it would be easier to, you know—" he flicked a quick look at Quin "—find stuff."

"So I just choke down a mouthful of ash and that's all there is to it?"

"Of course not." Elmo left us to go to the kitchen. He returned with a small blue bottle topped with a cork.

"You need to mix it with faerie juice first." He handed me the bottle.

I pulled the cork and took a sniff. Wrinkling my nose, I said, "I have to get drunk first?"

Elmo shrugged. "Dandelion wine. Makes the ashes go down a lot smoother."

seventeen

GHOSTS WERE EVERYWHERE. THEY SLITHERED out from between broken boards, floated over piles of rubble and drifted through stacks of brick that once encased the Vyantara fatherhouse. This place was worse than a cemetery.

Considering the number of sacrifices and murders that had happened here, it wasn't surprising to see so many specters. These ruins were their home. They had nowhere else to go.

Violence had shaken them loose from bodies that shed their souls at the time of death. The souls went one place and these shells of grief and terror stayed behind, but that was just my theory.

I walked up the front steps and peered through the gaping maw that had once been covered by a massive oak door. Black and gray ashes covered the floor of the gutted building. I stepped over broken glass and kicked aside chunks of charred wood and the twisted metal that had once been part of display cases for hundreds of cursed and charmed objects.

This area of the house looked well picked over. The staircase leading down to the basement was completely burned away. If I wanted to get down there I'd have to jump.

The sound of creaking floorboards above alerted me to the possibility I wasn't alone. I eased into a corner and pressed my back to the wall, standing as still as possible while I listened. I picked up two male voices, one of which I recognized right away. It was Evan, the wannabe sorcerer from the sewer rats.

The beam from a flashlight bobbed along the wall above my head and I ducked. It swept away from me and I exhaled a relieved breath. I wasn't in the mood for more confrontations with this guy. I didn't want to waste time volleying fireballs when I could be searching for charms and curses. I imagined Evan was here to do the same.

I could wait until he left, but if I did that there was a good chance he'd find me. My best bet was to assume my role of thief and make my rummaging quiet as a whisper, then get the hell out.

Ash blanketed the corner I crouched in so I scooped up a handful and let it sift down into Elmo's open wine bottle. Holding my thumb over the top, I gave it a couple of good shakes before tipping it to my lips. I held my breath as I took a giant swig of the stuff.

I stifled a cough and practically passed out in the process. Elmo hadn't mentioned how nasty it would taste.

Maybe the wine was okay without the ashes, but I made it a point to stay away from alcohol. It dulled the senses and I was afraid I might enjoy that a little too much.

I blinked and watched for a change through the fog that was my night vision. Within minutes the house appeared to rebuild itself, brick by brick and board by board. The entire structure reformed in front of my eyes, but not as the solid house it used to be. Like a transparent photograph, it superimposed itself over its own charred and scattered remains.

I wondered if others had tried the ash-eating trick, but I doubted anyone but the Vyantara knew the house had once been alive.

My gaze swept the room for any goodies that could have escaped the Vyantara's scrutiny. I recognized dozens. I spotted part of a coin jutting up through a crack in the floor. The ghost house confirmed it was a Chinese five-poison charm that protected against the venom of snakes, spiders, toads, centipedes and scorpions. I had to have it.

Dust and ash rained down on me as Evan and whoever was with him walked across the floor above. It was so unstable it surprised me that neither of them had fallen through yet. Maybe Evan used the flying charm to keep himself levitated. But what about his friend?

I crawled out from my corner and dashed to the coin. Grabbing it between thumb and forefinger, I yanked, but it wouldn't budge. I needed something to pry it loose.

A nail rolled out from under my foot. I wedged it in the crack and wiggled it until the coin popped free. When I heard a loud crackling sound over my head, I stuffed the coin in my pocket and just as I did, the ceiling caved in.

I'd barely rolled out of the way before plaster and planks of burned, brittle wood came crashing down where I'd been standing. A cloud of ash and dust exploded in the air around the boy who landed beside me. He didn't get up. The fall had knocked him out cold.

I looked up to see Evan hovering in the space where the ceiling used to be.

"I knew it!" he shouted at me. "They told me you'd come snooping around and try to steal more stuff."

It would be pointless for me to argue the fact that I'd been the one to steal most of this stuff in the first place. Though I wanted to recover everything I could find, there was only one object I couldn't leave without…if it was even here.

"You're not getting away this time," Evan said as he sprouted a fireball from his hand and balanced it on his finger.

Sheesh, this was getting old. There might still be some good shit in this house and I didn't want it erupting in a second blaze. Evan needed to rein in his ego and consider *what* he was doing and for *whom*. Stupid kid.

I held up my hands. "No more fire."

"Do you surrender?"

No. "Yes." As I said it I looked down, expecting to see a vortex open and swallow me whole. I darted my gaze around the room, searching for portal paintings, where Gavin might be spying on me from wherever dead sorcerers go when they die. But the paintings had all been fried to a crisp. The walls were bare except for some peeled wallpaper and large patches of scorch marks.

Evan lost altitude and hovered like a flying insect a few feet off the floor in front of me. He hadn't lost his fireball. The flaming orb bobbed in the palm of his hand.

"Tell you what," Evan said while tossing the fireball from one hand to the other. "Since you can see better than anyone I know, show me where all the objects are and I'll let you go."

The unconscious boy on the floor looked familiar. "I think your friend needs help."

"Hey, Duster," Evan said. "You okay, man?"

The boy groaned. I remembered him, Lilly's boyfriend. I wondered if he knew she was dead.

"He's fine. You should worry more about yourself." The fireball grew in Evan's hand.

I shrugged and darted my gaze around the room. "I'll help you search." *Like hell I would.* Whatever I found was mine. "But you really should call an ambulance for Duster." I listened to Duster's breathing and heartbeat. Both sounded strong. He'd be lucky if all he had were a concussion and some bruises.

Evan waved me ahead of him, using the fireball like a gun pointed at my back. I felt its heat through my coat.

My gaze swept the floor and walls and I tried to avoid being distracted by the double image of the ghost house and its carcass. I had to blink a lot and my eyes hurt from staring so hard.

Something slithered across the floor toward us, then stopped. Its bulbous form molded into something recognizable and my stomach clenched. Damn. The ghost of the fatherhouse's dead housemother, Zee. Hadn't she made my life miserable enough when she was alive? Cruel, jealous, power hungry, and Gavin's plaything all rolled up in one. Why couldn't the dead just stay…dead?

Her black eyes bored into me and her gray, ghostly lips peeled back in a sneer of contempt. I imagined she hadn't wasted her time wandering within these walls waiting for someone to haunt. Her having been a witch made it likely that she'd learned some new tricks as a shadow of her former self.

"Why did you stop?" Evan asked, and my back got a few degrees warmer. "Find something?"

"I sure did," I told him, and it was no lie. I backed up, angling to avoid his fireball, and pressed up against him. "Spooky old houses turn me on."

He snorted. "I just bet they do. Keep moving."

I stood on tiptoe so my face was inches from his. "My heart's beating so fast I can hardly breathe." I gasped into his ear to demonstrate, keeping an eye on Zee's ghost as I did.

"Do you believe in ghosts?" I asked him.

Zee's sneer morphed into a smile.

"I don't believe in anything I can't see," he told me, and nudged me away. "Like I can't see you and me together. I'm out of your league, babe. Pretty boy Duster is more your type."

I pretended to be insulted and stomped ahead, though I watched Zee from the corner of my eye. She puffed up, appearing to double in size, and I had a fair idea what she planned to do next. *Bring it on, bitch.*

I doubted she had any interest in the few trinkets left

behind inside the fatherhouse. Zee's shadow wanted life again and Evan would make the perfect vehicle for escape. Why not me? Because she knew that I had the knowledge and the means to expel her. Evan didn't have a clue. Most nonbelievers like him were easy to possess and Zee would take full advantage.

Part of me was concerned about this kid, but another part saw him as a threat. If Zee's possessing him helped me get away, I could always find a way to save him later. She wouldn't kill him, and I doubt she could even if she wanted to. But she could mess up his life pretty good. Sociopaths were like that.

Zee's ghost drifted toward Evan.

I stared, mesmerized. "Do you see that?"

Evan frowned. "See what?"

The ghost enveloped him like a melting marshmallow, folding around him before seeping in through his pores. He looked stunned, his mouth agape and his eyes so wide that only the whites of them showed. He jerked a few times, then his face went slack. I could see the ghost pulsing around him, its transparent mass larger than the kid's body. Zee squatted inside him like a toad.

Evan stood unmoving so I figured it was a good time to hop down to the basement and look for the changing charm. Evan-Zee would scram out of here the second she figured out how to move his legs. I'd find them later and do whatever I needed to set Evan free with a lesson learned: the dark arts are called dark for a reason. School, friends and sports should be his priority at this stage of his life. Dabbling was for grown-ups.

I was preparing to leap down into the dark hole of

the basement when a fireball hit me in the back and exploded. Sparks flew and my hair got singed, but some reflex part of Rusty's power warded off the brunt of it. I whirled around to face Evan-Zee, who had another flaming orb cocked to launch.

"Damn it, Zee. There's nothing here for you. Get the hell out." My hands sizzled with the flames sprouting from my fingertips. "I'm warning you."

"Aw," she said, pursing Evan's lips in a pout. "Are you mad?"

I glared at her.

She giggled. "Come off it, Chalice. You won't hurt this kid."

"You don't know that."

"Oh, yes, I do. I know what a sentimental idiot you are." She tossed the fireball in the air and caught it with her other hand. "I'm not as blind as Gavin. He had a soft spot for you just like he had for your mother."

Hold on. What the hell? She was trying to rattle my cage and did a darn good job of it, too. I blinked and hardened my eyes. I don't think she knew Gavin was dead. "Bullshit."

She cooked up two more fireballs and tossed them up with the first to juggle all three like a pro. "I don't want to argue with you, missy." The flaming orbs melded together, growing to the size of a basketball. "I just want to kill you."

Evan-Zee threw the ball at me and I raised my hands to catch it between my palms. "Missed."

Evan's eyes glowed with fire and I wondered if he was

even aware of what Zee was making his body do. "That's new."

I shrugged. "Yep. A lot's happened since you died."

Fire flamed from Evan's mouth when Zee said, "I'm not dead anymore."

I rolled my eyes. "Just because you stole a body doesn't mean you're not dead."

"Is that what you think?"

Zee's shadow didn't realize what it was. "You're too weak to hold on to this kid for long, so make the most of the time you have." I waved toward the front door. "Go out, have fun, get drunk and do whatever you did while you were alive."

Evan-Zee appeared conflicted for the first time. His eyes reflected doubt as they rolled in their sockets and took a fleeting glance at freedom. His chin dipped to rest against his chest. Maybe Zee had given up and decided to leave Evan's body, but then I saw the massive shape of Zee's ghost holding on. She wasn't going anywhere.

Blue flames shot out of Evan's mouth and melted the iron sconce on the wall. This was no ordinary fire. It was demon's breath, hot enough to turn solid rock to ash.

I seriously doubted the ability I'd acquired from Rusty was a match for a demonic inferno. I was a goner.

If I could make it down to the basement and stand at the center of the pentagram painted on the floor down there, I might be safe. I leaped toward the hole and flames from Evan's mouth caught the heels of my boots and set them on fire. I'm lucky Evan-Zee hadn't torched my entire leg.

I fell, bending my knees to take the shock of impact

on landing. The distance was far enough that I could easily break an ankle if I wasn't careful. About halfway down something with furry paws and arms caught me in midair. I struggled to break loose of whatever it was, vaguely aware that its wings beat the air to hold us aloft. Then I smelled him. It was Aydin.

I looked up at the opening in the ceiling, then at him, and he nodded. He knew what was going on and had probably been watching the entire time. Aydin was a better thief than me, and invisibility didn't hurt his skills of deception, either.

He gently flew us upward and used his body as a shield against the demon fire that flamed from Evan's mouth.

Aydin set me down on the floor, then turned to face our attacker and roared. It was the most god-awful, frightening sound I'd ever heard in my life. Not even Shui had sounded so terrifying.

Evan-Zee closed his mouth and backed up, eyes bulging. Aydin lunged forward in a feint attack, stopping with his open maw inches from Evan-Zee's face. His upper fangs were long enough to curl just below his lower jaw, and his tongue whipped out like a snake's as if tasting the air. He sniffed, his wide nostrils flaring, and saliva dripped from his mouth.

Evan-Zee screamed and dropped, unconscious, to the floor.

eighteen

I STOOD STARING DOWN AT THE UNCONSCIOUS Evan and looked for Zee, hoping she'd been scared out of Evan's body. No such luck. The plump specter curled around him, clinging with desperation. I think its survival instinct was stronger than whatever good sense it had.

Aydin wheeled around, his feline face set in a ferocious snarl. My heart jumped when I imagined him as the savage he pretended to be. He did pretend, right? His features relaxed and his jade eyes softened with a natural calm better suited to who he really was. My shoulders slumped as my tension melted away.

I watched him fade to his invisible form, and he took a step toward me. Nodding to let him know I was ready, I leaned forward and his body merged with mine.

The boy is possessed, Aydin said. *And Zee has no intention of leaving him without a fight.*

Not news to me. *Then let's fight her.*

The human Aydin I saw in my mind's eye shook his head. *Zee was a witch and her hooks are in deep. I've never exorcised a ghost, but I know someone who can.*

I hadn't met many exorcists during my thieving years, mainly because the Vyantara made it a point to exterminate every exorcist they found. Demon and ghost possession was good business for them. It was another way for them to control their enemies.

I don't like this kid, but I like Zee even less, I told him. *Besides, Evan doesn't deserve this kind of consequence for being a dumbass. A spanking would work better.*

He'd probably like that.

I smiled. *You're probably right.*

I'll fly the kid over to Gus Zenfieger's place. He'll pull Zee's ghost out of him and I'll get inside Evan's head to make sure he won't remember what happened.

You shouldn't fly in public. Panic coiled in my gut. *You'll have to be solid to carry him and someone might see you. We can't risk it.*

We have no other choice. I'll carry you, too.

Me? I was flooded with gruesome memories of Shui's talons puncturing my sides as he flew me around. The sadistic gargoyle had done it for fun. He got a kick out of my pain. I know Aydin would never hurt me on purpose, but the thought of being carried by a flying gargoyle terrified me. What if he dropped me? What if he ran me into the side of a building?

I won't leave you here alone. I can carry you both at the same time. Remember Shojin's harness?

I did. Aydin had made Shojin a special harness to carry people without injuring them. He'd even used it on Quin. *I remember.*

I brought it with me, just in case.

But if you strap in Evan, how will you carry me?

He grinned. *On my back.*

Better there than dragged underneath him. I nodded.

Your thoughts tell me you came here looking for one charm in particular, Aydin said.

The changing charm. Do you know of it?

Yes. He paused before adding, *I've seen it.*

It could make you human again.

Charms don't work on me, remember?

We can at least give it a try. I was so desperate to have him back that I'd try just about anything. *If we can't recover Shojin's heart, it can be our backup plan.*

I sensed his stubborn resolve and though I knew he wouldn't argue, I also knew he didn't agree. As far as he was concerned, it would *not* work.

The charm could be in the basement safe, which is where I was headed when Evan-Zee melted my boots.

Aydin released a mental sigh. *Stay here and I'll check.*

He withdrew from my mind and, still invisible, flew down the hole to the basement.

Evan lay unconscious, Zee along with him, and I suddenly remembered Duster. I ran to the pile of debris the boy had made when he fell, but he was gone. Smart kid. I hoped he'd been scared into going home and would be one less sewer rat to worry about.

Aydin flew up out of the hole and merged with me again.

The charm you want is still in the safe and appears unharmed, he said, though he didn't sound happy about it.

It's not for me, it's for you.

He had no response to that. *Saddle up. Time to go.*

Wait, I said. *We can't leave without the changing charm. I'll stay behind and crack the safe while you get Evan to the exorcist.* Which would also save me from having to be his passenger.

The safe is welded shut from the blast and you're not strong enough to pry it open, he said. *I'll do it, but not until after we get this boy to Gus's place. The longer Zee's shadow stays inside him, the harder it will be to get it out.*

Aydin backed out of me, and when he materialized, I saw the harness strapped around his back and chest. It was brown like his fur so it blended right in. He looked like a skydiver without a parachute, not that he'd need one.

We dragged Evan outside to the alley, where the asphalt was packed solid with ice and snow. Once hooked in, Evan's body hung forward like a sack of potatoes from Aydin's chest. The kid had to weigh at least 170 pounds, but Aydin didn't seem affected in the slightest. He motioned for me to hop on his back.

I sucked in a breath and jumped on, wrapping my legs tight as a vise around his waist. With one powerful flap of his wings we were airborne.

The freezing temperature had no effect on Aydin and our flight lasted only a few minutes. He landed us feather-softly behind one of the huge mansion-style homes in Denver's prestigious Capitol Hill.

I slid off his back and asked, "Gus lives here?"

He nodded and headed for the back door, his awkward gargoyle gait making him appear crippled. Evan was still hooked into the harness so the boy's feet dragged over the ground between Aydin's legs as he walked.

"He knows about your...you know." I spread my hands wide. "That you haven't been yourself lately?"

Still facing away from me, Aydin angled his feline head in my direction and jerked his chin at the door. Whether or not Gus knew Aydin was a gargoyle didn't seem to bother him. The alley behind the house was dark and all lights were off inside. I rang the bell.

Minutes later a porch light flicked on and the door creaked inward. Filling the doorway was an exceptionally tall man who had to stoop a bit just to peer out at us. His heavily lined face creased even more at seeing the sewer rat boy hanging like a rag doll from Aydin's chest. Any normal person would have run away screaming, but not this guy.

He wore a long, old-fashioned nightshirt complete with a floppy cone-shaped hat on his head. He glowered at me from below a set of bushy gray eyebrows. "May I help you?"

"We need an exorcism," I said.

He nodded. "Ghost, demon or elemental?"

Elemental? I didn't think elemental spirits were into possession. "It's a ghost."

He nodded and looked at Aydin, who was about equal to him in height. "My friend, I heard about what happened to you. What a handsome gargoyle you make." He stepped away from the door. "Come in, come in. All the heat is rushing out to melt the snow on my stoop."

Aydin slouched down to keep from scraping his head on the door frame. He slumped inside, dragging his burden along with him.

"I've heard of you, too, young lady," the old man said. "Chalice. You're the first person I know of to have survived the gargoyle's curse unchanged. Bravo."

I grinned. "Thanks."

He chuckled and walked through the kitchen, motioning for us to follow. He led us to a wood-paneled study that looked very much like an old-fashioned medical exam room circa 1800. It even had a nineteenth-century examining table with a hinged back that reclined and an elevated foot pedestal with stirrups on the side. I shuddered to think how stirrups were used in an exorcist's line of work. Though an antique, the wood table shone like new and even the metal parts gleamed silver in the dim light of a hurricane lamp.

Gus helped me release Evan from the harness and then bodily picked the boy up as if he weighed little more than a child. The man had to have been seventy if he was a day, but he moved like a twenty-year-old. He placed Evan on the table and strapped him down.

"I've never met an exorcist before," I told him.

He nodded. "We're a rare breed these days."

"Yeah, I know. It's a shame that so many have…moved on."

His head bobbed in agreement. He returned his focus to his patient. "When did the infestation occur?"

"Less than an hour ago."

"Excellent," he said before thrusting his hand into Evan's chest.

I gasped, then noticed that he hadn't broken the skin. Evan didn't flinch and there was no blood, yet Gus's hand vanished up to the wrist inside the boy's fully clothed body. He appeared to feel around, a look of concentration on his face.

"I never knew this was how an exorcism is performed," I said.

"Well, my methods are unorthodox." He continued fishing inside the boy. "Most exorcists chant and use incense and wave dead animal parts around, but I prefer a more straightforward approach. Aha!"

He yanked his hand out of Evan and something that look like a gelatinous organ writhed around his fingers.

"That's gross," I said.

"It's the ghost's physical form when it takes a body," he explained. "I imagine you're used to seeing the vaporous humanoid shapes the ghost projects on this plane."

"Well, yeah."

"Now you know what they look like in the fourth dimension, their true home."

"Home?"

"A number of energies exist in that dimension, but it's also a place for shadows of souls that have passed on. The ghost projects its nonphysical body on the human plane, in the third dimension."

Interesting. The fourth dimension is parallel to the third dimension we live in and can't be seen under normal circumstances. I was no physicist, but the Arelim told me all the veils existed in the third dimension of another universe. The objects there could be seen, touched, heard and smelled, but anything in the fourth dimension was supposedly intangible. At least in theory. Scientists had yet to prove anything.

"How am I able to see that gooey lump?"

He grinned. "Because I'm holding it and I exist in both dimensions at the same time."

"That's impossible," I said, staring at him more closely. I let down my visual shields to get a better look. He had no aura, so he was either dead or telling me the truth. He didn't look dead.

"It's not impossible if your mother was a sylph and your father was a necromancer." He chuckled. "My odd combination of parentage made me this way, as well as giving me my unique talent for exorcism."

"What will you do with her?" I asked.

"You know who this used to be?"

"A witch named Zee. Horrible woman when she was alive, and not much better now."

"Ah, well, no worries. She won't possess anyone else again." He held the ghost up over his head and leaned back, unhinging his jaw so that it opened wide enough to fit a soccer ball in.

Oh, my God. He was going to eat it. "Wait!"

His mouth snapped shut and he gave me a startled look. "What's wrong?"

"Um." Every race and every species had its own culture and dietary needs. That didn't mean I had to watch. "I'm sorry, but if you could put it away for later, I'd appreciate it. Watching you eat a ghost is like cannibalism to me."

"Of course. Didn't mean to offend." He looked sheepish. "The spirits I exorcise are payment for my services, and they're what I need to survive."

"Understood." I held up my hands. "No harm done."

He chose an empty jar off a shelf and peeled Zee's gloopy essence off his hand and dropped it inside. As soon as it left contact with him, it became a mass of vaporous smoke. He screwed the lid onto the jar and set it aside.

"How long have you been an exorcist?" I asked.

"Since I was two. I surprised both my parents by yanking out a ghost that had taken control of another child. No one knew he'd been possessed. That was…" He paused and scratched an ear. "One hundred and eighty-five years ago."

Holy crap. "You're a hundred and eighty-seven years old?"

"My mother is much older." He returned his attention to Evan, who still lay unconscious. "The boy will be fine now. Is he family?"

I shuddered. "Hardly. Just a wannabe sorcerer in training." I wasn't sure how much I should share with this guy, who I didn't even know. But he had done us a favor and seemed honest enough. At least Aydin knew him. "He leads a gang of teenage magic users and he's been getting instructions from the Vyantara."

Gus stiffened. "The Vyantara? And you let him live?"

"He's just a kid," I said, shocked that Gus would think him less deserving than anyone else. "If he gets himself killed, it won't be on my watch. I'd much rather he stay alive to use whatever skills he's learned in a positive way. There's always a chance he'll turn himself around."

Gus snorted and so did Aydin. I'd almost forgotten he was still here.

"You see?" Gus said, giving Aydin a friendly pat on the arm. "My friend here agrees with me. In my opinion, it's a fool's errand to help this man-child."

"Give him a chance. Kids like him are notorious for making bad choices. I just hope he grows up to make better ones." Speaking of choices, I should inspect Evan's clothes to see what he'd chosen to take from the ruins.

I patted his coat pocket and found the flying charm. "Eureka!" I held up the feather.

Gus frowned. "So that's what he was doing? Stealing charms?"

"And curses," I said. "The feather he got from somewhere else. But he was in the fatherhouse to take whatever he could find."

Gus's eyes sparked with interest and he ran a long-fingered hand along the inside of Evan's coat. Aydin watched him, his feline nose twitching with interest.

"If you find anything, hand it over," I told him, nodding at Aydin, who nodded back. We were both concerned that Gus might consider Zee's ghost less payment than he deserved. Especially since I wouldn't let him eat it in front of me.

Gus suddenly jerked his hand back. "Ouch!"

"What happened?"

When he lifted out the ebony mirror inscribed with some familiar symbols, I almost dropped the flying charm. It was the Aztec scrying mirror I had used to summon my father.

He handed me the mirror and stuck the side of his thumb in his mouth. "Cut myself on a sharp edge."

"Oh." I glanced down at the drop of blood he'd left on the mirror, but didn't stare at it for long. The last time I did that I was hypnotized by the enchantment contained inside the artifact. This was neither a charm nor a curse, but a tool for angel evocation. I had no clue how or why Evan had it, but I knew where it came from. The Vyantara.

nineteen

WE DROPPED EVAN OFF AT HIS "NEST" SINCE we didn't know where his parents lived, or if he even had parents. He wasn't conscious when Aydin carried him to the pile of ratty old pillows and blankets on the theater's abandoned stage. The rest of the rats had left. He gave Evan a mental suggestion to ensure he didn't remember being possessed. That way he had no recollection of a gargoyle, either. The less info he could deliver to the Vyantara, the better.

"But if they find out he no longer has the scrying mirror, that could be a problem," I told Aydin.

The two of us stood inside the basement of the father-house ruins. He'd remained solid in gargoyle form so that he could pry off the welded door from the safe. Being that he couldn't speak, our conversation was one-sided.

Aydin used a talon to make a circling motion over his head.

"Yeah, they're crazy enough to hurt him, or worse. But there's a chance they weren't the ones who gave it to him."

He held out his hands and shrugged.

"I don't know where else he could have gotten it from. Maybe he bought it on eBay."

Aydin folded his arms and tapped a clawed foot on the concrete floor.

"Okay, probably not. But he could have bought it off the black market. The Vyantara aren't the only ones who deal in the buying and selling of enchanted artifacts." I'd run into competition more than once during my years as a thief.

He sighed and headed for the melted safe.

My heart pounded. This was it. The changing charm would make Aydin human again and we could finally start living our lives together like we were meant to. So much of magic required belief to make it work. I believed, thanks to Aydin's encouragement, but I wasn't so sure Aydin thought this charm could help him.

He stood rigid with his feet apart to brace himself and hooked his talons into the space between the rock wall and the safe's door. Arms shaking, his muscles rippled beneath his fur and he growled so low and deep that I felt it vibrate in my chest. There was a screech of tortured metal followed by a loud pop, and then Aydin held a three-foot-square metal door in his fisted claws.

I rushed over to peer into the hole. The key lay apart from the small boxes and large envelopes stacked inside.

The old iron charm was pitted and showed signs of wear, and the distinctive wolf's head bared its teeth as it howled silently at an unseen moon.

A chill of both rapture and dread rippled through me. Though happy about this rare opportunity for Aydin, the magic was tainted by a dark curse thousands of years old. I only wished I knew more about what it did.

I found a tattered canvas bag sticking up from a pile of rubble and placed the contents of the safe inside. I didn't touch the changing charm. "I'll look through all this later with Quin. It could prove valuable enough to keep."

Aydin reached for the charm and I grabbed his paw. "Don't touch it."

He turned to face me and tilted his head sideways like a dog that's heard a high-pitched sound. His body faded to his ghost self and he took a step forward to merge with me.

You don't trust the changing charm.

I released a mental sigh. *No.*

His eyes crinkled slightly at the corners. *Me neither, but you already knew that. I don't know much about it, but I do know that werewolves have used it to force the change. It's been said the charm works on anyone, not just werewolves, but I imagine there are side effects.*

I hadn't thought about that. *What kind of side effects?*

He shrugged. *Maybe it changes more than physical appearance. What if it changes a person's personality? Or what if it turns them into something they're not prepared to be?*

I shuddered at the thought of Aydin's sweet nature becoming savage or cruel, or instead of human he became a were animal of some kind. It wasn't worth the risk.

I doubt it would work on me anyway, Aydin said.

Maybe, maybe not. I still wanted to keep it. Better it stay with us than go back to the Vyantara.

You must admit that lately I've been more useful as a gargoyle than human. How else could I have taken you away from the Canadian fatherhouse or helped you rescue that boy from the cellar? Not to mention today.

He had a point and I grudgingly agreed.

I felt like someone had let all the air out of my balloon. I'd been so hopeful that we'd found a cure, yet it could be an even worse curse than the one I'd survived. I hoped there was information with the other safe documents that told more about the charm.

I slid the iron key into one of my leather gloves and stuffed it in the bag.

After a good day's sleep, I was ready to review my treasures from the Vyantara's safe. Quin and I sat in the small storage room in back of Elmo's Coffee Shop. My recent discoveries were spread out on the cot Elmo kept there for guests, the last one having been Quin, who had been dead at the time of his visit. Now that he was alive and well, his living arrangements had been transferred to Elmo's home. But memories of him waking from death still unsettled me.

"Past history, Chalice," Quin told me as he leafed through the papers from one of the envelopes. "Stop letting it bother you so much."

"I can't help it." I slid a VHS tape from one of the envelopes. The label said it was a recording of a ghostly encounter three decades ago. "It feels like it happened only yesterday."

"You're not that far off," he said absently, and a slow grin spread across his lips. "Well, I'll be damned. Here's a recipe for perfume made from blood."

"Really?" I scanned the typed recipe card, its edges browned with age. A dark stain in the corner had me guessing it came from the perfume's main ingredient. What a great gift for the Vyantara to offer their enemies. A perfume or cologne this potent would attract vampires from hundreds of miles away.

"Hello." Quin snatched a page from the top of his paper stack. "What's this? Looks like a list of names."

I leaned sideways to check what he had found. The names at the top had a line drawn through them and one of those names belonged to Quin. "Appears to be a list of prospects," I said. Written beside each one was a supernatural ability or unique skill of some kind. These people had been targeted for recruitment. The list didn't surprise me, but the handwriting did. I recognized Gavin's pretentious scrawl. "This entire collection appears to have been Gavin's private stash. I bet the rest of the Vyantara don't even know it exists."

"That would explain why the safe's contents were still there when you found it."

"Yeah." I lifted a folder that had Maria's name on it. Too bad it was empty. "So Gavin knew about Maria. Figures."

"The man was filled with secrets. It's too bad he took most of them to the grave with him."

I wasn't so sure about that, at least not the grave part.

Which made me wonder what the Vyantara had done with his remains. After seeing his creepy shadow swirling around a vortex meant to suck me in, I now knew part of him had stuck around. Should I be worried?

I tugged the onyx scrying mirror from my jacket pocket and handed it to Quin. "We found this on Evan."

"Wow." Quin ran a finger over the carvings on the handle. "How do you think he got it?"

"No idea. I'm fairly sure Gavin was the last to have it. It should have been among his other supersecret goodies in the safe." *Now* I was worried.

"Anyone who was at the summoning ritual could have gotten their hands on this."

True. But everyone who had attended was now dead. With the exception of Barachiel and me.

"I need to know where this came from," I told Quin as I reclaimed the mirror. "The only one who might know is my father."

Quin pinned me with a serious stare. "You planning on performing another summoning?"

"Absolutely." I needed more from Barachiel than just to satisfy my curiosity. As a fallen angel, it was possible he could help me find Maria.

I went to my room and gathered the supplies I'd need for my journey and the summoning ritual.

Since I'd be venturing into a dangerous place, I felt obligated to let Rafe know my plans. He deserved that much, and I wouldn't have the chance to say goodbye to my grandparents or sister knights. Maybe Rafe could be reassigned to another knight because I certainly couldn't give him what he wanted.

It would be best to meet up with him at the cathedral where he could open the veil with no problem.

I wanted to walk there, but Quin insisted on driving me. We never knew when Maria would pop up, or even how she found the knights to begin with. It was like she had a homing device to track us. I figured she used black magic her father taught her.

"When will you be back?" Quin asked when he dropped me off outside the cathedral.

"I don't know." The concern on his face made him look like a lost puppy. "Time may work differently on the other side of the veil. I could be back in an hour or a year." *Or never.* But I felt no need to worry him.

Once inside Geraldine's shrine, I sent Rafe a mental message that I needed to speak to him. The silver surface of the veil appeared almost immediately and Rafe walked out into the peaceful garden room looking like a million bucks. He hadn't scrimped on the finest in men's fashion: sports coat with a turned-up collar, thick wool scarf, twill pants, neatly pressed, and a cable-knit sweater thick as a blanket. He smelled good, too.

"I was hoping you'd call," he said, his smile only a bare grin. "I wanted to apologize for what I'd said to you."

I shrugged. "I've already forgotten." Which was partly true. Our friendship was now strained thanks to him, but I'd been too focused on recovering charms and finding Maria to think much about our fight. I had more important things on my mind. "I thought I should let you know where I'm going."

He scowled. "Don't tell me you're running off to do something stupid."

"Not stupid, just necessary." I took a step toward the doorway and tilted my head in a request that he join me. "Walk me to the ruins and we'll talk along the way."

He hesitated, then matched my steps as we made our way up the stairs and out the door into the frigid night. "Thank you for allowing me to guard you for at least a little while."

I laughed. "There's only so much you can do, Rafe. I'd ask you to come with me, but you can't go where I'm going. You'd self-destruct or melt or something."

He grinned. "Or something."

I hooked my arm through his as we walked down the street. "Try not to worry. I have Rusty's fire and my knives to protect me."

"The squires have been asking about you."

"That's nice."

He nodded. "You made quite an impression."

"Let them know their training is far from over. There will be homework and tests."

"I'll be sure to tell them."

We walked in silence for a few blocks, Rafe's eyes turning to look to the side and behind us almost constantly. He'd get a kink in his neck if he kept that up. But the night was quiet, traffic was light, and the streets were empty of people. My senses told me we were alone, but that didn't stop Rafe from taking his guardian duties seriously.

"Is he going with you?" Rafe asked me.

"If you mean Aydin, yes, he is. He shouldn't have any trouble crossing to the other side. We each have one foot over there already." I glanced up at Rafe's face. He wasn't amused. "Lighten up and don't be so jealous."

"I'm not jealous." He sounded like he meant it. "I'm traditional. I have an obligation to the Arelim and to the knights to maintain proper order within our ranks. You make that very difficult to do."

I sighed. "Rafe, times have changed. You need to change with them or you'll get left behind." We had arrived at the ruins and I stopped to look up at him. "Tell my grandparents that I miss them and I'll see them soon."

The weight of his stare made me uncomfortable. "Be careful," he said.

"I will."

A rustling noise came from the broken steps leading up to the fatherhouse entrance. Dark as it was, I had no trouble recognizing Maria's faceless silhouette and her hooded cloak billowing around her ankles.

I grabbed my throat and gasped for air, but there was no need. Shock at seeing her is what took my breath away, not Maria herself. She appeared to study me as if watching me under a microscope. Like the specter of death itself, she stood still and completely unconcerned. Why should she worry? She had nothing to fear because no one could hurt her. At least not as far as I knew, though everyone had his or her kryptonite.

Rafe tensed beside me and I tightened my grip on his arm. "She's not doing anything," I whispered.

"Yet." His body hardened and I knew he would sprout wings and grow a foot taller at any second.

"Don't make a spectacle," I told him. Even from this distance I sensed Maria's loneliness. Arrogant and thoughtless, yes, but there had to be more inside that sociopathic head of hers. After centuries of life spent in darkness, this world outside the veil must be new to her. It intrigued her. Though I marginally understood how she might feel, it was no excuse for murder. "She's not surprised to see you with me, Rafe. She doesn't feel threatened and she apparently has no plan to take action."

I took a step toward her and Rafe grabbed me by the elbow to pull me back.

"It smells like a trap," he said.

I sniffed the air. "Funny. I don't smell anything." I yanked my arm free and turned to head up the steps. The second I did, Maria vanished. A single black feather fluttered in the empty space she left behind.

"If that was a trap, it was a poorly planned one," I told him. "But I think you're half-right."

"About...?"

"She's teasing me. She wants me to chase her, like it's a game."

Rafe's jaw muscles clenched. "I accept that you will do whatever it takes to stop this menace. But *you* must accept that I don't like it."

I bobbed my head in a slow nod. "Understood." I folded my arms and looked up at him. "It is what it is, Rafe. I'm the only practical choice."

Rafe dipped his head to stare at the ground in silence. I understood his feelings of helplessness, but his role as an Arelim angel was more valuable now than ever.

"We need to look to the future and not let Maria make this chapter of our lives the final one," I told him. "While I'm gone, you can help by continuing to recruit new squires. I'll be back to teach them what they need to protect themselves."

"Promise?"

I smiled. "I'll do my best."

twenty

I TIED THE ROPE I'D BROUGHT ALONG TO what was left of the banister on the staircase leading to the basement. After lowering myself to the bottom, I blinked in the foggy darkness until I could make out the outline of Aydin's ghosted gargoyle form.

He knew my plans for summoning my father and had no objections. Aydin was a pragmatic man and rarely let his emotions rule his thinking like some people I knew. He understood that Barachiel was our best chance of crossing to the other side of the black veil. The only question now was whether or not Barachiel would agree. I wouldn't know until I asked.

Once the giant pentagram on the floor was cleared of all debris, I filled the bowl I'd brought along with herbs I'd collected, adding natural resin and a generous shot of absinthe to the mix. I lit a match over the contents. The mixture ignited and a flame shot toward the ceiling.

I positioned myself at the head of the pentagram. Heavy smoke swirled from the bowl and I offered it to the north, south, east and west. After dropping five Celestine crystals into the bowl and coating them with ash, I set one at each point of the pentagram.

My balisong blade stung my flesh when I used it to cut my palm and dribble blood into the smoking bowl. The last time I'd performed this ritual I had added Quin's blood as well. Since then I'd learned that because my own blood came from a fallen angel, it was all I needed.

I mixed the bloody mixture with my fingers and touched my forehead to draw an X there. Once I set the mirror at the center of the pentagram, I focused my intent on breaching the boundary between realms and spoke the words that would bring my father here.

"The blood of an angel's spawn serves as conduit to cross the barrier between two worlds." I touched my bloody fingers to the scrying mirror and smeared the symbol for creation onto its surface. "I summon my father, the fallen angel Barachiel."

A cyclonic spiral of sparks rose from the ash on the mirror. It grew bigger as it lifted in the air and hovered a foot or so above the ground. A powerful hum vibrated at the core of my body as a chill coursed down my spine and raised goose bumps on my arms. The magic felt strong, and it even felt right, which was unusual for me. It must be because it came from my own blood, from my family. Fallen or not, Barachiel was, and always would be, my father.

My heart pummeled my ribs as I watched the giant angel take shape in front of me. His enormous black wings spread out as if ready to take flight, but he folded them in close to his body. Barachiel looked as though carved from white marble and his black hair fell over his shoulders in thick glossy waves, wisps of it floating around his face on an unearthly breeze.

"Greetings, my child," he said, his baritone voice reverberating against the basement walls. "I'm happy to see you again."

I gazed up at his obsidian eyes that sparkled like a starry night sky. He wasn't evil. Not all fallen angels were necessarily bad. They were ostracized from their Arelim counterparts for committing the sin of fornication. Having fallen from grace made them predisposed to taking the wrong path, and many were bitter enough to do so. Barachiel was not.

"It's good to see you, too," I told him.

"Are you still angry with me?"

I shook my head. "No, not anymore. Only disappointed. I'm still trying to understand why you chose to fall rather than become human to marry my mother."

He closed his eyes and sighed. "I sense that's not why you called me here today."

"It's not," I said, though he wasn't getting off that easy. He may not tell me today, but he *would* tell me. I'd make sure of it.

"Is it because of the mirror?" he asked, peering down at the artifact he stood on.

I frowned. "Of course not. The mirror is my tool for calling you here. Why?"

He crouched down to pick it up. The mirror looked like a child's toy in his big hand. "It has been used recently by someone else."

My heart gave a jolt. "Who?"

"Unknown," he said. "But it wasn't used to summon an angel. It was used as a vessel for a soul."

What the hell? "How do you know?"

He shrugged. "I come to you through this mirror and I feel the absence of a presence it held. Perhaps a day or two ago."

"Where is it now?" I asked.

"Gone."

Obviously. I racked my brain trying to think of who it could have been, how it got there, and where it was now. Evan came to mind since he was last to have the mirror, but he'd been possessed by Zee. I had watched her glob of mucus-like essence drop into one of Gus's "food" jars. I considered Evan the only logical new vessel for whatever stowaway soul had been inside the mirror.

"If not about the mirror, why else am I here?" Barachiel asked.

I blinked and struggled to push the mysterious soul problem to the side. We had a more immediate dilemma. "I need your help."

"I promise to do whatever I can. Chalice." My name lingered on his tongue like a precious thing and it made my heart swell. Could he feel love for his child? Could I feel love for my father? I doubt either of us knew those answers.

I reached up to touch his cheek and he covered my hand with his. "What is it you need?" he asked.

"I want you to take me through the black veil."

He took a step back and pulled my hand gently from his face. "That is no place for you."

"Barachiel, my sister knights are dying. They're depending on me to stop the killer and I know where she is. You have to take me there." My tone sounded more pleading than I meant for it to, but I felt desperate. He was the only one I knew who could take us there.

"I must know more about this murderer you speak of." He cupped my head in his huge hands and closed his eyes. I felt him probe my thoughts as memories fluttered through my mind like a shuffling deck of cards. He released me seconds later.

"I know of this Maria, though I didn't know what she was until now. I have never seen her." His lip curled in disgust. "All I know is that she drinks the blood of the Fallen."

I shuddered. "So I heard." Staring hard at him, I asked, "Did she drink from you?"

His eyes widened. "Of course not. It would only have added to that broken doll's pain. She is damaged. I would have helped her, but her father stands guard constantly. You wish to end this woman's life?" he asked.

"Not if I can help it." I honestly hoped it wouldn't come to that, but considering how she had annihilated an entire order of knights, killing her was a possibility. It was all about survival now.

"I won't be going alone," I told him.

Aydin materialized one second later. Barachiel looked surprised.

"The warrior is now a gargoyle," he said with an approving grin. "I remember when Pharzuph cursed you with invisibility and immortality. I did not know you were afflicted with the gargoyle's curse as well."

"Aydin fought Shui to save *me* from having to suffer his fate." I cupped Aydin's feline face with the palm of my hand and he nuzzled into my caress. "I promised to reverse his change."

"Chalice, you cannot. Not without the heart of his bonded gargoyle."

I smiled. "I have it."

"You killed his beast?" Barachiel blinked. "Well done. But then why does Aydin retain the gargoyle form?"

Shame replaced my pride and I stared down at my feet. Not only had I not struck the killing blow, I'd lost my prize. "Because the heart was stolen."

An uncomfortable silence made the air hard to breathe and I was afraid Barachiel's disappointment would make him leave. I glanced up to see him still there, the expression of pride on his face reviving my hope.

"Is that on the other side as well?" he asked.

I nodded. "I believe so. Maria kidnapped one of our squires, the one who I think stole the heart."

Barachiel scowled at Aydin. "When you are a man again, will you continue to care for my daughter?"

How did he know about us? Aydin gave a quick nod.

Barachiel grinned. "Then I will help you."

I exhaled in relief. I had a feeling he'd come through for us. After all, I was the child he'd abandoned before I was even born. He owed me.

"One more thing." I pulled the ugly old horn of breath

from my nap sack. "Do you know if this can be re-charged?"

He stared at it and scowled. "That's the Viking horn for breathing. You have used it?"

"I saved a sister knight with it after Maria sucked her breath away."

"Ah, yes." He plucked the horn from my fingers. "I'm quite familiar with old Norse magic. I have made these before."

"*You* made them?"

When he saw the look of disgust on my face, he cleared his throat. "I make many things. I will tell you all about it someday."

I wasn't sure I wanted to know. A fallen angel making charms was bad enough, but my own father? What did he do with them? Who did he give them to, and why? Now I had one more thing to worry about.

Barachiel created a cocoon with his hands and blew into the crack he made between his thumbs. I jerked a quick look at Aydin as I remembered him doing the exact same trick with a caterpillar. Except the caterpillar had turned into a moth. I wondered what this horn would become.

When Barachiel opened his hands, the horn lay centered in his palm. It was no longer old and chipped, but whole and shiny white. He handed it to me and I hesitated.

"What's wrong?" he asked. "Isn't this what you wanted?"

"It still works?" Though what I should have asked is *what's it going to cost me?*

"Of course."

"Thank you." I wrapped my fingers around the horn, which still felt warm from Barachiel's breath. I tucked the charm back into my knapsack and included the scrying mirror with it.

"One thing we must do before we go," Barachiel said.

"What's that?"

He took hold of my hand and turned it over so that my palm faced up. He traced my sigil scar with his index finger. "This will prevent you from crossing."

I stared down at the brand Rafe had given me while I recuperated behind the silver veil. Without it, I'd no longer have access to that realm. I wasn't even sure I'd have access to Rafe.

"But it's part of my body."

Barachiel shrugged. "I'll remove it."

I jerked my hand away. "It's a scar. You'd have to cut it away."

"No." He gently retrieved my hand. "But this may hurt a little."

He rubbed his thumb over the sigil and the scorching heat of his touch burned my skin. I winced and gritted my teeth, the sound of sizzling flesh making my stomach turn. But it was over quickly. When he took his thumb away, a fat blister remained. My sigil was gone.

"May I?" Barachiel nodded at the knife still in my hands and I handed it to him. He pricked the sigil on his palm and red blooms welled from the cut. "My offering to the veil. Now we may cross."

My father held out both his hands. "Take my hand."

Aydin took the uninjured one and I took the other. Barachiel focused on a basement wall and the bricks began to shake. I braced my legs, expecting what was left of the house to fall around us, but nothing else moved. The bricks appeared to soften like rubber, the surface bubbling and then popping with sparks. Very different from the silver and green veils I was used to.

Barachiel stepped toward the rippling black surface. It was hard to imagine myself walking through that without melting.

I balked and Barachiel tugged me closer. "Chalice, are you certain you want to do this?"

I peered over at Aydin, who jutted his chin at the melting wall. He waved his hand forward to encourage me and I mentally exhaled in relief. Having him with me made all the difference. I could never do this alone.

"What's it like over there?" I asked Barachiel.

"It's been a while since I've crossed, but it never changes." He paused as if to think. "You know of Vikings, yes? It's much like that. Perhaps the veil influenced the ancient Norse way of life."

I tightened my grip on my father's hand and plunged ahead.

Passing through the gelatinous barrier between worlds wasn't as bad as I thought it would be. It was very similar to how it felt passing through the silver veil. Beyond the silver curtain I'd encountered nothing but white fog, as if the vacancy of senses helped the Arelim focus without distractions.

Where the realm of angels was shrouded in a cloud of mystery, the black veil lay exposed for what it was. The paintings of Hieronymus Bosch came to mind, but that wasn't accurate. It was more like the realistic oils created by Sir Thomas Francis Dicksee. Beautiful and dark, brutally honest in its savagery, and scary as hell.

Because, in a sense, this *was* hell. Now I understood what Barachiel had meant about the ancient Norse having been influenced by the black veil, as every detail could be linked to the Middle Ages. It was like time stood still here, the clock having stopped during the Crusades of the first millennium.

The scars of battle lay all around us. Wounded soldiers wandered the dirt streets and alleys between crude buildings made of mud and brick. Straw roofs shed clumps of thatch and strange-looking animals trampled over them while dragging wagons filled with filthy men, women and other things.

Most everyone wore armor. Cloaked figures trudged in and out of stalls that appeared to sell a variety of hand-made goods from clothing to tools, herbs, potions and what I guess could be food, though I wasn't sure. Demons walked out in the open, as did fallen angels and gargoyles. This was a city of miscreants.

"Is this hell?" I asked Barachiel.

"In a matter of speaking, though its citizens are very much alive," he said. "You can see why I don't come here."

"It's quite…medieval," I said.

"Some things never change." He turned around slowly and made a wide sweep with his hand. "As you can see, we fit right in."

I zeroed in on a display in one of the stalls, but my eyesight wasn't cooperating. What was happening to me?

I blinked and refocused. It didn't help. I sniffed the

air. Hay, animal droppings, dirt, but nothing out of the ordinary. My senses weren't working.

"Barachiel," I whispered. "My abilities. They...they're not working."

He scowled. "I don't understand."

"It's like my senses are muffled. My eyes, my sense of smell, they're...normal."

He nodded slowly. "I believe I know why."

"What?"

"Humans are powerless here. They serve the dark ones. Your abilities have been stripped from you so that you may be a better slave."

"Slave?" Panic gripped me. "I'm no one's slave, not now and not ever."

"Of course you're not," Barachiel soothed. "I'm just explaining how it works here. Humans do not normally have supernatural powers. The knights may be different in that respect, but you're still human."

I glanced at Aydin and he shook his head. He held up his claws to look at them, front and back. I think he was trying to tell me his abilities weren't working, either.

"Look at Aydin," I said. "He's not human, yet he can't become invisible."

"Ah, but he *is* human at his core. That's the difference."

Damn it. Now what? Without our abilities, we were helpless as kittens. At least Aydin still had his strength. All I had was my knife and a few charms that wouldn't work for me.

He flattened his palms against his chest. "I'm unaffected and can watch out for you both."

I appreciated his reassurance, but it was a struggle to

smile. My abilities were gone and I felt…exposed. I'd
have to rely solely on my smarts and my knife skills.
Aydin's brute strength and wing power would have to
be enough. And there was something else: he and I now
had no way to communicate.

"Though I'm mostly a stranger here, I know my way
around." Barachiel held my hand gently between his. "I'll
guide you."

I wanted to ask where he'd been for the past twenty-
six years. Who knew what can of worms that question
would open, so I shelved it for now. I hoped we'd have
time to catch up later.

"This is one village among dozens," he said. "It is the
largest and is called Yngvar."

I knew of Yngvar, at least in human terms. It was the
Scandinavian name for a fertility war god. A fitting village for Pharzuph, considering the type of fallen angel
he was.

The three of us left the road to gather behind a village structure that reminded me of the old chapel in the
Lebanese monastery where I grew up. This village, and
possibly the entire realm, was a conglomeration of cultures with one thing in common: destitution.

I clung to Aydin and he draped a furry arm protec-
tively around my shoulders. He pulled me close, letting
me know in his own way that he loved me. I so needed
that right now.

Though my eyesight wasn't nearly as good as I was
used to, my power of observation hadn't wavered. I studied the people moving about their daily chores, buying
and trading goods, cooking over open fires, haggling

over purchases and arguing. Lots of arguing. No one appeared content and they all seemed to have issues with one another. Perhaps that's what made *their* world go round. The three of us may blend with the populace in appearance, but our congenial attitudes had us sticking out like flowers in the weeds. We'd have to get out of here before we drew attention to ourselves.

I was about to say just that when my practiced eye spotted a familiar vagrant in one of the food stalls. She wasn't dressed in the typical peasant attire, though she appeared as dirty as the rest of them. Her razor-cut white hair was what tipped me off. Xenia.

I had to clamp a hand over my mouth to keep from shouting her name.

Barachiel spun me around to look at him. "What is it? What did you see?"

"The kidnapped girl we're looking for," I whispered. "She's in that stall buying bread or something. It's Xenia."

He scowled and nodded. "Do not be alarmed with what I'm about to do."

Which of course made me anxious. "What *are* you going to do?"

"Bring her to you." He turned and went over to the stall, where Xenia was having a heated debate with the cook. His forceful strides made him appear menacing and Xenia's head jerked up at his approach. Her eyes widened and she stiffened as if recognizing who he was. Or what he was. Fallen angels were obviously not new to her, at least not anymore.

Thanks to my lousy human hearing, I couldn't hear what was said, but I saw her cower when Barachiel grabbed her arm and jerked her away from the cook. The man she'd been talking to acted like nothing had happened. He went right back to flinging globs of dough onto a hot iron and verbally sparring with the next person in line.

When Xenia spotted me, her face contorted in a mix of shock and relief. She struggled to free herself, then halted the second her gaze landed on Aydin. She looked between the three of us and her face fell, her brows tilted with worry, and she turned to pull away in the opposite direction. Barachiel grabbed her firmly by the shoulders and pushed her toward me.

"What the hell are you doing here?" Xenia asked, voice shaking. "And with them? I thought you'd come to rescue me, but now I see you're on her side."

"I'm here to take you home, Xenia." I studied her from head to toe. There were bruises on her bare arms, a cut on her cheekbone and her scraped knees showed through her torn jeans. She'd been beaten. "Who did this to you?"

Xenia clamped her mouth shut as she scorched me with a hateful glare.

"The only side I'm on is the Hatchet knights'," I told her. "All of us are. This fallen angel is my father, Barachiel. He came to help, and so did Aydin."

Xenia spit on the ground by Barachiel's feet. "The Fallen. I know what *you* are."

I grabbed her away from my father and clamped my hands roughly to her shoulders. "You know nothing." I'd had all I was going to take from this girl and gave her a firm shake. "You're a thief and a liar. Don't presume anything! Mistakes like that can get you killed."

Aydin laid a paw on my shoulder and I slid him a sideways glance. He slowly shook his head and I lightened my grip.

Her eyes filled and a tear dripped off the lashes of one lower eyelid. She snuffled loudly, but whispered, "I'm sorry. I'm so, so sorry." But I caught a flicker of uncertainty in her eyes. Was she that confused?

My heart reached out to her. How could I stay angry with this girl? She had screwed up and suffered consequences I wouldn't wish on anyone, least of all a sister knight. Now we had to get her home. But first I needed to know what she'd done with Shojin's heart. "Where is it, Xenia?"

She lowered her eyes to stare at the clumps of dry mud around her feet. "I sold it."

My heart dived to the pit of my stomach. "All of it? Even the heart?"

She gazed into my eyes and scowled. "Heart? What heart?"

I huffed in exasperation. "The bright purple stone I buried under the tree. You took it, remember? Whom did you sell it to?"

Xenia shook her head. "I don't know what you're talking about."

I growled and lunged at her, but Aydin curled a furry arm around my waist and hauled me off my feet. My fingers tore at the air inches away from Xenia's face. I could have scratched her eyes out right then. She ducked away from me and Barachiel got hold of her again.

At least now we blended in with the rest of the snarling riffraff fighting in the streets. No one gave us a second glance.

"Stop lying!" I screamed at Xenia.

"I swear I'm telling the truth!"

I relaxed, but only for a minute. "Then who took it? And where is it now?"

"I don't know."

The heart was gone. My final hope for a future with Aydin was gone.

"Do you wish to cross back now that you have the girl?" Barachiel asked me.

I gritted my teeth as I stared at Xenia. I had to redirect my rage at who was really responsible for the hell we were going through right now. Perhaps it was Maria who'd stolen the heart. After all, she was there the night I reburied it. She could have been watching me before I ventured beyond the safety of Halo Home's wards. She could have unburied the heart and taken it while I was mind-linked with Aydin, just before she nearly suffocated me to death.

"Maria has the heart," I told Barachiel, and explained my reason for thinking so. "I have to get it back. And she's going down when I do."

My father's mouth softened slightly with the beginning of a smile. I think he approved of my plan.

"Xenia," I said. "Take us to Maria's lair."

Xenia swallowed and her pleading gaze jumped between the three of us. "Don't make me go back there. The dark ones. They'll hurt me again."

"We won't let them touch you," I told her.

"You don't understand," Xenia said. "There are at least a dozen fallen angels with her and one of them is her father." She flicked a frightened look at Barachiel. "And there are women there, too."

I frowned. "Human women?"

She nodded. "They're very chummy with the Fallen. Paired up. They, um…" Looking embarrassed, she said, "They make out a lot."

None of this sounded right. Fallen angels paired up with human women? It couldn't get more wrong than that.

"Who are they?" I asked.

She shrugged. "I don't know. We've never been introduced. But you know what's really scary?"

I waited for her to answer her own question.

"They're pregnant."

twenty-one

I FELT SUDDENLY NUMB. THE SPAWN OF THESE fallen angels would have powers like the Hatchet knights.

Barachiel shook his head. "This can't be. The Fallen are unable to father children."

"Which means they hadn't yet fallen when they took their mates," I said.

"So they were Arelim as I had been." Barachiel's eyebrows tilted in a worried frown. "No ordinary human woman can bear the child of an angel. They must either be a Hatchet knight, or one who can speak with the Arelim."

"Angel whisperers," I said. Just like our squires. And more to the point, just like Xenia. That must be why Maria had kidnapped her. But why her and not the others?

"Xenia," I said, smoothing away the steel edge from my voice, or at least trying to. "I remember you telling me you were special, better than the other squires. Where did that come from?"

She blinked and darted her gaze left to right. "It's what I was told."

"By whom?" I asked.

She bit her bottom lip and winced. "An angel. He didn't tell me his name and I thought he was my chosen guardian, the one I'd be introduced to on my birthday. He said I was destined for something better than the Hatchet knights."

Damn. He couldn't have been one of *our* Arelim angels and he obviously acted on Maria's behalf. She could be gearing up to start a new order of knights on her own.

Xenia's eyes filled with tears again. "He acted like he understood what I was going through. He knew I was motherless, that I'd had a tough life growing up, and he sympathized with my fears. He made me feel like I mattered."

"How did Maria get you to go with her?" Barachiel asked.

"She promised me a better life and a husband who wouldn't leave me or my baby. She said I'd be treated like a queen."

Brilliant. Maria had used the guardian-as-mate card to play Xenia. Girls groomed to be squires knew they'd lose their guardian the minute they conceived. He would either become human or fall. The Fallen were forced apart from their knights, but this new order apparently allowed them to stay together.

"Maria found me after I'd sold all the charms I'd stolen from you. She brought me through the veil," Xenia said.

"I hate it here and I'm treated like anything but a queen. She's made me her slave."

To say I was furious at this point would be an understatement. My ears burned and the pulse in my neck beat hard enough to make my entire body shake.

"Calm yourself," Barachiel told me.

I clenched my jaw and heaved in deep breaths. Maria wouldn't get away with this. I'd die before letting her use and abuse more girls like she had Xenia.

"I take it you're in the village running errands for Maria?" I asked.

Xenia nodded. "I was sent for supplies."

I focused on regaining control of my temper so that I could think more clearly. Maria knew I'd come here. She had taunted me to get my attention and as soon as we arrived, I conveniently ran into Xenia on the street. Convenience, my ass. I'd been set up.

I wasn't about to change my plan. We would still go to Maria's lair, but we'd be more prepared than she expected. She didn't know I had a fallen angel on my side, too.

"Xenia, did you get a chance to talk to the other women?" I asked.

"No," she said. "They were off-limits to me, but I caught a glimpse of them when I walked by the big room where they'd all get together and, um…you know."

I didn't like the sound of that. "You mean an orgy?"

She nodded.

I hated to ask this next question, but I had to know if these women were being held against their will. "Did they act like they enjoyed it?"

"Chalice!" Barachiel's widened eyes made him look like a shocked dad.

"We have to know if they're prisoners or willing participants," I said. "It's not for my own interest. Sheesh. I'm not a pervert."

"I didn't watch, so I wouldn't know. Besides, what difference does it make?" Xenia asked.

"Because we need to get them out of there." These women were carrying the children of Arelim angels. Those babies were related to the Hatchet knights, and that made them our family. "I want to take them home. With us."

Aydin threw up his paws and began to pace. I guessed he wasn't too keen on that idea.

"It's not like we can click our heels together and chant, 'There's no place like home,'" Xenia said. "We're stuck here. There's no way back."

Of course there was a way back. I pulled Maria's fallen angel feathers from my knapsack. "If Maria can cross back and forth, so can we."

"You only have three feathers," Xenia said.

Barachiel spread his wings. "I have plenty more."

"How many fallen angels are with her?" I asked.

She squinted, appearing to mentally calculate her answer. "Ten. Maybe eleven. I know Maria's father is one of them, but he hasn't been around."

There's no way we could stand up to a small army of immortal fallen angels. We would have to return with reinforcements to take the women away. It was time to scope out Maria's crystal cave and see what we were up against. And then I would find where she had stashed Shojin's heart.

After Xenia collected her supplies, she led us out of the village. The four of us looked like the little troupe from *Wizard of Oz,* minus Toto. The road wasn't paved with yellow bricks, but made of dirt, and it took us through a maze of towering rock formations and a forest of creepy trees. The trees moved and it wasn't the wind that thrashed their branches. Their bark rippled and they seemed to strain against the roots holding them in place.

"Don't get too close," Barachiel warned. "The trees are carnivorous."

"No one has to tell me twice," Xenia said, shoving herself closer to me. "Maria warned me not to touch them. Now I know why."

A leafless branch shot up to snag a bird that looked like a crow, but it had no beak. In fact, it appeared to have a human face, though I couldn't be sure. I was starting to miss my super senses. I felt blind without them.

Aydin took the lead as we walked, with Xenia a pace or two behind him and well out of earshot. I thought it a good opportunity to chat with my long-lost father. "Where have you been all this time?"

Barachiel shrugged and hesitated too long before answering, "Not a place you'd know."

I realized the human realm wasn't the only world that supported life. If there were three veils, why not four? Or five? "Another veil?" I asked.

"No." He heaved in a breath and let it slowly out his mouth. "Another dimension."

I nodded, remembering what Gus had told me. "I know of the fourth dimension, but I've never been there."

He raised his eyebrows as he turned his head to look at me. "You never cease to amaze me."

Now it was my turn to shrug. "I haven't been a knight for long, but I was involved with charms and curses for over a decade. So I've been around the supernatural block a few times."

He nodded. "Indeed you have."

"What were you doing in the fourth dimension?"

"Perfecting my magic."

It wasn't that long ago that I detested anything having to do with magic. But with Aydin's help I'd come to finally accept it as a natural part of my life. There was good magic and bad. I'd seen plenty of bad, but good? Not so much.

"What kind of magic?" I asked, worried how he would answer. I couldn't handle it if he practiced the dark stuff like Gavin, who was all about greed and power. Barachiel didn't seem the type, but I didn't really know him yet.

"It's nothing evil, Chalice. Not much different from what the Arelim practice. But some of my defensive magic can be lethal, which is why I'm perfecting it. Putting my own spin on it, so to speak."

"Why?"

"Magic has always been a part of who I am."

I could see where this was going. "And that's why you didn't want to stay with my mother. You didn't want to become human and lose your powers."

"Partly, yes. But Chalice, even though your mother and I respected each other and I cared very much for her, we were never in love." He ran a hand through his hair, looking frustrated as if searching for the right words. "I didn't abandon her. She and I both agreed that my leaving would be best for all of us, including you."

I sighed. I supposed he was right, but I couldn't help remembering back to how badly I'd wanted the American dream. A mom and dad, brothers and sisters, a house with a garden, a real school with friends... But that life was never meant for me. I'd been forced to make the most of what I had.

"There's another reason, too," he said. "I do not ever want to die."

I hadn't thought about the immortality angle. "Does death bother you that much?"

"I may be an angel, but we don't know everything. The Arelim are the lowest order of angel, just above the Fallen, so I was never privileged with the knowledge of such a divine mystery as death."

My mind still tried to wrap itself around the whole immortality thing. "If angels can't die, how will we get rid of Maria's horde or coven or whatever the hell they are?"

Barachiel twitched his eyebrows. "Angels can be banished."

That was an unfamiliar concept for me. "Really?"

"It rarely happens and very few know how to do it."

"Have you ever banished anyone?"

"Never had a reason to, but I know how it's done. The spell for banishment is linked to what I did at the fatherhouse the night you summoned me."

That was the night he stopped time so that I could

escape. I'd never forget the image of Shui frozen in mid-flight about two feet off the ground.

"The spell connected to that one will banish an angel to an area of the fourth dimension that does not move."

"Doesn't *move?*" That made no sense.

"It's difficult to explain." Barachiel narrowed his eyes and used his hands to form a cocoon like the one he had made around the horn. "It's a pocket of time that goes neither forward nor backward. It acts as a prison of sorts."

"Inertia." Though my knowledge of quantum physics was a bit fuzzy, I knew the fourth dimension had something to do with time and space. So what he just said *did* make sense, but from a magic point of view.

"Is it permanent?" I asked.

"I believe so, but I'm not certain."

I wondered how many angels had been banished there and what crimes had caused their punishment. It was comforting to know that if bad angels couldn't be killed, at least they could be contained.

Xenia stopped and pointed to a large hill up ahead. "The crystal cave is in there."

The four of us huddled behind an outcropping of rocks on the opposite side of the road. I watched Aydin, whose nostrils flared as he sought out a scent. I knew what he was looking for.

"Is it here?" I asked him.

He hung his head and wagged it from side to side.

My shoulders slumped in defeat. Maria could have hidden the heart anywhere, including the human realm. We might end up searching right back where we started.

I wished I could see through the thick rocks that encompassed the cave. I also wished I could have a conversation with Aydin to discuss my plan. The only option left at this point was to scope out the cave and spy on the women being kept there. I could take that information home to share with the Arelim. They would know what to do.

"I'm going in," I told the others as I slid my balisong from the sheath on my back. "This won't take long."

"No!" Xenia grabbed my arm. "Let me go first. They're expecting me. Maybe I can distract Maria while you find a way to sneak inside."

"Maria expects her back anyway," Barachiel said. "It makes sense."

Aydin slapped a hand against his chest.

"You want to go with me?" I asked him.

He nodded and, after a minute's hesitation, Barachiel nodded, too. I appreciated how protective they were, but I'd been in far worse situations than this. They shouldn't worry so much.

"You'll stand watch for us then?" I asked my father, and he nodded again.

Xenia stepped away from us and strode with confidence toward the cave entrance. She didn't look one bit worried, her back straight and head held high. It contradicted the frightened girl we'd confronted only an hour ago. I gave a mental headshake. Xenia was an oddity that I doubted I would ever figure out.

Aydin and I crossed the road to get closer to the cave, using the tall rock formations to shield us from view. I guessed about a hundred yards lay between us and the front entrance, where Xenia had already disappeared. I searched for a back entry and found a small opening on the side of the hill. Peering inside, I was shocked at how dark it was. I never imagined I could be so visually impaired.

"Can you see?" I whispered to Aydin.

He nodded. I wasn't surprised. Gargoyles had excellent night vision.

I held on to his tail as he stealthily moved up ahead. I stumbled over a rock in my path and Aydin reached back to steady me. We wound through a narrow tunnel that led deep into the hill and I hoped it ended inside the cave. Anxiety seeped through my skin and crawled around the pit of my stomach. Was this how it felt to be claustrophobic? A faint light shone ahead and I wheezed out a relieved breath.

I tugged Aydin's tail to get him to stop, then stooped down to crawl between his legs so I could get ahead of him. Even with his wings folded close to his body, he was a very tight fit.

The knapsack strapped to my back was impeding my efforts so I shrugged it off and dragged it along behind me as I crawled over shards of sharp rock and clumps of dirt. It was hell on my knees, which would be bloody by the time I could stand up again.

A flat round stone had been rolled in front of the opening to the cave. I gave it a tug, but it wouldn't budge.

Aydin grabbed hold of one edge and gently, almost soundlessly, rolled the stone aside enough for me to see in.

I handed Aydin my knapsack and mashed my back against the rock wall to make myself as small as possible so I could gaze into the open room. It appeared to be a bedroom occupied by five small beds. The linens were clean and quite pretty for such a dismal place. There were even decorative rugs on the floor and stained glass sconces with low burning flames on the walls. Bouquets of red roses sprouted from ornate vases positioned on dainty whitewashed tables beside each bed.

I saw four women huddled on one bed, arms around each other as if to console one another. The fifth woman lay alone on a different bed, her bare back facing me. Even my ordinary eyesight let me see the bleeding gashes that striped her flesh.

That clinched it.

Without a second thought, I squeezed my way through the slender opening and sprinted for the blood-soaked bed.

As I ran across the stone floor to the bleeding woman, I heard a collective gasp from the others. One even screamed.

When I got to the bed, I held my fingers to the woman's throat. No pulse. And her skin was cool. She was gone.

"Why didn't you help her?" I asked the others, who all sat gawking at me. "She's dead."

"We know she's dead," one of them said. "We *did* try to help, but it was too late. She'd lost too much blood."

I gazed down at the body again and saw that most of the blood soaking the sheets came from below her waist. "Did she miscarry?"

The one who'd spoken up nodded.

"And she was punished for it," another one said before

breaking down into sobs. "Her husband whipped her, over and over, until she passed out."

Oh, my God. This had gone far enough. These women were leaving with me right now. I stood and waved them toward the opening in the wall. "Come with me."

They sat frozen, eyes big as a deer mouse cornered by a cat. Then they all began shaking their heads at once. So I asked, "You want the same thing to happen to you?"

Each of them stared down at their pregnant bellies. Some were further along than others, but all were heavy with child.

"There's not much time. I have a place to take you, somewhere safe." I grabbed one by the arm to pull her to her feet and she yanked away from me. "What the hell is wrong with you people? Can't you see the danger you're in?"

"Not nearly as much danger as you," said a voice from the other side of the room.

Xenia stood staring, her heavily made up eyes trained on me like I was a morsel of food she craved. She moved toward me and I instinctively stepped back.

"What's the matter, Chalice?" Her words sounded deeper than usual. She sounded just like… "Scared of your own sister? You hurt my feelings."

twenty-two

"XENIA?" I STARED HARD AT HER, LOOKING for the lost girl who was too frightened to dedicate her life to the knighthood. What had happened to her?

She shook her head. "I'm afraid you have me mistaken for someone else."

"You can't be her."

"Oh, yes I can." She bent her head and gazed up at me through her lashes, her grin sinister and playful at the same time. "You people are so much fun to play with. I'm amazed how gullible you are."

I was too stunned for words. I blinked, trying to clear my mind of the image I had of sweet, obstinate, troubled little Xenia. But that girl was a lie. Xenia never existed. It had been Maria all along.

"You lived in our house," I stammered, my head pounding with the shock of having believed her lies.

"You laughed with us, cried with us, grieved with us. Yet you were the cause of that grief."

There was a subtle shift in her features, a softening of her stormy eyes. Then she firmed her jaw and her lips stretched into a wicked smile. "Fooled ya."

"How could you?"

She shrugged. "How couldn't I, you mean. After everything I've been through? Come on, get real."

Oh, I'd come on, all right. I moved toward her, my knife heavy in my hand. "You murdering little bitch."

She laughed. "Oh, my. Brave words from someone whose life could be over with one snap of my fingers." The second her fingers snapped, all the air left my lungs.

I grabbed my throat and crumpled to my knees, my knife clattering to the floor. It didn't seem possible. How could her ability function when mine did not?

"Don't forget who and what I am." Her fist opened slightly and a wisp of air cooled my throat. "I'm hardly human anymore. My body has been nourished by the Fallen's blood since I was a baby. I'm more angel than human now, and much stronger than you'll ever be."

"You mean you're more demon," I rasped through my constricted throat.

She squinted at me and nodded. "You could be right about that." When her hand opened all the way, so did my lungs. I swallowed as much air as I could heave in all at once.

I gagged on my dry tongue and lunged for one of the vases to snatch out the flowers it held. I downed the water in greedy gulps.

"So tell me, Chalice." Maria swayed from side to side

like a child listening to a favorite tune, her black cloak billowing at her sides. "Is my mother well?"

I coughed before saying, "Your mother is in pieces."

She offered a comical lift of her eyebrows. "Oh, that's right. She got hacked to bits for heresy."

I had no response to that because it was true.

"She could have lied and lived." Maria stopped her swaying and her voice sounded wistful now. "But instead she martyred herself and threw me away like a piece of garbage."

"Geraldine did *not* throw you away."

"That's not what my father tells me." She stood still now, all playfulness gone from her voice. "He rescued me from the midwife who planned to make her slave."

"He lies as badly as you do. That's *not* what happened."

"You better watch what you say about my father."

I needed to play this right and antagonizing her wasn't the way to do it. A troubled girl lay somewhere underneath Maria's demonic facade. This was Geraldine's daughter, a Hatchet knight, and in spite of what she'd done she was still family.

Brute force wouldn't work against her, seeing as how I had none, so reasoning with her could be my only hope. Speaking of brute force, where was Aydin? I hoped he saw what just happened and went to warn Barachiel.

Maria flashed me a sudden smile. "Where are my manners? Let me show you around."

Spinning on her heel, she headed for a doorway that I assumed led to the rest of the cave.

"Xenia...I mean Maria," I said, saying her name as gently as possible. Her mind was obviously unstable and I needed her to believe I was open to whatever she needed from me. The lies Pharzuph had told her poisoned her against her mother and against all of us. Once she knew the truth, she'd realize that what she had done was wrong. "The woman on the bed is dead."

"Oh?" Maria stepped over to the corpse and the four remaining women cringed at her approach. They were scared to death of her. "So she is. Do you know what she did?"

Unsure how to answer, I just nodded.

"Killing a knight is punishable by death," she said without inflection. "Her unborn child was a priceless life we couldn't afford to lose. Now it's gone."

I wanted to say the child's death was no one's fault, but I doubted Maria would agree. She would only get more angry. "I understand," I said, trying my best to sound agreeable. "Hatchet knights sired by the Arelim are precious and—"

"No!" she shouted. She turned on me, her eyes blazing with fury. "Not a Hatchet. The Hatchets are dead. This child was intended for a new knighthood."

Confused, I frowned and shook my head.

Maria's demeanor flipped back to charming as she calmly said, "*My* knighthood. The Order of the Darkest Knight."

The woman was stark raving mad.

She narrowed her eyes at the frightened little group on the bed and flicked a hand at the body. "Clean up this mess. Your husbands will be here soon and I suspect Ravachiel will be in a foul mood. Poor angel is mourning the death of his child. Let this be a lesson to all of you!"

She stomped off toward the exit. "Chalice, I have something to show you."

I gritted my teeth and offered the women a sympathetic glance, then mouthed the words, *I'm getting you out of here*. None of them looked convinced.

I followed Maria out into the cave. It was huge and dark and magnificent. The walls glittered as if made of stars and the floors were carpeted in enormous animal hides larger than any beast I'd ever seen. Tables made of ceramic tiles held works of art from cultures I never knew existed. I would have studied them more closely if my eyes worked like they were supposed to. Even if they did, I was too distracted by what Maria had to show me. It was enough to make me wish, if only for a moment, that I'd gone completely blind.

"I'd like you to meet my pet, Shameena," she said, grinning at the female gargoyle chained to the wall beside a red velvet throne trimmed with gold and onyx. The creature snarled at me, its large hairy breasts making its broad chest appear even broader. It had a distinctive baboon face and I could have sworn it was related to my deceased gargoyle, Shui.

"Poor Shameena has been lonely without a companion, so thank you, Chalice, for bringing one for her."

Ice flowed through my veins right then, but when I saw Aydin chained to the opposite wall, my heart almost stopped. I ran toward him, but a black winged angel lunged out of the shadows to stop me.

"Are you mad? They can't be in the same room together!" I yelled at her.

"Are you jealous?" Maria asked, a grin splitting her

deathly pale face. "You can have him back, you know. On one condition."

My heart raced and my mind was speeding to catch up. Where was my father? "I won't bargain with you," I told her. "Where's Barachiel?"

She shrugged. "He's here with his brothers. They have a lot of catching up to do."

I felt sick. I held on to my stomach and it was all I could do to keep from retching. I stared hard at the squire who had made a vow to her sisters only to betray them. I wasn't as angry as I was disgusted and disheartened. And very much alone.

"Now," Maria said, brushing her hands together as if to rid them of dirt. "Let's get down to business."

My hopes had been dashed and from what I could tell since arriving here, my life was as good as forfeit. Things couldn't possibly get any worse.

"I would very much like you to join my order, to become a Darkest knight," Maria said.

My answer was a no-brainer. "No."

She tilted her head to one side. "And I want you to wed your guardian angel and conceive his child."

I barked a laugh. "Not only no, but *hell* no."

Maria nodded and paced in front of me. "Then you leave me no other choice but to bond you to your gargoyle, Aydin."

"What?" She couldn't be serious. I'd been there, done that, and was determined not to let it happen again, ever. Aydin's curse would lift as soon as he ate Shojin's heart. "You can't do this."

"I sure can," she said. "And I will. I have a shaman

standing by to tattoo your neck and commence with the ritual. You do remember how that works, don't you?"

I swallowed. I remembered only too well.

There came a loud clanging of chains as Aydin thrashed against his constraints. He'd heard Maria's bargain.

"If I take Rafael as my mate, you'll let Aydin go free?" My heart sank even further. What would I do without him? I wasn't sure I'd have the will to go on. However, if I made this promise to Maria, it would buy me time to figure a way out. The tiniest flicker of hope warmed my heart.

She nodded. "I'm giving you a choice and it's a win-win for you either way. Use your angel-mate to conceive and bear a child for my order, or live out the rest of your life *with* a gargoyle or *as* one. Winged or not, it makes no difference because your love will keep you together." She laughed and sang the last bit like it was a nursery rhyme.

My eyes burned and the answer I was about to give scorched my tongue. "Okay, I'll do it. I'll take Rafael as my mate."

"Excellent!" Maria clapped her hands like an excited child.

I glanced over at Aydin, who stared at me silently for a few seconds before his head drooped to his chest. I prayed he realized I was working on a plan to fix this. He knew me well enough to know I'd not give in without a fight.

"Why now?" I asked Maria.

Maria leaned forward as if hard of hearing. "Excuse me?"

"The Hatchet knights have existed for centuries. Why did you wait until now to kill us all?"

She nodded slowly. "Well, you see, it all has to do with my mother. Everything starts with her. Everything."

It was true that Geraldine started our order, was the first to mate with her guardian and bear a child, and the first to be condemned for her actions. I didn't know what that had to do with Maria's murder spree. "So?"

"As long as her remains were in the mortal realm, I was stuck on this side of the veil, inside this beautiful cave my father made for me." She waited for me to say something, but I only listened. "I tried to leave, to go to her and learn the whereabouts of my sisters, but a barrier lay between me and the outside world."

"Why?"

Her laugh was bitter. "Isn't it obvious? My mother didn't want me. She hates me because my father loves me and she made sure I could never leave this place."

That made entirely no sense. Geraldine wasn't a sorceress and didn't have that kind of power. Her only power was, and is, her psychic link with the Arelim. She was the most humble, gracious and loving person I'd ever known. "Maria, your mother thought you were dead."

Maria stiffened and her stormy eyes widened with rage. "Liar!" She pointed at me and marched up to stand before me, her face barely an inch from mine. Her finger jabbed me in the chest as she said, "She deceives you. She deceives everyone. My mother is a vicious, hateful woman who thinks of no one but herself. I wish she was dead."

Wow. Pharzuph was the deceiver and probably the one who had kept Maria imprisoned here from the start. He wielded that kind of power, not Geraldine. He'd only let Maria loose now so that she could kill the competition before Geraldine had a chance to become whole and live again. Pharzuph was afraid of her. I wish I knew why.

Maria shook her head and sighed. "Let's not quarrel, Chalice. We're sisters. We have a new knighthood to prepare and we must do it together. Wouldn't you agree?"

A smile twitched falsely at the corner of my mouth. "Of course."

Her answering smile was sweeter than I expected. "I'm so happy to have you here with me. I really enjoyed getting to know you at Halo Home. You and I are so much alike and I've been so lonely…." Her eyes filled and she blinked quickly while turning her head to look away. "It's getting late and I'm famished. You look a bit peckish yourself. Can I offer you some refreshments?"

I shook my head. "No, thank you."

She shrugged. "I hate to eat alone, but I never actually do." She clapped her hands. "Let me introduce you to my companion for the evening."

Following the direction of her gaze, I zeroed in on a curtained doorway. The drape opened and a black-winged angel stepped through leading another dark angel on a chain attached to his bound wrists. My breath caught and I gasped. It was Barachiel.

I lunged forward, but the angel leading Barachiel caught me before I could touch him. He wrapped an arm around my waist and lifted me up, my legs kicking out at whatever I could reach. He held me like I weighed no more than a loaf of bread. Barachiel didn't meet my eyes when I called to him. He stared stoically down at his feet.

"You keep doing that," Maria said to me. She waved

her hands in a rush of motion. "Do you always swoop in like that?"

"Only when the people I care about need help," I said through gritted teeth. "You're hurting my family!"

She scowled and folded her arms. "Well, I was hurt first."

She stomped over to her velvet throne and threw herself onto it, then leaned back against the cushions. Waving her hand at the angel holding me like a sack of potatoes, she said, "Bring them to me."

He obeyed, setting me down at her feet and jerking Barachiel over to an iron ring mounted on the cave wall. There was too much space between my father and me to reach each other. I knew Barachiel had strong magic he could use to free himself, but something or someone prevented him from doing it. I bet Maria had threatened to hurt me if he didn't comply. I would never forgive her for that.

She held her hand open and the dark angel who did her bidding placed a slender, curved knife onto her palm. "Thank you, Soriel."

Leaning over the armrest of her throne, she reached out to grab hold of Barachiel's bound hands. "You won't feel a thing," she told him before slicing the blade across his wrist.

She yanked his hand up to her mouth and greedily clamped her lips over the wound. The sucking sounds she made while feeding echoed against the cave walls and sent a shudder of revulsion through me. I again looked at my father's face. He was resigned to fulfill whatever bargain he had made, but I saw deeper thoughts in his eyes. He wasn't about to let this go. His set jaw and the sneer on his lips told me someone would pay for his humiliation.

Maria finally released him and sat back, her lips red with blood. A drop of it dribbled from the corner of her mouth and she swiped the back of her hand across her chin. She smiled with teeth stained from her meal. "Take him away."

Soriel unchained Barachiel from the wall and led him back the way they'd come. My father didn't stumble, didn't look up, just dutifully trudged beside his fallen brother. But I could tell by the stiff way he moved that he was furious.

Nausea burbled in my stomach and I couldn't hold it back a second longer. I leaned sideways and threw up what little was left of the breakfast I'd had at Elmo's that day.

Maria cringed at the sight of it. "That's disgusting, Chalice." She stood and yelled, "Soriel, get one of the squires to clean up this mess."

"I'll do it," I said, searching for something I could use to mop it up.

"No, you won't. It's unbecoming for a knight to belittle herself with drudgery. You're royalty now."

I didn't feel very royal, and I felt even less so when one of the pregnant women arrived with a bucket and mop. I'd never felt so ashamed.

Maria sighed loudly, making sure everyone could hear. "I'm bored."

My gaze flitted around the room as my mind started working on a plan of escape. Aydin still slumped against the wall and made no eye contact with anyone. Soriel was the only fallen angel in sight, and as soon as the squire finished her chore she was taken away.

I heard a shuffling behind Maria's throne and turned my head to see her gargoyle skulking toward Aydin.

"Stop!" I shouted at the creature, but it ignored me.

"Oh, dear," Maria said, not moving a muscle. Her gaze followed the gargoyle as it slithered purposefully toward Aydin. "How did Shameena get loose? Soriel?"

Her angel slave stepped out of the shadows to show himself.

"Never mind." She waved him away.

"Aren't you going to do something?" I yelled at Maria, whose rapt attention had been caught by her ugly pet.

"Hmm?" She tried to ignore me.

"If you don't stop her, one of them is going to get killed."

"You think so?" Maria scooted to the edge of her throne and clasped her hands together, her eyes bright with excitement. She didn't care. She *wanted* them to fight.

Aydin heard the other gargoyle approach and his body visibly tightened. A warning growl rumbled in his chest. His legs were chained together at the ankles and he was barely mobile. He stretched the length of chain binding him to the wall, but it didn't reach very far. Shameena drooled as she got closer to him, her eyes gleaming with malice.

Aydin crouched low and stayed so still I thought he might have put himself into a meditative trance. Shameena slowed, cocking her head to the side and appearing confused. She was obviously unused to a docile opponent.

The female gargoyle's nose twitched and she snarled, taking another cautious step forward, then another. Her muscles bunched and I saw the tendons in her scaly legs tighten as she prepared to spring.

If she got hold of him, he'd have a really hard time fighting back. Both gargoyles had wings and she could easily evade him, whereas he was like a sitting duck with wings that wouldn't take him anywhere since his legs were shackled. My heart ricocheted inside my chest and I could hardly breathe. I knew there wasn't a thing I could do, but I had to try. I leaped to my feet, but Soriel swiftly grabbed me to hold me back.

My sudden movement distracted Shameena and her eyes jerked away from Aydin for a fraction of a second. It was enough. He was on her in an instant, his arms wrapped around her neck and his legs squeezing her middle like pincers. She screeched and tried to tear herself away, but Aydin was motivated to put an end to this game. I sensed he'd had enough of Maria's shit and his mood was darker than ever. I'd never seen him behave with such ferocity, not even in his bloody battle with Shui.

His jaws unhinged and his roar split through the air, making my ears ring. The rows of razor-sharp teeth glinted in the faint light offered by the sconces. He arched his neck back, then thrust his head forward with so much force it knocked Shameena off her feet. They both rolled in a tangle of wings, arms and legs, and I struggled to see past the giant angel who held me back.

Blood flew around the fighting pair like crimson rain. I couldn't see who was injured and my breath caught as I waited agonizing seconds for what was surely the end of one of them. Both gargoyles became still. I couldn't tell them apart now. There was as much blood as fur and both had their heads down. Then I heard that familiar sound, the same one I'd heard in the cathedral after I killed Shui. I'd heard it again soon after Shojin ripped out his own beating heart. It was the resonance of death that only a gargoyle can make. The sound of stone being made.

I watched, breathless, to see which one would come out the victor. Such a senseless battle. Maria could have stopped it, but she wanted even more blood than what she'd already swallowed. When Aydin reared up and kicked the dead chunk of rock that had been Shameena, I cried out in relief. Maria screamed in rage.

twenty-three

I FELT OVERWHELMED WITH RELIEF AND terror, and my defiance was starting to wear thin. I needed rest. I needed time to think. I had to get away from Maria or I'd rip out her throat and that would get us all killed.

I slumped against Soriel and he had to hold me up by the shoulders to keep me from falling. I felt weak from lack of food and sleep and my legs would no longer support me. The dark angel lifted me up to carry me like a baby, then trudged toward the curtained doorway.

My eyes struggled to stay open, and they worked hard to focus on what little I could see. The black walls glittered and colorful rugs like runners led down a long hallway that got darker the deeper we went. Soriel strode forward with confidence, though I had heard no command from Maria as to where to take me. It must have been prearranged. The angel still hadn't said a word and I wondered where he stood in all this. Sycophant or slave? Food or fun? Probably all of the above.

My heart hurt like someone had squeezed the life out of it. I missed my grandparents, especially my grand-mother, whose tough love and compassion I sorely needed now. I missed Natalie and even Rusty. My life with the Hatchets had barely started and I'd already been forced to defect to the hellish Order of the Darkest Knight. My head was so full of rebellion that it ached. My soul knew this wasn't right, that I didn't belong here, and neither did Aydin or Barachiel. The deceived pregnant squires shouldn't be here, either. Not even Maria belonged on this side of the veil. Insane as she was, her heart bruised with darkness, she was still Geraldine's daughter. I would never forgive her for what she'd done, but I'd help her leave it behind if she let me.

We stopped suddenly in front of a door that Soriel kicked to open. The wooden plank swung in and banged against the wall. I peered inside, blinking at the darkness, my nose twitching at a faint scent of incense and candle wax. He stepped closer to the center of the room and dropped me.

I stiffened, expecting to land on the hard rock floor and have my breath knocked out of me, but I connected with something much softer. A fluffy pillow or cushion broke my fall. I stared up at Soriel, and I suddenly wor-ried that he had more lascivious plans for this bed.

When Soriel moved to one of the wall sconces to light it with a flame from his finger, it brightened the room enough for me to make out a few pieces of furniture.

Sparse, but elegant, and that surprised me. Why had Maria put me in such nice quarters? From the way she had treated me I expected to be tossed in a dungeon, not a palatial boudoir.

"Thanks," I told Soriel because I didn't know what else to say. I *wanted* to say get lost, but wasn't sure how he'd react to that.

The dark angel twitched his wings and stepped toward me. I shrank back against the pillows. He shook his head and his eyebrows tilted up in an expression of worry.

"Why won't you talk to me?" I asked him.

He was a handsome angel, darker-skinned than my pale father and much darker than the Arelim angels I'd seen. His black hair was tied back in a ponytail and he had thick scars all over his chest, back and arms. His eyes were mesmerizing, very large and greenish-blue like the ocean. He pointed to his lips and shook his head.

I frowned. "I don't understand."

He opened his mouth and showed me where his tongue used to be. I closed my eyes and heaved in a breath to calm myself. Was there no end to the cruelty in this place?

Soriel turned his back on me and walked from the room, closing the door softly behind him.

The spicy incense that lingered here had a tranquilizing effect. I yawned in spite of the flutter of nerves dancing in my stomach.

I grabbed a pillow and hugged it close, wishing it were Aydin. Could he come to me in my dreams here? Probably not, as he'd have to be physically close for that to happen and I didn't know where he was. I only hoped he was safe and healing.

I heard a click and focused on the doorknob as it twisted in slow motion. I instinctively reached for my knife, but I'd been relieved of that weapon right after Maria snatched my breath. So I crouched on the bed and prepared to spring at whoever, or whatever, entered my room.

The door creaked open and Soriel stood staring at me. He brought a finger to his lips and pushed the door closed. From behind his back he brought out my knapsack, the one I'd left with Aydin inside the tunnel.

Knowing he was one of Maria's pawns, I narrowed my eyes and whispered, "I don't trust you."

He stared without expression as he handed the bag to me and I wondered if Maria was setting me up again. So I asked, "Did you look inside?"

Soriel nodded.

I checked the knapsack to make sure everything was there. It was. My shoulders slumped in relief. "Does Maria know you brought this to me?"

Again the stare, but he followed it with a quick shake of his head. Silent though he was, he had learned how to express himself with body language and facial tweaks. It was as if he spoke without saying a word, but I knew what he *wanted* to say. He was asking for help, and not for himself. He wanted me to help Maria.

I peered in the knapsack at the ornate iron key and an idea sparked in my mind. I suddenly knew how to defeat Maria.

I slept surprisingly well after spending the night in the

home of my nemesis, where both my father and my boy-friend were chained up like animals. The cave appeared brighter today, possibly because my brain had lit up with an idea that could save us all.

There was no daylight on this side of the veil because the sun didn't shine here. Neither did the moon at night. The only source of *natural* light was an odd greenish glow on the horizon. I had no idea what caused it or why it was there, but its cyclic appearance indicated a passage of time. How that time related to the human realm remained a mystery, but solving it wasn't high on my list of priorities.

I tried to leave my room, but the door was locked. I should have known. The room might look pretty, but it was still a prison cell. I hid my knapsack between the bed's box spring and mattress. Just knowing it was there gave me comfort. Feathers to take us home, the horn of breath to give us life—should we need it—the changing charm and the scrying mirror. Life was good, or at least it would be good again.

Footsteps outside the door alerted me to company. I checked to make sure the knapsack was well hidden, then climbed up on the bed and waited.

The door opened and Maria stepped inside with a tray. There were a couple of steaming dishes on it and they actually smelled pretty good. She set it on the nightstand. "I brought you breakfast," she said brightly.

I gave the plates a sideways glance. It looked like scrambled eggs and fried meat of some kind, plus a buttered roll sprinkled with nuts. My stomach growled, but I was too suspicious to eat any of it. I wasn't a stranger to hunger so I had no problem ignoring the food, however I didn't want to appear rude. I wasn't sure how she'd react to being offended. For all I knew, she blamed me for the death of her precious Shameena and wanted to poison me as payback.

"Thank you." I dipped the fork into the eggs and pushed them around. "Will you join me?"

She shook her head. "I don't need to eat solid food."

I frowned. "But you're still human. Or at least part of you is." Though from the looks of her, that was debatable. Her skinny physique made her appear undernourished and life-deficient.

She shrugged. "I'm fine without food. As long as I always return to this side of the veil."

Now that was interesting. Because she was no longer completely human, she needed whatever this side of the veil would give her to survive. Fallen angel blood had nourished her, but I imagined she took in other sustenance as well.

I brought a forkful of eggs up to my mouth and sniffed, but didn't take a bite. I wasn't that brave. "These look like eggs. Smell like them, too," I said.

She nodded. "They *are* eggs, but not from a chicken."

I scrutinized the food. "Oh?"

"It's a bird we call a craven. It's a lot like a raven."

"What's the difference?" I asked.

"Instead of beaks they have noses. They have human faces."

I dropped the fork and gently replaced the plate to the tray. I'd seen one of those birds yesterday. A tree had eaten it. I blotted my lips with a linen napkin and said, "I'm sure it's delicious, but I'm not that hungry."

"It's okay," Maria said. "You need to get used to your new home. There are quite a number of new experiences for you to try."

Instead of rolling my eyes like I wanted to, I tried to look interested. "You said before that you were fine as long as you stayed on this side of the veil."

"That's right."

"Well," I said, leaving a meaningful pause before going on. "Your body has changed, grown accustomed to this side. But my body isn't used to being here. I may not survive."

She smiled. "Don't worry about that, Chalice." She sat on the bed and turned to face me. "We'll do like I did while pretending to be Xenia and go back and forth through the veil. You won't have to stay here all the time."

That was a relief, though I didn't intend to stay here at all. "Good to know."

"We'll have a cave in the human realm that's just like this one and my Fallen will fix it so that it's easy for us to cross back and forth." Her cold fingers closed around mine as she peered into my eyes. "We're sisters, Chalice. We'll share everything."

I didn't like the sound of that. "Like what?"

"Like eternal life." She hesitated before adding, "You can live forever. All you have to do is feed off the Fallen."

I yanked my hand away from her and stood from the bed. I hugged myself as I paced in front of her. "No."

"It's really quite nice and very natural," she said. "The Fallen are our family. They're our fathers."

I shuddered and hoped she hadn't noticed. The last thing I wanted was to upset her. She appeared rational when calm, but out of her mind the rest of the time.

"Think it over," she told me as she slid off the bed. "It will make life so much easier."

Of course it would. Having my mind and body twisted like Maria's would surely make *her* life easier. She'd finally have a like-minded companion, a replacement for her pet Shameena. It was a good thing I hadn't eaten those eggs, because they'd be coming up right now.

"Oh, before I forget." She stepped over to the dresser and slid out one of the heavy wooden drawers. "I have a gift for you."

Maria was full of surprises. I watched her lift out a folded bundle tied with a shiny silk ribbon. "Your wedding dress," she said as she handed it to me.

I backed up a step. "My what?"

"Surprise!" She giggled. "You're getting married to your guardian angel today."

To say my blood turned to ice would be an understatement. My entire body went numb, but only for a second. She surprised me, yes, but that's because I thought I would have more time to prepare. Rafe coming here was a good thing. He was the main ingredient for making my plan work.

I smiled and pretended to be eager as I accepted her gift.

"Put it on," she said.

"Isn't that bad luck?"

"Nah, your guardian won't see you until it's time."

I studied Maria's face and saw the sadness in her eyes. I wondered if she'd ever had a mate among her Fallen entourage. She'd certainly had plenty of time to go through more than a few of them. I shifted my gaze back to the folded garment in my hands and plucked at the ribbon. It loosened and then fluttered to the floor. "This gown used to be yours, didn't it?"

She blinked and looked away. "That was a long time ago."

"Want to talk about it?"

"Not much to say," she said. "My father found me an Arelim angel to mate with me, but it didn't work."

"The relationship didn't work?"

She laughed. "What relationship?" Her eyes had that crazy gleam in them again and I was afraid I'd gone to far. "His seed didn't work. I never got pregnant."

I had a feeling it didn't work out so well for the angel, either. "What happened to him?"

"He fell, as was expected. After all, he had committed the sin of sex and had to face the consequences. My father threatened to kill him if he chose to become human, so his feathers turned black instead." She smiled sadly. "He was such a beautiful angel."

"I don't understand. The Hatchet knights…" I stopped when I saw her narrow her eyes at me. "Women like us *will* conceive her guardian's child. That's how it's always been."

"True," she said, picking up the silk ribbon from the floor and twirling it around her finger. "But it turns out it wasn't his seed that was the problem. It was me. I'm not human enough to conceive. I'm barren."

"You know that for sure?"

"Oh, yes." She fidgeted with the ribbon and retied it in a knot. "I tried again with the other Arelim angels my father brought for me, but it always ended the same. They fell, and I added them to all the others who feed me with their blood."

What a waste. "Are they still with you?"

"Where else would they go?"

I pondered her point, which was a good one.

"In fact, you've met one of them. He was my first, the one for whom I wore that wedding dress." She waved a hand at the flowing gown of black and red silk in my hands. "It was Soriel."

My breathing hitched. Soriel's scars. His missing tongue. Pharzuph must have punished him for not fulfilling his breeding duties.

Maria unknotted the ribbon and waved it in the air. "That's all in the past now. I've accepted who and what I am, and my father and I figured out a way to create a new order of knights who will be as dark as we are."

She was going about it the same way the Hatchets were: recruiting angel whisperers as squires to partner with their guardians and procreate. There would be two supernatural orders of knights at odds with each other. Maria and Pharzuph were planning a war.

Though I assumed deception was involved in their recruitment effort, I wanted to know how they did it. "What do you say to convince the angel whisperers to join your side?"

She shrugged. "They don't know any other side exists."

Of course they didn't. The Hatchet knights were a secret order. The Arelim wouldn't share that knowledge with just anyone, not even a whisperer unless she was destined for knighthood.

"We have friends among the Arelim who sympathize with our cause. They're the ones we have contact the whisperers," she said.

I thought of Harachel and remembered what Quin had told me. I bet Harachel was one of Pharzuph's sympathizers. "The Arelim have a hive-mind. They would know who among their ranks would betray them."

She grinned and tilted her head to the side. "Angels are individuals with free will. Their hive-mind communication is for the sake of convenience and not a requirement." She started playing with the ribbon again. "The Fallen are only a notch below the Arelim and have amazing power they won't hesitate to use for personal gain. Never underestimate an angel."

I thought about my father and what he'd told me. He had said falling from grace didn't automatically make an angel a demon. It was the angel's choice which way to go and Barachiel had kept his wings so he could continue honing his magic, not to pursue evil interests. Both sides were magicians in their own right, and I supposed one or the other could wield a dark power for good, or a good power for bad. Pharzuph was a bad egg who knew how to manipulate good people.

"The whisperer is told about magic and how she'll be a mother to an exquisite child with powers beyond imagination. Not all of them are won over, of course," she said with a sniff. "But some are. We have five here now, all pregnant with our first generation of Darkest knights."

"Four," I corrected.

Her eyebrows furled in thought. "That's right. We lost one, didn't we? Pity." She clapped her hands, startling me, and said, "Let's see that lovely wedding gown on you now."

I stared at the dress draped over my arm.

"Don't be so modest, Chalice. We're all girls here." Her gaze roamed the room and I sucked in a breath when she stared down at the bed. But her focus switched back to me. "The dress is very sexy," she said with a sly grin. "I'd wanted to be alluring for Soriel's first time."

I just bet she did. I laid the dress on the bed and kicked off my boots before shrugging out of my T-shirt and jeans. I peeled off my socks and wiggled my bare toes against the icy floor.

Maria stared at me as I lifted the dress to shake out the creases. I imagined my naked breasts were somewhat of an enigma for her as she was too skinny to have more than mosquito bumps on her chest. I didn't mind her staring and hoped it reminded her of the humanity she had lost and might find again someday.

The only times I'd ever worn a dress were as a disguise. In my thieving days, I'd often wear whatever was needed to fit the part I was playing. A princess from a remote village in Northumberland, an aspiring model, an heiress, and even a pixie queen to show off to prospective clients the Vyantara's connections with the fae. So it's not like I'd never worn a dress, I just didn't feel comfortable in them.

I slid the silky mass of fabric over my head and adjusted the bodice—what little there was of it. The shiny black-and-red fabric was loose as liquid and I wondered how it was made, but didn't ask. I was afraid of the answer. The skirt's hem puddled at my ankles and flowed around my feet like a lapping stream.

"Are you cold?" Maria asked, still staring at my chest.

"As a matter of fact, I am."

She went to the door and opened it slightly to stick her head out. I heard her speak to someone before pulling herself back in with something black and furry in her hands. It was moving.

"Wrap this around your shoulders. It may smell bad, but it will keep you warm." She handed over the writhing strip of fur, but I pushed it away.

"No thanks," I said, peering at the creature to search for its face. It didn't appear to have one.

"Suit yourself." Maria slung it over the back of her neck and it coiled around her like a snake. She took a step back to study me. "That looks truly lovely on you, Chalice. You're going to make Rafael a very happy angel."

"How will he get here?" I asked, knowing the tainted veil wouldn't allow a celestial being to cross.

She plucked a long black feather out from beneath her cloak. "With this."

I had figured the Fallen's feathers were a method of travel through the veil, but I thought it only applied to crossing from here, not the other way around. "When?"

Maria swiped the feather down one side of her face. "When? Now. He's already here."

"I need to speak to him," I said. I had to tell him what I planned. He needed to know or it wouldn't work.

Maria tsked and shook her finger at me. "No, no, no, my dear. Now *that* would be bad luck. You're not allowed to see each other until the ceremony."

twenty-four

UNLIKE MOST GIRLS, I'D NEVER IMAGINED what my wedding day would be like. However, if I were ever to have one I'd assumed it would involve a lacy white gown with a frothy veil and pretty flowers gathered in a handheld bouquet. This wedding was nothing like that. There was no church, no flower arrangements, no white gown and no congregation of tearful wedding guests to wish the bride and groom a happy future together. The groom in his white-winged splendor and pristine white tunic looked very much out of place. And very unhappy.

Rafe and I stood side by side in front of Maria's throne. He stared down at his feet, his face full of despair. He never looked at me. Not once.

I tried to call him with my mind, but like my abilities, it didn't work on this side of the veil. I was one hundred percent human here. He must know me well enough to believe I'd never willingly go along with Maria's scheme. But he must also think his life as an Arelim angel would soon be ruined forever. And it was all my fault.

The throne sat at the center of a pentagram surrounded by an enormous circle. This must be where Pharzuph held his rituals and wielded his magic. The circle protected those within its boundaries and prevented anyone outside from interfering.

I was pleased to see Aydin inside the circle, but not so pleased to see the stranger standing beside him. I knew what he was and why he was here, and the hair at the back of my neck bristled around the scar of my old tattoo. This man was a shaman, and not the peaceful healing kind from American Indian lore. The markings on his arms and face identified him as a shaman of darkness, a doctor of curses. His black gaze burned into me, letting me know he would bond me to Aydin if I didn't make good on my deal.

Bondage to a gargoyle was bad enough, but to be bonded to one who used to be the man I loved would be torture. The longing for a physical union would haunt us both. We'd be close in proximity, but miles apart in every way that defined us as human. Loving each other would never go beyond the memory of what that love could have been. Aydin might end up resenting me for failing my promise to bring him back. And I would resent him for my enslavement.

I tried to catch Aydin's attention, but he was back in that trance again. Had he totally shut down? I wanted so much to run to him, hold him close to me, let him know that no matter what happened, I'd always love him. I hadn't given up on us being together and never would. He just needed to keep the faith.

I saw Pharzuph, his hair whiter than snow and his skin a deep ebony that shimmered in the glittering light of the cave. He practically blended in with the rock walls like camouflage. But his eyes shone phosphorescent-green. I remembered Aydin telling me Pharzuph's skin had been white when he met him, so I wondered if it had darkened with the passing of centuries or with the accumulation of his evil deeds. Possibly both.

My father was here as well. I wondered if Maria would let him give me away to my betrothed. If only I could talk to him. It felt strange being so near the people I cared about without getting to touch them. Barachiel was shackled, but I was not. I could use that to my advantage.

Outside the circle were Soriel, the four pregnant squires, and a few nameless fallen angels I hadn't met and didn't want to know. Maria hadn't arrived yet. Was she primping for her debut as the knighthood's grande dame? My gaze darted to Pharzuph, who hadn't even breathed, not that he needed to. He looked chiseled out of the very rock he'd used to create this cave.

I took a risk and lunged toward Barachiel, literally falling on top of him. He jerked as he startled, but took barely a second to recover and grabbed on to me, holding me close. His mind delved quickly inside my head as he searched my thoughts. It didn't take him long. He responded: *Excellent, Chalice. Very clever. She will believe it and it will be her undoing. I will create a distraction to give you time to—*

A rough hand, cold as frozen granite, grabbed me by the neck and yanked me away from Barachiel. Pharzuph held me aloft with one hand while using the other to pummel my father until he lost consciousness.

I kicked at him and struggled to break his hold, but he only tightened his grip. I saw Rafe from the corner of my eye and he strained against the iron ring attached to his ankle that chained him to the floor. There was confusion mixed with anger on his face. Instinct had him wanting to protect me, but logic made him analyze the situation and weigh his options. Smart angel. However, he didn't yet know the motive behind my decision to marry him.

Someone was shouting now and from the screeching falsetto I guessed it was Maria.

"Stop it! Father, put her down right now. You'll ruin the gown!"

He dropped me and I sprawled at his feet, the dress hitched above my hips. It didn't appear to be ripped, but it was badly rumpled.

Maria reached down to help me up.

"Honestly, Father, what were you thinking?" She smacked his bare chest and he didn't flinch. "Ugh! You'll spoil everything!"

She stared up at her father, who was at least a foot taller, and seemed to listen to whatever he was saying. I hadn't heard him utter a sound. Stomping her foot, she said, "I don't care! So what if he hugged her? He's her father, damn it. You know how special the relationship is between father and daughter." She pushed out her lower lip in a pout.

So Pharzuph no longer spoke verbally to his daughter.

Telepathy had become his chosen form of communication and I wondered if Maria was okay with that. I knew I wouldn't be.

Maria fussed over my spiky black hair and smoothed the wrinkles from the dress. "There. Much better."

"Barachiel was only wishing me happiness," I told her.

"Of course he was," she said in a soothing voice that I only half believed. It was hard to tell with her. "I considered letting him stand at your side during the ceremony, but I'm having second thoughts now."

"I understand." I had achieved my goal and felt satisfied now that Barachiel knew what I was going to do. "It won't happen again."

I glanced over at Aydin, who was fully alert now. From the intent look in his eyes I could tell he had watched what just happened and picked up on my ruse. He was the one who taught me how to lie, so he knew better than anyone when I wasn't telling the truth.

Maria hopped up to sit on her throne and heaved in a long breath. "Shall we get started?"

I went to stand beside Rafe again. He still refused to look at me, staring solemnly down at his bare feet instead. Maria hadn't provided him with ceremonial garb for this auspicious occasion. I supposed his angelic wings were enough.

This wasn't a real wedding so I didn't take it to heart. It was a charade, a parody, and the childish whim of an immortal who had chosen to never grow up. We were her entertainment for the day. I'd go along with all of it as long as I didn't have to eat or drink anything because that could tie me to this side of the veil. I was still human, or mostly human, and I had every intention of staying that way.

"Rafael and Chalice, will you face each other?" Maria asked, her tone imperious.

We did as we were told, and Rafe finally looked at my face, his gray eyes filled with sorrow. He was my friend, my mentor, my guardian, and I hated that this was happening to him. But I swore on my life that it wouldn't last for long.

"Hold out your hands with your palms up."

We did. The blister that had once been my sigil for accessing the silver veil had healed to a white scar the size of a quarter. I gazed down at Rafe's palm and saw that he had a similar wound, the rim around the puffy blister still an angry red. They had stolen his only way back home.

I swallowed the growing lump in my throat. There was no joy in this forced union, only pain.

Footsteps approached and I stiffened when a shadow fell over our extended hands. It was the shaman. He held a steaming rod with a circular iron at the end of it, which he tilted down in our direction.

Maria's somber words echoed against the cave walls as she said, "The brand of our knighthood shall seal your union, and the blood you share will strengthen the bond between angel and child. Thus marks your loyalty to the Darkest knights until the end of days. Let it be so."

Seal. Union. Loyalty. All sentiments I associated with Aydin and not this twisted farce Maria called a knighthood. Rafe continued gazing into my eyes, his own filling with tears. A single drop poised at the corner of his eye and slid slowly down his cheek.

The iron dropped onto my hand, the sound and smell of sizzling flesh making my stomach lurch. Then it burned into Rafe's. The shaman grabbed both our hands and pressed our palms together.

Though our branding shed barely a drop of blood between us, it was enough. Rafe's angel blood burst through me like an explosion and I struggled to stay on my feet. From the expression on his face I could tell something similar was happening to him. It was neither sexual nor intimate, but incredibly powerful. Our family bond intensified, but our relationship didn't change.

The minutes of silence that followed were deafening, compounded by the throbbing pain in my hand. I glanced down at my bleeding palm to see the new symbol that branded me. It looked like a knife pierced through a winged heart. The crest for the Darkest knight.

"And now you may consummate the union," Maria said.

Rafe scowled, then blinked. He finally spoke his first words since arriving here. "I beg your pardon?"

Maria sighed and folded her arms across her chest. "The mating. It must be done in front of witnesses."

"I think not," Rafe said.

The Darkest knight's grande dame stiffened her spine and leaned so far forward I thought she'd tip right out of her throne. "What did you say to me?"

He cleared his throat. "My dear woman, you are mistaken if you believe I can perform in front of an audience."

"You will perform and you will do it now!" Maria's

voice had reached an alarming pitch and I had a feeling she was seconds away from losing it.

Rafe gave me a hard look and I caught something in his eyes. He sensed I was up to something. He knew I had a plan for escape and he was doing his best to stall an act we'd both regret for eternity.

I was too shocked by Maria's expectations to think beyond the words *consummate* and *witnesses*. A public coupling? Stunned didn't begin to describe how I felt.

"I require privacy," Rafe said. "Without it, I cannot possibly do what you ask."

Maria's eyes bulged in their sockets and she looked ready to explode. Rafe didn't react to her rage. He stood calmly waiting for her judgment or her orders. If she wanted what she asked of him, she had no choice but to comply with his demands. As for me, I was merely the vessel. My job was to lie there and accommodate my mate, but that wasn't going to happen. Maria would get her fallen angel, but not the way she thought.

Like a switch had been flipped inside her ancient brain, Maria relaxed. She leaned back and crossed her legs. "Very well. Have your privacy, and sire a knight before you fall." She snapped her fingers and Soriel stepped to the edge of the circle. "Escort them to Chalice's room and wait outside until they finish."

Soriel nodded.

"You have ten minutes."

Rafe squinted at her. "Fifteen."

Maria closed her eyes as if praying for patience. "Fine. Fifteen. But you better be worth it. I'm famished."

Yet another humiliation Rafe must endure. A newly fallen angel was bound to be on today's menu.

Once in my room with the door closed, Rafe grabbed my shoulders to pull me toward him. He glanced back at the door and whispered harshly, "What are you doing?"

"Saving our lives," I said, and grabbed the bodice of my gown. I yanked at the fabric, trying to rip it, but I barely left a crease. "We have to make it look good."

Rafe scowled so hard his forehead bunched down over his eyes. "Explain."

I gave up on the gown and lunged at the bed, where I crouched to bury my hand under the top mattress. Yanking out the knapsack, my hand shook as I reached inside. My fingers touched the cold iron of the changing charm. I stood and held it out to Rafe. "Take it."

He did. "What is it?"

"A very powerful charm that will change you into whatever you want." I knew what he really wanted to change into, and maybe he still could after this was over. Right now I needed him as one of the Fallen.

Understanding sparked in his eyes and a dozen different thoughts reflected there all at once. So many emotions, two of which were shame and regret. What was he ashamed of? And what did he have to regret?

"You planned to give this charm to Aydin so he could become human, didn't you?" he asked.

Avoiding his question, I said, "You have to trust me, Rafe." I closed his fingers around the iron key and held his fist between my hands. "And I trust you to change into the black-winged angel we need to fool Maria."

"And then what?" he asked.

"Barachiel creates a distraction so we can get away."

"To where?" He looked genuinely confused.

I held up the three black feathers I'd removed from the knapsack. "Home. With these." I had three feathers that were originally meant for Aydin, Xenia and myself. Now that I knew Xenia was Maria, I no longer needed the third one for her.

Rafe studied the charm in his hand. "How...?"

I shook my head. "I'm not sure how it works so you'll have to wing it." I stepped back to give him room. "Clear your mind and concentrate on what you want to become."

"What if it doesn't work?"

"Then we're screwed," I said. "Or at least I am. It means I'll get bonded to Aydin and once again be a slave to the gargoyle's curse." I shrugged and tried to smile, but my lips felt numb. "Maybe it won't be so bad this time around."

"Your only other choice is out of the question," Rafe said with conviction. "I know that now. I'm sorry I failed to realize it sooner."

Though I already knew his answer, I had to ask the question. "Do you love me, Rafe?"

His eyes filled with sadness again. "Of course I do, but as a brother loves a sister. You and I are family and I'll always look out for you."

I rushed to him and wrapped my arms around his neck to give him a fierce hug. He gently hugged me back and planted a light kiss on the top of my head before pushing me away.

He bowed his head and closed his eyes, the changing

charm clutched in both hands. The blood from his new brand would be enough to invoke the spell inside the key. Were we doing the right thing? I wasn't even sure it would work on an angel, or if the change would last. Scariest of all, I didn't know if there were side effects to using this charm.

There was a slight rumble beneath our feet and the air inside the room heated as if a fire burned at its center. Rafe's body glowed with angel light that suddenly turned red, as did his wings. I started to panic. The Fallen's wings were black, not red. My anxiety swelled and just when I thought the change was over, his feathers turned raven-black like his Fallen brothers.

twenty-five

RAFE BLINKED HIS EYES OPEN. "DID IT WORK?"

I stepped up to him and my hands shook as I ran my fingers over his gleaming black feathers. "Yes."

"It's only temporary?"

I nodded, though I wasn't a hundred percent sure. "As long as you have the charm, you can turn into anything you want."

A wistful look crossed his face and I knew what he was thinking. He idolized my ex-angel grandfather. Though he could disguise himself as human whenever he wanted, Rafe could never actually be one. The charm would allow him to *become* the human he so desperately wanted to be.

We were running out of time. I needed to save all the contents of my knapsack, but the sack itself was too obvious not to get noticed. I grabbed my filthy T-shirt from the floor and tore it into strips. After lifting the hem of my dress above my hips, I used the rags to tie the feathers, scrying mirror and horn of breath to my upper thighs. I shoved the empty knapsack in a bureau drawer and slammed it shut.

Holding out my hand, I said, "Give me the changing charm and I'll hide it for you."

Rafe reluctantly dropped it in my palm, and when he did, his feathers turned white again.

I thrust the iron key toward him. "Quick. Take it back!"

Eyes puzzled, he grasped hold of it and his feathers returned to their glossy black hue. "Why? What happened?"

"The change won't hold unless you keep the charm with you."

"Where will I put it?"

I glanced at the white tunic he was wearing. "Can you tuck it under there somewhere?"

He nodded and lifted the fabric to slide the key down the front of his loincloth.

I suspected our allotted time had expired and expected the door to open at any second. Rafe took hold of the front of my dress and dragged me so close that my breasts pressed against his chest.

"Hey!" I slapped at his hand. "What are you—?"

He made a long, jagged tear down the center of the gown.

"There. Think that's believable?" he asked.

I'd never been ravaged before so I really couldn't say, but I didn't have to. The door flung open and Soriel stood staring at us, his eyes taking in the view. He glanced from one to the other and nodded, though he didn't appear happy with what he saw. I thought I knew why. He had done what he assumed we just finished doing and look where it got him.

When Soriel presented the unhappily wedded couple to Maria, her eyes brightened with sheer joy. She barely gave me a second glance, but her gaze raked Rafe from head to toe and a drop of drool glistened at the corner of her mouth.

"Magnificent." The word escaped her lips on a breath. I couldn't argue with her there. The stark contrast between his black feathers and porcelain-white skin made Rafe a stunning fallen angel.

"Come to me." She leaned forward on her throne. "I'm thirsty."

I tasted bile at the back of my throat. What had I done? Saved myself and Aydin, but what about Rafe?

My gaze jumped to my father, who was fully conscious now. Though his beating happened less than an hour ago, the bruises on his face had already yellowed in healing and the skin around his scabbed lip appeared pink and healthy. I heaved a sigh of relief, but his furious expression gave me a jolt. He stood behind the throne, still shackled, and glared daggers at Maria's back. He wanted revenge for his indignity and for my capture. Pharzuph stood about fifteen feet from him with his attention on his daughter and nothing else.

Aydin watched in silence, his large gargoyle head held high, his powerful body tense. Though his expression was impossible to read through his feline features, his eyes were not, and I sensed what he must be thinking. He waited, knowing a time to act was minutes away. The shaman appointed as his keeper stood just out of Aydin's reach. Heavy circles of iron manacled Aydin's ankles, and though this kept his wings from taking him far, they could still extend. I wondered if the shaman had considered a gargoyle's wingspan when he chose where to stand.

"Kneel," Maria told Rafe, who stiffly complied. I couldn't see his face at this angle, but I observed his rigid posture and the bunching of his shoulders. He knew Maria fed on the Fallen and that he was about to become today's feast.

I refused to watch so I studied the audience—our wedding guests—to divert my attention. The squires stood beside their fallen angel husbands, their faces slack as if having already given up. Definitely not knight material for the Hatchets, but perfect for Pharzuph's plan to have half-angel offspring he could control. Each squire was in a different stage of pregnancy, from the baby bump to ready-to-pop. One squire's shoulders shook with quiet weeping and she brought her hands up to cover her face. The angel beside her grabbed her wrist and yanked her hands down. She stood stoically still after that, the tears drying on her face. I had to get her out of here. I had to save them all.

I looked away from them just in time to see Maria's mouth latch onto Rafe's bleeding wrist. Her face appeared serene, like a suckling baby, and she moaned with pleasure. Then her forehead creased with concern and her eyes stretched open in surprise. She dropped Rafe's wrist as if his flesh burned her mouth.

She screamed. A long, wailing scream that reverberated against the walls of the cave and made my ears ring. Rafe stood and backed up a step. He appeared puzzled while watching Maria choke and gasp, his blood still wet on her lips.

When Pharzuph saw what had happened and lurched toward the throne, Barachiel splayed his fingers and the air inside the room went completely still. Maria's Fallen entourage jumped to attention and made a move to rush at the throne, but abruptly froze in place. My father had stopped time outside the circle. Inside the circle was a whole different story.

Time continued unabated within our bubble of protection, giving Pharzuph the opportunity to attack my father again. But Barachiel was ready for him. His manacles slipped off his wrists and he clutched Pharzuph with the ferocity of an enraged beast. Both dark angels glared at each other with red eyes that glowed with hatred. Their bodies pulsed a vibrant green light.

The shaman searched through the pouch he wore, probably looking for a magical instrument of some kind to stop my father. The tip of a long bat wing smacked him on the back of the neck and he flew forward, his bald head cracking against the back of Maria's throne. He collapsed and never got up again.

Maria clutched her throat, her eyes staring wide at me in a silent plea for help. I had no idea what was happening to her.

"It's my blood," Rafe said in a flat voice while staring

at Maria. "She's been nourished by the Fallen for centuries and now my Arelim blood is…" He swallowed and turned his attention on me, his brows tilted in sorrow. "I never meant for this to happen. She is Geraldine's child…" His chin quivered and he caught Maria in his arms as she toppled from the throne.

Barachiel and Pharzuph were wrapped tightly together in a wrestling match for power. The strain on Barachiel's face was mirrored on Pharzuph's and both angels struggled to win. My father's gaze flicked to me as he yelled, "Finish it!"

I felt confused, unsure what I was supposed to finish. I knelt in front of Maria, whose lips were turning blue, her face even more pale than before. Rafe's blood had dried to a brown stain on her chin. The whites of her eyes had turned as red as her father's and her tears made crimson streaks down her cheeks.

"Please," Maria breathed, the word followed by a gasp. "Chalice, help me. Don't let me die."

I saw Xenia then, the frightened young girl on an uncertain path. She was the real Maria underneath the insane facade of a life her father had forced on her. She wasn't meant to be the bitch queen Pharzuph had created.

I'd never had the chance to meet my mother, but Maria could still meet hers. She deserved to know the miraculous woman who'd given up her own life for the truth. The woman who started an order of knights dedicated to helping, not hurting. Maria should be one of us.

I heard an anguished cry and jerked a look at the two battling angels so magnificent in their primal struggle for dominance. Someone had to lose and Pharzuph's determined expression made it clear it wouldn't be him. "No!" he screamed as he watched his child go limp in Rafe's arms.

Pharzuph tried to wrench away from Barachiel, who redoubled his efforts at clutching him in a bone-crushing embrace. My father caught my eye and his sadness was so profound I nearly collapsed myself. Red tears streamed down his face as he mouthed the words, *I love you*. And then both he and Pharzuph vanished from sight.

"Barachiel?" I shouted, and jumped to my feet. "Father! Where are you?"

I ran to where the two had been fighting and felt the air quiver where I stood. It had a viscous quality, and it sucked at me like it wanted to take me wherever it had taken my father. That's what I wanted, too. I had to find him!

Rafe grabbed my arm and yanked me back to the throne. "My God, Chalice! What were you doing? Your body was fading and I could see straight through you."

And then I knew. Barachiel had banished Pharzuph, but while wrapped in the same spell he had banished himself as well.

"He's gone," I said numbly, then saw Aydin, who stood with his arms held open to me in invitation. I ran to him and he folded himself around me like a wall of protection. He comforted me with his strength and his faith. I needed him so bad I could hardly stand it.

Barachiel's hold on time was slipping. I watched over Aydin's shoulder as the Fallen gradually found movement again. They stood silent and lost in the sudden absence of their leader.

Soriel was the first to approach the circle. His anxious eyes took in the damaged woman still draped over Rafe's arms, her eyes open and staring. Her spirit was gone.

Face contorted with anguish, Soriel collapsed to his knees and his head drooped forward as his shoulders shook with grief.

The other angels appeared confused. They stared at Rafe, assuming he was now one of them. If they only knew, and I was glad they didn't. The squires gazed dumbfounded at the aftermath of the scene they had missed. Though time moved on, paralysis remained. They were all waiting for the next shoe to drop.

"I know what to do." I moved out of Aydin's embrace. "I can bring her back."

Rafe shook his head. "Not even the Arelim can bring her back. Even if we were on the other side of the veil, Maria had so much Fallen blood running through her veins that it's beyond our ability to help her."

"It's not beyond mine." I lifted my gown and slid the horn of breath out from under the rag tied around my thigh. I crouched beside the throne. "Lay her down, Rafe."

"I'm not sure this is wise," he told me.

"Maybe not, but I'm doing it anyway." I positioned the tip of the horn between Maria's blue lips. "I owe it to Geraldine. She deserves the chance to see her daughter again."

I remembered how this had worked with Rusty so it didn't surprise me to see her chest rise and her ashen skin begin to pink. The dark circles under her eyes faded to pale lavender instead of the deep purple that had been there before. Even her lips seemed to warm from the energy flowing inside her and now looked more rose than gray. Maria appeared more human than I'd ever seen her, even while she masqueraded as Xenia.

She coughed lightly at first, bloody foam dribbling from her mouth. She started to gag and I tipped her to her side so she could expel the blood she had swallowed. Rafe's blood.

Her eyes blinked open and she asked, "What happened?"

I answered with a question of my own. "Do you know where you are?"

Fluttering her eyelids, she turned her head one way and then the other, her eyes swiveling in their sockets. They brimmed with tears, normal tears, not bloody ones. She shook her head. "Who are you?"

I frowned. "I'm Chalice, remember? We're inside your father's crystal cave on the other side of the black veil. This is your home."

She rose to her elbows and Rafe reached out to brace her arms so she wouldn't fall. One look at him and her face contorted with fear. "A demon!" she yelled.

Maria had seemingly forgotten everything. Did she even know who and what she was?

"Maria, this is Rafe. He's an angel and wants to help you," I said softly.

She shook her head. "His wings are black. He's a demon. And why do you call me Maria?"

"Because that's your name."

Appearing confused, she said, "No, it's not. My name is…"

I waited for her to go on and when she didn't, I prompted, "What *is* your name?"

Maria rested her back against the cushions of the throne. "I don't feel well."

She was disoriented. We had to get her away from here.

The dark angels outside the circle appeared agitated now. Seeing their mistress alive had inspired them to talk amongst themselves and they didn't look encouraged by what they saw.

I stooped down to rummage through the dead shaman's pouch and found the key to Aydin's manacles. "Rafe, say something to them," I said as I unlatched the loops of iron that bound Aydin's ankles to the floor.

"What should I tell them?" Rafe asked.

"Make something up to pacify them until we can get away." I had three fallen angel feathers and I needed at least four to get us to the other side of the veil. I gave Rafe a cursory glance, then dismissed using one of his feathers, which were nothing but a disguise. My gaze swept the floor inside the circle and I spotted a plume on the ground where Barachiel and Pharzuph had fought. Good enough.

Rafe cleared his throat. "Pharzuph had an errand," he told the small gathering. "He asked me to let you know he'll return soon."

"Barachiel stopped time," one of them said. "Where did he go?"

"Pharzuph has taken him away." Rafe turned to look at me and whispered, "Now what?"

I handed him one of the black feathers. "We leave." I

slid a feather inside Maria's cloak and told her, "Hang on to this and don't let go."

She frowned and her lower lip quivered. "I'm scared."

My heart went out to her. "Me, too."

Aydin took a feather for himself and we joined Rafe at Maria's throne.

"Can you stand?" I asked her.

She looked confused again. "I don't know."

"Rafe, you should be the one to pick her up," I said. "The Fallen consider you one of them so I doubt they'll mind if you help their mistress."

He took a feather from me before lifting Maria in his arms. When he stood, the changing charm fell out from underneath his tunic and clattered to the floor. The second it did, his wings returned to their original snowy white.

An enraged shout erupted from the tight group of dark angels outside the circle.

twenty-six

"WHAT JUST HAPPENED?" RAFE ASKED ME.

I bent to retrieve the iron key from the floor and held it up to show him. "You dropped this."

Soriel was watching, his eyes intent on Maria. I sensed he wanted to help *us* so that we could help *her*. As long as the circle held, we were safe, and he knew that as well.

The squires frantically grabbed their husbands to pull them back, using every seductive move imaginable to divert their attention. They'd seen Rafe in his unadulterated glory and I believed the sight had renewed their hope for rescue. Yet I couldn't take them with us now. Not only was I out of feathers, but we couldn't break the circle. I'd have to come for them later and I only hoped they'd be safe while I was gone.

His gaze locked with mine, Soriel jerked his head at

the women and nodded. He was trying to let me know he would do his best to protect them.

I looked from Rafe to Aydin, marveling at how close they stood to each other without fighting. This was the first time the two had ever had to cooperate and neither appeared awkward or uncomfortable.

I focused on the feather in my hand and experienced an intense feeling of having done this before. But I hadn't. I'd never crossed the veil before Barachiel brought Aydin and me to this side. Nevertheless, I knew exactly what to do to go back. A pang of understanding hit me in the gut. Maria. When I used the horn of breath to revive her, I probably took her ability the same way I had Rusty's. It made me wonder what else of hers I had absorbed.

I knew precisely where I wanted the four of us to appear on the other side. It was time to go home. Halo Home.

The energy inside the feather flowed through my fingers, up my arms and curled around the back of my neck. My body hummed with it. Though I wanted to go home, I knew that arriving inside the house would be impossible. The house was protected by the Arelim and had a direct link to the silver veil, so the black veil would never open there. But it would outside the perimeter of the warded property.

I closed my eyes and visualized the snow-packed road in front of the house, then expressed my desire for the four of us to be there. When I opened my eyes, we were still inside the crystal cave, but its walls were fading. The group of angels and their wives faded, too, and were replaced by a swirling fog so dense I could no longer see the ground beneath my feet.

Less than a minute later, the fog lifted and we were all standing in the exact spot I had pictured in my mind. The sun was out, and after two days spent in near total darkness, I'd never been happier to see blue sky. Unfortunately, the impact on my retinas was like having twin ice picks stabbed into my eyes. I pressed my palms over my closed lids and waited to regain control over my senses. Painful as it was, I welcomed them back.

I checked on Maria, who lay limp in Rafe's arms with her eyes closed.

Either she'd passed out or was too overwhelmed to say anything.

Aydin appeared lost and uncomfortable. He knew he wasn't wanted here, at least not by my grandparents or the Arelim, but I believed it only temporary. If I had my way, he wouldn't be a gargoyle much longer.

Both my grandparents appeared through the invisible boundary that surrounded Halo Home. My grandmother rushed toward me, her face stricken with worry and tears streaming down her face. I couldn't tell if she was happy to see me or if a new catastrophe threatened the order. I didn't think I could handle another one so soon. She didn't wait for a greeting, just barreled into me and wrapped me in a tight hug, her body shaking with sobs.

"Grandmother, what's happened?" I asked, a sinking feeling in my gut. "Is everything okay?"

"It is now," she said into my hair. "You've been gone for over two weeks."

I pulled away from her. "What?" That was impossible. "We crossed over only two days ago."

She shook her head and wiped at her eyes. "I've been worried out of my mind. I was afraid I'd never see you again."

I smiled sadly and smoothed my hand over her shoulder to try comforting her. The gesture felt awkward. Showing affection wasn't my strong suit. "I'm fine, see? And so are Rafe and Aydin. And we also brought—"

"Xenia?" My grandmother covered her mouth with her hands. "Oh, my God. I thought for sure Maria had killed her."

This would be difficult to explain, so I just blurted it out. "Xenia is Maria."

Aurora's forehead creased with confusion. "I don't understand."

I gave her a brief rundown of what had happened, but left out the faux wedding between Rafe and me. That was a long story best left for another time. I wasn't sure how an added shock would affect my grandmother's blood pressure. "When Maria came back to life, she apparently lost all memory of who she is and where she's been for the past nine centuries."

"We know who she is." Aurora began to pace in short, angry steps. "She's a killer who practically exterminated an entire order of knights. She masqueraded as a Hatchet squire here, inside *my* home, with the intention of..." She gritted her teeth and stopped to stare me in the eyes. "This is a matter for the Arelim to decide."

"What's there to decide?" I asked, genuinely puzzled

by her venomous hatred of a fellow knight. "She's here with us now, where she belongs."

Aurora shook her head. "Her offenses are far too great for her to be accepted into the knighthood."

"It wasn't her fault," I said. "Her father turned her into a monster. She doesn't even remember any of it."

"How can you be sure?" She glared at the unconscious woman in Rafe's arms. "This could be another one of her tricks."

That was a possibility, but I wasn't willing to give up on Maria so quickly. Forgiveness was the first step toward healing our order and making it stronger. "Won't you at least give her a chance?"

"It's not for me to decide," Aurora said stiffly.

"All I ask is that you allow her asylum until she gets her strength back." I gazed at the woman I once knew as Xenia. "She's not a danger to anyone."

Aurora shot me a look.

"I have her ability now." I held out the horn of breath.

My grandmother heaved a sigh, either of relief or exasperation, I couldn't tell which. "Fine. But only until the Arelim pass judgment on what's to be done."

I nodded as I watched my grandfather relieve Rafe of his burden. He turned around and carried Maria across the boundary, disappearing from sight.

"Come inside," my grandmother told me. "Let's get that ghastly dress off you and clean you up, then feed you some proper food. You must be exhausted. What a nightmare you've had to endure."

She didn't know the half of it. I waved a hand toward Aydin. "I still have unfinished business to take care of."

"You haven't found the heart?" she asked, her face softening with sympathy.

I shook my head. At least she didn't hate him, but he was still a gargoyle and not allowed beyond this point. And I would never leave him behind.

"I believe I can help you with that," Rafe said.

"Excuse me?" I looked Rafe up and down, then studied his face to see if he was teasing. I knew there was no love lost between Rafe and Aydin. Despite our recent nuptial experience, I wasn't convinced he'd given up his goal to sire a knight for the order. However, Rafe wasn't a conniver. He had never lied to me before and I didn't think he'd start now.

"I have something for you," he said, then walked through the property barrier and vanished from sight.

"What's going on?" I asked my grandmother.

"I'll go find out," she said, and disappeared, too.

I went to Aydin, wondering if now would be a good time for us to talk. We hadn't had a chance to communicate since crossing the veil, and now that he had his power of invisibility back, we could link minds again. He must have been thinking the same thing because he abruptly faded to his ghost form. Just as he took a step toward me, Rafe reemerged through the barrier carrying a small iron chest.

"This is for you," he said, handing me the box.

I accepted it and lifted the lid. Inside was the vibrant, shiny purple jewel of Shojin's heart.

My own heart leaped with joy at the sight of it, but a dozen questions beat it out of me when I realized what Rafe had done. "You've had it all this time?"

"I didn't understand our relationship until we faced each other in your bridal chambers." Looking sheepish, he added, "I'm sorry. Before that, I thought I was protecting you."

"By lying to me?"

"I didn't lie." His gaze avoided mine as he focused on the line of trees standing on the opposite side of the road. "I simply kept the truth to myself."

"You watched me dig under the tree where I'd hidden it and you saw how devastated I was to find it gone." My fury cooked up a fireball in my hand that I hurled down to the snow. It sizzled as the ice melted around it. "How could you?"

"As your guardian, I did what I thought best for you and the knighthood."

"No, you did what you thought best for yourself. You didn't want to give me up."

"No, I didn't. Not then. But that's changed now." He finally looked at me and tears stood in his eyes. "You were right and I understand now that a union between us would be wrong. Your true mate is standing right there." He nodded at Aydin, who had rematerialized the second Rafe came into view. "I promise to no longer stand in your way."

I narrowed my eyes at him, hating him and loving him at the same time. That's how it was with family. "I thought you couldn't touch this," I said, balancing the heavy box on one hand.

"I found an empty iron box in the charm storage room," he said. "I used it to scoop up the heart and then replaced the box in the room. No one knew it was there but me."

Clever angel. But I was still angry. How would I ever trust him again?

"I apologize," he said softly.

I gritted my teeth. "What's done is done, Rafe. We have the heart now and that's all that matters." At the moment, anyway. I knew nothing could ever be the same between Rafe and me. I would never forgive him.

Eyes shadowed with shame, Rafe nodded at us both, then spun slowly on his heel and headed back to the house.

I peered inside the iron box again, remembering the day Shojin had torn his beating heart from his chest and given it to me. The heart was beautiful, but even more beautiful was the loving sentiment behind it. I gazed on it one last time before presenting it to Aydin.

Aydin stared into the box, his human eyes filled with affection for the beast he had been bonded to for over eight hundred years. This gem was all that was left of his friend. We both knew that when Aydin took it into himself, Shojin's memory would live on. The two would be as one.

He reached his paw inside the box and scooped up the heart as if it were fragile as an egg. It fit perfectly in his giant palm and I knew from handling it myself that it was hard as stone. Gargoyle stone.

Aydin opened his mouth, unhinging his jaw like a snake does to swallow its victims. He slid the heart between his lips and pushed it to the back of his throat. Then he swallowed it whole.

Nothing happened at first and I suddenly feared we had been fooled into believing the impossible. Until I noticed a change in Aydin's expression. He blinked as the fur on his face receded into his flesh, which reformed around his shrinking head that morphed into a more human shape. His wings shriveled down to nothing, his tail vanished, his claws retracted, and his body lost its fur as bones and muscles restructured to the normal shape of a man. A naked man whose skin was turning blue from standing in the snow so long.

It didn't seem to bother him. His purple lips widened in a white-toothed smile as he shivered. He thrust his fist into the air and shouted, "Yeah!" He yelled it several times, in fact. It was the first word he'd been able to say for weeks and I imagined it tasted delicious.

I was so overcome with relief and joy I could hardly move, but I didn't have to. Aydin lifted me up and twirled me around until I became so light-headed I nearly passed out. But the spinning wasn't what made me dizzy. My head spun with happiness at finally being in the arms of the man I loved.

I had my Aydin back.

★ ★ ★ ★ ★

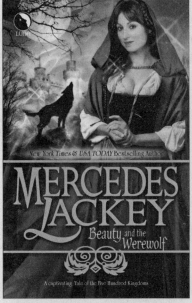

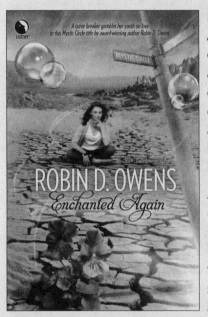

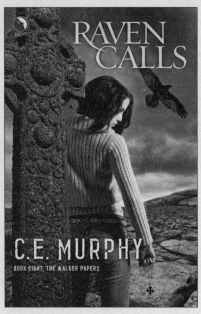